FINDING SANTA

ALMOST A BILLIONAIRE SERIES, BOOK ONE

BRIDGET E. BAKER

❀ Created with Vellum

For my darling husband, Whitney.
The snap and crackle I felt when we met over that table of grapes didn't prepare me for the lovely life you and I would create, one day at a time. Even now, more than thirteen years later, you still pay careful attention to all the little things: acts of service, thoughtful notes, and heartfelt gifts. That's why I love you in such a big way.

CHAPTER 1

By the time my friends turned seven, not a single one of them actually believed in Santa.

Ironically, that's the year my faith in the big guy began.

I was skeptical from the start. A fat, bearded man shoots down chimneys or climbs through windows to deliver presents to lots of kids he doesn't even know? He travels via a sleigh that's powered by flying deer?

Yeah, right.

I always gravitated toward science and math, because their clear-cut answers helped make sense of the world. I learned about Occam's Razor while preparing my science fair project in second grade. It dictates that all other things being equal, the simplest explanation is probably the correct one. That's why, the Christmas after I turned seven, when all my friends were catching up to what I'd known all along, that Santa's a big, fat, phony, I began to believe.

After all, that year I woke up to a decorated tree with blinking lights, and a whole truckload of fancy, beautifully wrapped presents. My options to explain this baffling event were: 1) a red-suited man who lives in the North

Pole brought me toys in a magical sack; or 2) my dad actually saved some of the money he would otherwise spend on beer to buy the presents for me as a surprise. I could count on one hand the number of times Dad left the house, if I exclude walking around the corner to the auto-repair place where he worked, or walking to the convenience store for more alcohol.

In fact, if I hadn't learned to steal tiny amounts of cash from my dad's paycheck stash, my little sister Gertrude and I wouldn't have even had hotdogs and ramen to eat. Trudy and I still twitch every time we pass a hotdog stand.

It was clear, given what I knew, that Santa must exist.

I stand up, and clear my throat. Almost a hundred sets of eyes turn toward me, and the thrill I feel every year when Sub-for-Santa season commences fills my chest. Large nutcrackers stand guard by the door, and faux holly garland drapes along every surface. A sparkly, rainbow lit tree covered in ornaments we've been given by grateful parents as thank yous over the years decorates the conference room. It looks cheerier than usual, but it's still essentially one big table with a podium up front, and a hundred folding metal chairs in rows toward the back.

"Welcome to the organizational meeting for this year's Sub-for-Santa program, sponsored locally by the United Way. I'm delighted you're all here. We can't wait to work with you to bring a little wonder to a lot of children who haven't had enough of that in their lives. My name is Mary Wiggin, and I'm the President of the Sub-for-Santa program here in Atlanta."

Smiles sprout on the faces of volunteers all around me, which is more impressive given the fact that they're all sitting on hard, metal chairs.

I continue. "We are here to uplift the lives of as many kids as we possibly can. I'm proud to say that this program has grown consistently each of the eight years that I've been in charge, and I hope to be able to say the same next year."

Everyone claps and I wait for them to finish.

"Many of you are familiar, and I'm so pleased to see you returning year after year. Do any of you repeat sponsors recall the number one rule?"

Three hands shoot up. I point at a lady in a bright pink sweater sporting a reindeer wearing magenta lipstick.

"Only nominate families who are super poor?" she asks.

I nod my head. "We do want to ensure the families placed on our list are in need, mostly because our resources are limited and we want to help as many people as we can, but it's not our number one rule. Anyone else remember that?"

Now that one of them was wrong, they're all nervous about answering. Only one hand stays raised, the green polished fingers waving wildly, like a kid waving down an ice cream truck. "Yes, Paisley?"

My perky secretary from work is helping me run the program for the third year in a row. She's paid for some of her time, but at minimum wage. Ironically, she doesn't seem to care about anything at our real job where she's paid far, far more, but she's my most enthusiastic volunteer with Sub-for-Santa. Paisley's just made for Christmas, I guess.

She beams. "Don't ruin the magic."

"Exactly, yes, that's rule number one. We do not want any of these children, not a single one, to know where these presents really originate. The reason this program works is that these kids believe in the cultural fiction that a jolly fat man with a loving, hardworking wife supervises a host of tiny elves. The kids need to believe that someone has noticed the kind things, the good things, and the right things they've done this year. They need to believe that someone cares about them. If they think these presents stem from pity, how will they feel instead? "

Paisley's hand shoots up again, and she bounces up and down in her chair. I suppress my grin and call on the heavy-set man sporting a full beard with his arm raised behind her.

"But isn't that kind of a lie?" he asks. "I mean, eventually they'll figure it out, and they'll either be mad or feel like idiots."

I frown. I should never have trusted a man with howling wolves on his t-shirt.

"Were you ever a recipient of Christmas gifts, something like the Sub-for-Santa program?" I ask.

He shakes his head. "Nah, my parents didn't need handouts."

I grit my teeth. "As someone who was a recipient, trust me. They won't be angry when they find out people cared enough to keep their donation a secret."

"You're only one person. You don't know how everyone will feel."

Note to self: install ejection seats before next year's opening meeting.

"I can't speak for everyone," I say, "but neither can you. Respectfully, speaking from ten years of experience with this program, I think you're wrong. I've seen a lot of reactions and heard from a lot of children. I've heard from kids who were participants year after year on both sides. Many of them are involved to this day, just like me. We aren't lying to these children, and anyone who believes that Sub-for-Santa is perpetuating a lie should leave."

I pause and glance meaningfully toward the back door. No one stands up. "If you're all staying, I'd love to share something with you that might help you understand how this will work. When I was younger, my mom left our family. My sister was not quite four years old. After Mom left, our dad started drinking heavily. Now I have a label for what he was: a poorly functioning alcoholic. Those were difficult times in the Wiggin household."

Paisley gives me two thumbs up and I want to stop this presentation to hug her.

"That Christmas I was old enough to know that Santa wasn't real. He was a lie, and I knew we'd wake up Christmas morning the same as every other morning. I'd make ramen for my sister, and we'd pretend it wasn't the crappiest day of the year."

I make eye contact with a dozen people, making sure they're all listening.

"Except that's not what happened. For the first time in a very long time, something great happened to us. Santa Claus was real, and he brought us a beautiful tree with multitudes of presents underneath it. Once a year, I knew that even if my parents thought I was worthless, someone somewhere cared. When I did finally discover that it wasn't Santa, but in fact a group of extraordinary people who wanted me to have a fantastic day, that meant more to me than the fiction of Santa."

A tear springs to my eye, as it always does this time of year when I think back to that first Christmas. I wipe it away.

"Sub-for-Santa," I say, "is a program that allows good people to give to those who need love, for no benefit to themselves. We should be doing things like this all year, but that's too tall an order, so we settle for one day a year of selfless service and love to children who will truly appreciate the gesture. The real reason we never, ever, let the children know where the presents come from is that—"

Paisley's waving so frantically I'm worried she's going

to poke the guy next to her in the eye. A lawsuit would eat up all our funds and the program would collapse. I sigh, but the corners of my mouth turn up a little anyway.

"Yes, Pais?"

"If the kids figure out it's coming from a charity, they'll feel patronized. We want them to feel like someone values them, like they're worthwhile, not like they're getting presents out of pity or guilt. Eventually, they'll be old enough to realize that there may be a real Santa somewhere, but he can't really reach everyone, so other people help out and do some of his work for him."

There may be a real Santa somewhere? I can't help but smile, because other than her small delusion, she's spot on. If she exhibited half this much zeal in the tax office where we both work, she wouldn't still be my secretary. She'd have been promoted to office manager.

"Well said Paisley, thank you. If these children believe in Santa, they also believe that they matter to someone. If these children know rich people are donating things to poor kids who aren't loved, they'll feel lesser. That's obviously the opposite of our goal."

As I work my way through the rest of the rules, my heart lifts and it finally starts to feel like the holiday season is upon us. Eventually, it's time to pass out nomination forms and sponsor requirements.

"I have a list of volunteers that we've collected from several church groups and businesses, as well as employees, friends and neighbors. You're all here because you offered to sponsor a family, or be part of my core team to help administer the entire operation, or both. I appreciate that greatly. We still have one more week to collect volunteers and then I'll finalize the nominations for participants. Please write down the information on anyone you have now, and bring it to me. The sooner we have nominations, the sooner we can contact them for permission, and request the documentation we need to ensure our efforts go to the right place. Last year, we helped five hundred and thirty-two families, with more than eleven hundred children. My goal for this year is to reach six hundred families and fifteen hundred children. If you'll all help, I think we can get there."

Paisley passes out nomination forms, and cards with the website URL where they can submit nominations once they've left tonight. "Thank you all, and please feel free to call me with any questions. My phone number and email address are both on that card, below the website listing. I try to reply as promptly as possible during the holiday season. I don't want details to impede our desire to bless these children."

Pais and I each take a door and people hand us nomination forms on their way out. Once the last person waves and walks out the door, I lock it behind her and blow out all but one of the Christmas Cookie candles. Paisley and I buckle down to work immediately, compiling a list of people to contact. A few people added names to the volunteer column as well, and my heart swells. Several others indicated they'd be willing to sponsor more than one family.

"We're almost done with the nominations," I tell her. "Why don't you take the volunteer names and update that spreadsheet for me. I'd love to send out the introductory email tomorrow. We always get a flurry of new sponsors when that goes out, plus maybe you can post our numbers and our mission statement to the Facebook group and hopefully get some shares that way."

Paisley is a whiz with lists of any kind. Sometimes I think she manages lists better than the computer. Whenever I comment on it, she says her parents had her working on lists of things before she could even talk. I've never asked her about her parents, and she's never volunteered much more than that.

"Sure boss, right away."

"I'm not your boss here, Pais. You're a volunteer same as me."

She rolls her eyes. "Except you're the Chair, and I'm still getting paid. But whatever you say, boss." She salutes me.

Paisley hops on the computer with a saucy grin on her face, and the clacking of her fingers on the keys soothes me. After a long and exhausting tax season, it's a relief to be focusing on the one thing I love more than taxes for a few weeks before we start all over again.

"Umm," Paisley says, "I found something a little odd on this list."

I tilt my head sideways. "Odd? What does that mean?"

"Well, I need to compare something first." She walks across the room and peers over my shoulder at the list I'm finishing up of nominated families. "There." She points. "That says Lucas Manning, right?"

I squint at the screen of my laptop and nod. "Yes, Lucas Manning, at 236 Sunset Cove."

"Can the same person be both a nominee and a volunteer?" she asks.

I scrunch up my nose. "No. If they're a legitimate participant in the program, they shouldn't be able to afford to sponsor a family."

Paisley walks back over to the desktop, and I follow. About a third of the way down her list, there's his name again. Lucas Manning, 236 Sunset Cove."

"Gah," I say, "what a mess. We must've included his name by accident. We'll have to go over the initial forms and figure out which one he really is."

We search and search, but sure enough, we didn't make

a mistake. His name and address are listed here on the nominee form, and someone filled his name and address out as a sponsoring family as well.

"Now what?" I wonder out loud.

"Has this ever happened before?" she asks.

I shake my head. "Not that I know of."

"What do we do?"

Take the bull by the horns, I suppose. "I'll call him and set up an appointment to discuss the program. I don't think it's a subject I should broach over the phone, because if he's a sponsor, he'll be offended someone nominated him, and if he's a nominee, he'll wonder if other people disapprove of him taking things as evidenced by his name being listed as a sponsor. What a snarl. Hopefully the answer will be glaringly obvious once I reach his house, and I can play it off as a standard preliminary meeting either way."

"Good idea," Paisley says.

I dial the number listed, and the phone rings and rings. Finally it goes to voicemail. Lucas Manning has a deep voice with a faint accent I can't place, at least, not from hearing only ten words. I leave a message asking him to call me at the United Way office.

Not five seconds after I end the call, my phone rings and the words UNKNOWN CALLER pop up on the screen. Probably Lucas returning my call.

"Wow, that was fast," I say.

"Mary?" My boss Shauna's voice, even just saying my name on the phone, is unmistakable. "What was fast?"

I cringe, not that she can see it. "Your phone number came up as unknown, and I thought you were someone with Sub-for-Santa returning my call." Which was stupid, because I only gave him my office number.

"Ah, okay. Are you busy tonight? I was hoping you

could meet me for dinner. I need to talk to you, and it's important."

"That sounds ominous," I say.

She laughs. "Well, we do have a lot of data to review. I got our analyst's reports on numbers and performance for the year."

My stomach turns. "You're not firing me, right?"

"I'd hardly do that over dinner. I'd have to wait until the end of the meal to tell you, which would be beyond awkward when I finally got around to firing you."

She also wouldn't be making a joke about it if it were happening. I relax a little bit. "Where did you want to meet?"

"Bentleys, eight sharp. Dress nice." Shauna hangs up the phone.

"Was everything okay?" Paisley asks.

"I'm wearing black pants and a red sweater. Does this count as 'nice enough for Bentleys' do you think?" It's one of the premiere steakhouses in Atlanta, and I've only been once.

Paisley scrunches up her nose. "Well, I've never been there, but. . ."

"That bad?" I sigh. "Shauna wants to see me, and she said to meet her there. She reminded me to dress nice, like I need someone to tell me how to pull my pants on the right legs."

"Bizarre. Although you are her rising star. Probably just another client that asked for you specifically. If she's giving you more work, I know it goes against every part of your character, but you need to demand a raise. You already work harder than everyone else in that stupid office."

I wish. "No way is she calling me over to give me a raise. In any case, I have forty-five minutes until I'm supposed to arrive, and it's fifteen minutes to get to my house for a change of clothes. Bentleys is a solid twenty minutes away from home. I'm sorry to ditch you, but I better run."

"I have a cocktail dress in my trunk. If you ask nicely, I might be persuaded to share."

I raise one eyebrow. "Do I even want to know why you have a dress in the back of your car?"

She grins. "I'm single, and I like to be prepared. You never know where the night may lead."

I always know where mine will go. My nights beeline toward a TV dinner in front of an episode of Gilmore Girls. But that's kind of pathetic. I should have a cocktail dress in my trunk. I should be spontaneous and fun.

"I'm single too," I say, "and the only thing in my trunk is dust bunnies, hiding amidst old tax files."

"You want the dress, or not?" she asks.

"I might. Lemme see it." I follow her out to her car.

She lifts the trunk and slides a black bag out. She pulls the zipper down to reveal a blood red sheath dress with black piping. I gasp. "Yes, I'd love to wear that, but I doubt it'll fit me."

Paisley eats like a bird and it shows, but one quick try on won't hurt. If by some miracle it fits, I'll spare myself a lot of anxiety about traffic and changing in time to reach Bentleys.

Paisley snorts. "It'll look better on you than on me I imagine, especially with your coloring. I mean come on, this vibrant red with your blonde hair and hazel eyes? Not to mention your golden tan. Remind me why we're friends again?"

I don't bother correcting her, but my skin isn't actually tanned. My dad's half Italian, so my skin's darker than your average white person.

I roll my eyes. "Obviously I've been using you this

whole time for the day I would need a cocktail dress with no notice."

I leave the conference room and walk around the corner to try on the dress in my office. Paisley stands guard by my door just in case. It's late enough that everyone who normally works here is gone, but I'm not taking any chances on janitorial staff. The dress is red satin, with panels that alternate between shiny and matte in vertical stripes. It's a little snug, which means it shoves my chest up near my collarbones.

"I don't think I can go out in public looking like this."

"You have to at least show me." Paisley whines. "Come on, lemme see it. I have no exciting news, so I need to live vicariously."

I step out of my office.

Paisley whistles and claps. "If you were going on a date instead of to meet our boss, I'd totally force you to wear that. Since it's just a work thing, it's your call. You're welcome to borrow it as long as you dry-clean it afterward."

I bite my lip while I think about it. "It will be way easier than trying to drive home first, so I'll borrow it if you're sure it's okay."

She nods. "Totally fine."

"Thanks." I slide into my boring black pumps and grab my purse. "Actually, I should probably use the time I'm saving to help you finalize the nominee list."

Paisley shrugs. "I can finish the last few up here, no problem. Order the most expensive thing on the menu. Frank & Meacham owes you a nice meal for coming in on no notice, and late at night. Not during tax season." She scowls. "Those guys abuse your work ethic."

"I'll order the lobster and the steak."

"Oh man, then bring me leftovers. And to pay me back

for the loan, text me and let me know what's going on. I love firm gossip."

"Will do." I pull my light brown leather jacket on over the stunning red dress, and walk out the door.

I run through a list of things Shauna might need to tell me. It can't be a promotion, because I'm a senior associate, which means she's got the only position above mine. I can't imagine she'd fire me. My hands shake. Could she be transferring me? There's a rumor going around that the London office is struggling. I can't leave my baby sister Trudy here in Atlanta alone, and she'd never follow me to London. If that's it, I'll have to tell her no. Can I tell her no?

I'm deep in thought, and only a few steps away from the comfort of my Honda Accord when I bump into someone.

My heart accelerates and I stumble backward, blinking my eyes in the cold air to help focus them. Strong hands wrap around my upper arms, steadying me. "Mary?"

I look up into the face of my ex-fiancé, Foster Bradshaw. He looks every bit as aristocratic and perfect as ever. I shouldn't be surprised to see him here, since he runs United Way's Atlanta office, but he's not usually here after hours. His dark hair falls softly over his forehead and ears. His deep blue sweater exactly matches his eyes. He knows it, too. With Foster, nothing is ever a coincidence.

"I'm so sorry, Foster. I didn't see you."

"Obviously." The humor in his tone rubs me the wrong way, or maybe it's my body's reaction to his cologne that makes me cranky. "Do you have a few minutes to spare? I need to talk to you about something."

Get in line, buddy. "Sorry, I don't actually. I just got a call from my other boss, the one who pays my bills. I've gotta run."

"Always working, even after tax season has ended. Typical Mary. Well, don't let me stop you, but I'd love to touch base sometime in the next few days before things get crazy." He releases me and steps back. "Be careful. It's icy out there."

I practically sprint to my car. Whatever my boss has to say, it can't be worse than spending another second with Foster.

CHAPTER 2

Traffic is light this late in the evening and I arrive more than twenty minutes early. I slide a little on a patch of ice behind a Range Rover, but this isn't my first winter here. I regain my balance and head toward the doors. The enormous pine bough wreaths create a festive atmosphere, especially in conjunction with the white twinkle lights. When the greeters open the door, holly bushes in enormous, rough-hewn pots sitting on either side of the double door entrance come into view.

"I'm meeting my boss. Reservation for Shauna? Eight p.m."

"It's only seven-forty, and you're the first to arrive. You could wait at the bar until your party is here," the perky hostess suggests.

I hate that they always say my "party," like people with balloons and cake and presents are on their way. How about, wait until your people have arrived?

I climb up on a barstool and whip out my phone to text Paisley.

MADE IT. SHAUNA NOT HERE YET. THANKS AGAIN.

I check my email too, since I'm waiting anyway. The IRS finally responded on our request for a private letter ruling. I'm downloading it when the bartender asks for my drink order.

"Can I get you a drink?" he says.

I don't bother looking up. The bartender's got a very light Australian accent, but the letter ruling popped up on my screen and it looks like good news for my client. "No thanks. I don't drink."

"Wow, you didn't even look at my face before shutting me down. That's a new low."

I glance up from my screen, and realize the offer came from the barstool next to me, not from behind the bar. The man smiling at me has light bluish grey eyes, and short, caramel hair with a hint of grey at the temples. His grey polo shirt stretches tight across his chest, the sleeves barely containing his biceps. Which I should not be staring at. Dressed that casually, he's either out of his element here, or he's so stinking rich he doesn't care what anyone thinks. Based on the heft of his biceps, I'd say out of his element. In my experience, very few wealthy men bother working out consistently enough to bulk up. Certainly Foster and his buddies didn't.

My eyes dart back up to his face, and I blush. "I'm so sorry. I thought you were doing your job."

He lifts his eyebrows. "Doing my job? Rejected and insulted in two sentences, even after you took a moment to check me out. I guess that means I have an unattractive voice and a smarmy look."

I roll my eyes. "You're Aussie, right? I'm guessing you get a lot of mileage out of that voice."

"I've been here for fifteen years, now. Most Americans don't recognize it anymore."

"Maybe I can pick it up because I've been to Sydney," I say. "I loved it."

"It's been a decade since my last visit, but it is a beautiful city."

"In any case, I apologize. I thought you were the bartender asking for my drink order."

"Now that you know I'm not, does that change your mind?" He chuckles. "Any interest in a free drink from me?"

"Sorry, I don't drink alcohol. Never have," I say.

"Never have? So you're not in AA, then. Are you Mormon or something?"

I raise one eyebrow. "If I was ever in AA, I certainly wouldn't tell you, and if I was Mormon I wouldn't talk about anything else. For me, it's neither of those things. Actually, my dad should've been in AA and never joined up. Thanks to his shining example, alcohol never held any charm for me." I glance behind him at the door.

"You're waiting for someone. I get it."

"What makes you think I'm waiting for someone?" I ask.

He glances down. "Other than the toe tapping, the purposeful glances at the door, and the phenomenal dress?"

I suppress a smile. "Yes, other than those things."

"Most people who are looking to meet new people in a restaurant bar make eye contact, and you were clearly engrossed in your Facebook post until I propositioned you."

I huff. "I don't even have a Facebook account. I was replying to a client."

"Ah, a working woman, maybe even a boss lady. Now I'm even more devastated you shut me down. Twice."

I can't quite contain my smile this time. "Fine. It's not very festive, but I'll take a virgin piña colada."

"A milkshake with a twist for a woman of refined tastes. I like it." He holds up two fingers to the bartender and tells him our order. "Virgin piña colada and Scotch on the rocks with peppermint."

"Peppermint?" I ask.

He taps the bar. "It's festive, right? So tell me, what's your name?"

"Mary. Which is a festive name, now that I think about it."

He chuckles. "And who are you waiting for? A shepherd? An angel? Someone named Joseph? Please tell me you're not also looking for a hotel, because that would be too obvious." His eyes sparkle as he shifts sideways, one arm up on the wooden bar.

"How about you?" I ask. "You're at a nice steakhouse, clearly killing time for a bit. You must be waiting for someone, too."

He grins. "My cousin-in-law's running late, but even if he wasn't, he wouldn't mind being left alone for a minute, not once he saw who I was talking to."

Oh please. Let him chew on this one. "I'm meeting a woman."

His eyebrows rise. "In that dress? So I'm seriously barking up the wrong tree, huh?"

I purse my lips and watch him squirm for a moment before saying, "She's my boss."

"Mary?" Shauna's high, clear voice carries from the hostess stand. "Are you ready?"

"She looks tough. Cracks the whip, huh?" he says.

"Before you go, I'd love your phone number, Virgin Piña Colada Mary."

I roll my eyes.

The bartender brings us our drinks. I take a sip of mine and look him over. He's probably too good looking for me, and way too tall. I barely top five foot. He's over six for sure. "If we're meant to date, I'm sure fate will push us together again."

He shakes his head. "Fate's a heartless jerk. I prefer making my own luck."

I stand up and push my stool forward. "I don't even know your name."

"It's Luke, which fits Mary well, I might add. Both of them are in the New Testament, and both are short."

"Luke," a booming voice calls. "Sorry I'm late, but I'm so hungry I could eat a whole cow. You ready to go?"

Luke turns his head toward the man calling him, a large barrel chested man with a full beard. I take advantage of the break to slip away and join Shauna. When I reach her side, the hostess grabs three menus and walks toward the back of the restaurant. A grey haired man in a gorgeous charcoal suit walks alongside Shauna.

My eyes widen. "Oh, I didn't know anyone else would be here."

The man switches his grip on his briefcase to his other hand and extends his right one to me. "Peter Meacham."

My mouth drops. One of the two founders of our accounting firm is eating dinner with us? "Wonderful to meet you, sir. What brings you all the way to Atlanta?"

He doesn't speak until we've been seated, but then he wastes no time. "I don't believe in small talk or meaningless chatter. I'm here because Shauna will be taking over the London office at the first of the year. It's drowning, and thanks to her organizational prowess and work ethic, the Atlanta office runs like a well-oiled machine."

I frown. "That's bad news for me, sir. I've absolutely loved working with Shauna."

Shauna smiles. "I'll miss you Mary, but I hope tonight's dinner isn't a sad one for you once you hear what we have to say."

"I'll try to keep my chin up," I say.

The waitress brings us menus and we all look over it and place our drink orders.

"Actually, I'm ready to order now," Shauna says.

"Me too," I say.

The waitress takes our orders and disappears.

"Two decisive women," Peter says. "Which is exactly why we've asked you here tonight, Mary."

I glance from Peter to Shauna and back again. Peter pulls out a piece of paper from his briefcase, placing it carefully on the table.

"What's that?" I ask.

"Frank & Meacham employees love figures, balance, and order. Once a month, Shauna sends me updates, as I'm sure you can imagine. But beyond that, at the end of each tax season she provides a chart for me with a lot of relevant statistics. Do you know how many CPAs work for our firm at present in the Atlanta office?"

I tally my co-workers in my head. "Eighteen, including me."

"How about the total accountants?" Peter taps the table absently.

I shake my head. "Twenty, give or take? I don't know them as well, because since my second year, I've focused on taxation."

He points at the paper. "This line is you, Mary. You're our

top tax preparer for volume, total returns, and refund amount. You're also the fastest worker, and your co-workers regularly report that if they have a question or concern, you answer it for them without complaint and in a snap. Your peer reviews and your end of year reviews are off the charts."

I open my mouth, but I don't know quite what to say. "Thank you sir. I love what I do, and maybe that shows."

"In spite of that, you never complain, you've never demanded a raise for helping your co-workers, and Shauna reports that you pick up any extra work and audits that no one else wants."

"She's far and away my best employee," Shauna says. "And everyone in the Atlanta office knows it."

"We've asked you to dinner today because we have a proposal for you," Peter says. "When Shauna leaves, we need someone to steer the boat here. We all agree you're the best one for the job."

My heart sinks, and my head begins shaking involuntarily. "I can't do that."

Peter's eyebrow rises. "You can't?"

Shauna sighs. "I wondered about this. Something I hadn't mentioned was that Mary spends all her vacation and most of her free time each year running a program for the United Way. It's called Sub-for-Santa. They provide gifts and food for families who can't afford to provide for themselves."

Peter steeples his hands over the report. "I don't see the connection between that, admittedly admirable effort, and our promotion."

"Running the program takes up fifty hours a week for the three weeks leading up to Christmas and at least fifteen hours a week for the three weeks before Thanksgiving. I can do it as a tax preparer, and even have time left to schedule a few audit defenses during December, but if I'm running the office. . ."

"The accounting end picks up around the holidays," Shauna says, "with all the year-end reporting requirements. She can't dedicate enough time around the holidays to run her charity if she's filling my position."

Peter grunts. "It's an impressive thing you've done, young woman, but I'm sure they'll thank you for your many years of service and wish you well. Besides, we haven't even gotten to the best part yet. Your current salary is just under eighty thousand a year. Your pay will go up to nearly a quarter million, and on top of that, you'll become a partner, eligible for the profit share. It really isn't something you should turn down."

I clench my napkin in my lap. "You have no idea how flattered I am at the offer sir, but I love my job. I enjoy preparing returns, and I don't want to give that up. And the average CPA here makes around eighty-thousand, but I've been making closer to a hundred thousand, based on my speed."

Shauna puts her hand over my forearm. "Peter hasn't even mentioned the bonus."

Peter clears his throat. "Typically new partners are required to buy in, but it's a nominal fee of ten thousand dollars. However, we do allow them to participate in the profit share in the year they become partner. For you, that will be locked in on December 30. This year's bonus should be nearly a hundred thousand dollars."

My eyes widen. "Into a retirement account?"

Shauna shakes her head. "No, the retirement plan for partners is generous as well, but it's a separate track. We can sit down and go over those numbers tomorrow. You're still coming in to meet with Bargain Booksy, right?"

"I am, and that's exceptionally generous," I say, "but for me it's not so much about the money."

Shauna grins. "That's one of the many reasons we appreciate you. Your priorities are nothing short of phenomenal, but think of all you could do with that extra income."

"The United Way would need to hire someone in my place, and that would cost them as much as I could donate, or awfully close after taxes."

"Accountants." Shauna shakes her head. "Take some time to make your decision, Mary. It's a big one, and we won't even announce my departure until the firm Christmas party. As long as we know the day before that, we'll have plenty of time to select another candidate or bring someone over from another office."

I'm relieved when our food arrives and the conversation shifts to the quality of the steak and accuracy of the requested temperature. I ask Shauna about her plans when she moves, and whether her daughter's excited. We discuss the plans for the expansion of the Atlanta office, and the hiring program. Clearly Shauna's dying for me to accept this position, and extra money's always nice, but at the end of the day, I don't need it. And the Sub-for-Santa program gives me a reason to wake up in the morning, a purpose, a goal.

I shake Peter's hand again after dinner. "It was a pleasure meeting you, and I'll give your offer a lot of thought."

He nods. "You do that. If you turn this down, it won't come around again, at least not anytime soon."

I'm walking out to my car when I hear my name.

"Mary," a deep, barely Aussie accented male voice yells.

When I turn around, Luke's smiling at me, his dimples visible from here. He waves at me wildly and jogs toward me. He looks even better with a black leather jacket on than he did inside. "Mary, what a coincidence to bump into you here. One might even go out on a limb and call it fate that threw us together again."

Oh good grief. "Maybe not such a coincidence, since you were eating dinner at the same time and place as me."

He shrugs. "What if I told you I finished eating half an hour ago, and I'm only here because I forgot my phone?"

"Really?"

He shakes his head. "No, although that does make for a more interesting story. The truth is, I waited on that bench by the door for no more than ten minutes. I probably would've waited half an hour, fair warning."

"I walked right past that bench."

"Yep, you did. You were so busy shaking hands with that old guy that you didn't even notice me. Does that count as my third rejection?"

I count them off on my hands. "Well, number one was refusing your drink. Number two was thinking you were a working man. Number three was not giving you my phone number when you asked. So I think that makes this number four. If you're keeping track."

"Since you weren't actually calling me a working man, I don't think that one counts. And I hear the third time's the charm." Luke smiles and I can't help but notice his adorable dimples. I don't want to get involved with anyone right now, not with so many other things going on, but he's unbelievably good-looking.

"Oh, fine." I dig an old receipt out of my purse, along with a pen, and scrawl 'Mary' and my number on the back.

Our hands brush when he takes it, and an electric zing travels all the way up my arm. It's such a strong reaction, that I don't know what to make of it. I almost snatch my number back. I don't have time to deal with a smooth operator anytime, much less at Christmas.

"I'll call you tomorrow," he says. "I'd love to take you to lunch."

I should tell him I'm busy. I shouldn't agree. For one thing, it's not how the game is played, but for another, he's altogether too eager. I decide to tell him no.

"I've been craving French food." The words fly out of my mouth in spite of my plans, but when he smiles again, I decide it's almost worth the risk.

"I'm guessing McDonald's fries don't count?" he asks.

I snort. "Uh, no. I was thinking more like La Madeleine's."

"I have no idea where that is." He whips out his phone. "If I text you, can you hit me back with an address for it?"

"Subtle," I say. "Making sure I didn't fake number you."

He shrugs. "Not my first rodeo, lady."

My phone bings. "I'm not a bronco, and I wasn't trying to buck you off."

"Good to know. Although a little bucking doesn't bother me."

I raise one eyebrow. "As long as you're respectful and listen."

"Yes, ma'am I always do."

"Then I guess it's a date."

His perfect, white teeth, and his beautiful eyes aren't a bad image on which to end the night. I hop into my car and close the door, but it doesn't stop me from watching him walk away.

CHAPTER 3

Peter and Shauna asked me to keep the offer a secret, so my text to Paisley is a lie. WENT OVER MY NUMBERS. THEY MAY WANT ME TO MOVE TO ACCOUNTING.

She texts me back right away. IF YOU'RE GOING, TAKE ME WITH YOU.

I smile. If I did take the promotion, Paisley would move up with me. OF COURSE. ALSO, I MET A GUY.

WHAT?!?

I THINK IT WAS YOUR DRESS. HE'S HOT, THOUGH, SO THANKS.

Paisley's been bugging me to go on a date for over a year, ever since Foster and I split. LIKE HOW HOT?

I roll my eyes, not that she can see me. HOTTER THAN FOSTER.

Her response is all emojis, heart eyes, the wow face, and party confetti. I swear, Paisley texts like a thirteen year old. A moment later, three dots appear, and she texts again. DOES HE HAVE A BROTHER?

I shake my head. HAVEN'T ASKED YET. PROBABLY NOT.

I CAN'T CATCH A BREAK. YOU OWE ME A PHOTO. HE LIKES YOU BECAUSE OF MY DRESS. ARE YOU SEEING HIM?

I can't mention that we've got a date tomorrow. She'd probably follow me to the restaurant to try and get a look at him. HE ASKED FOR MY NUMBER.

I STRONGLY PREFER SUMMER WEDDINGS.

I don't even reply to that. I can't encourage this sort of madness. The next morning, after my jog, I drive over to the United Way office. Over the holidays, I split time between United Way, and Foster & Meacham, coming here in the morning, and doing my real job in the afternoons. It's only eight in the morning, but Foster's always in early and I need to talk to him.

I wave to his assistant Heather as I pass her desk. She lifts one eyebrow, and I shake my head. "Is he busy?"

She smiles. "Mr. Bradshaw's always busy, but he's not in a bad mood."

"Thanks." I tap on the door and walk inside.

When Foster turns to face me, my heart skips a beat. His hair curls a little around his ears and at the base of his neck when he's overdue for a haircut, and I want to touch it, tuck it back in place. I miss having someone in my life, someone whose hair I'm supposed to fix. It's been a year, but it still stings a little bit at the strangest times. Sometimes he asks if I'm free for dinner and I wonder if we should give things another try, but I'm always busy even when I'm not really busy. Because he wants kids, and I'll never have any.

Foster leans back in his chair, his designer suit shifting along with him. Most presidents of a charitable organization wouldn't wear two thousand dollar suits every day, but Foster's a trust baby, so he owns nothing else. "I'm glad to see you made it safely home on the icy streets last night."

"There wasn't any ice, no need to worry." I sit down in one of the plain black chairs facing his modular desk. Foster's determined to pull the United Way out of the stone ages, and he started with the furniture.

"When I said we needed to talk, I didn't mean you had to rush in this morning before work."

I shrug. "As it happens, I need to talk to you too."

"Oh?" His eyebrows rise. "What about?"

"You can go first if you want."

"Ladies always go first." Foster may be a little old fashioned, but no one contests that he's a gentleman.

"Okay, well, I have a question I suppose. This is confidential, but last night I was offered a promotion at Frank & Meacham."

He scrunches his aquiline nose. "To what? Even better CPA?"

"Senior Partner, and head of the Atlanta office."

He whistles. "That's amazing, Mary. Major congratulations."

I shake my head. "I told them no."

He leans forward and braces his hands on this desk. "Why would you do that, Mary? I don't know anyone who loves their job as much as you do."

"Actually that's a large part of it. I love my job, preparing returns for people and businesses. I love the certainty, the absolute answer, the beauty and balance. I love helping people save money, and helping them fulfill their financial goals. But that's not all of it. If I took this job, I couldn't run Sub-for-Santa anymore."

Foster breathes in slowly through his nose. "You told them no already, like absolutely no?"

"I tried," I say, "but they told me to think about it for

three weeks."

His shoulders slump a little, and his eyes fall to his desk. "It's not great timing then, for my news I mean. Or, I don't know. Maybe it is."

Uh oh. "What's up?"

"The President of the United Way has been phasing out the Sub-for-Santa programs in various locations for years. They feel it doesn't reflect well on us, and makes us seem to support Christian beliefs at the expense of other religions and cultures."

"Wait, what? That's stupid. Santa isn't even a Christian construct."

Foster sighs. "Don't make this difficult, Mary. Santa is short for Saint Nicholas."

I close my eyes and force myself to count to ten.

"Don't be so melodramatic," he says. "If there hadn't been an enormous anonymous gift two years ago, they'd have cut the program then."

The substantial anonymous gift, otherwise known as my entire life savings. It was that, or no more Sub-for-Santa. It's nice to know my entire savings fund bought us two years. I've been replenishing my accounts ever since, but it's nowhere near recovered.

"Stan has asked me to provide him a timeline for phase out. He understands we can't halt it for this year, but he'd like us to develop a press release to issue just after the holidays. It should give the community time to process its termination before the holidays hit again next year."

I groan. "We've heard this before, and we've kept it going. Tell him you'll phase it out over five years or something. He'll quit or be fired in the next few years and we'll tell the new boss what a great program it is."

"I've pushed back before because I always had a strong leader willing to make things happen. We made sure it remained net neutral from a resource pull, and you've worked for free. If you leave, I'd need to hire a replacement, and that means a bigger chunk of the budget. I think we need to be realistic about this."

I grit my teeth. "Are you punishing me with this?"

The veins in his neck stand out. "It's been more than a year, Mary. Of course I'm not punishing you. This is about limited resources and allocating them in the best way possible. A way that allows United Way to grow and serve the community well into the next hundred years. This is off brand for us now, anyway."

"I can't see how bringing Christmas cheer will stymie United Way's growth. It's still good PR, right?"

"You're looking at this all wrong. This is an escape hatch for you. You can't make life altering decisions around a once a year charity," he says. "You've worked so hard at your job and at this, but it's time to focus on the one that matters to you."

"Sub-for-Santa changed my whole life, Foster, and if you can't see that—"

"I know it did. And you've paid it forward for a decade, running the whole thing yourself for the last seven years."

"Eight." I cross my arms over my chest.

"Fine, eight. But the point is that over time, things change and we have to accept them. There are plenty of other charities, some that run year round, where you could make a tremendous difference, but to do that, you have to let go of this obsession."

I no longer believe we're talking about Sub-for-Santa. "I have moved on, Foster. This decision has nothing to do with you, believe me. It's not like I'm holding on to this as an excuse to see you. I ran this program for five years before you even got the job you have now. Not everything is about you."

He stares at me. "Are you sure?"

I roll my eyes. "Are you kidding me? Yes, I'm sure. In fact, if your news was that you were offering me your job because you've been offered a transfer, I'd take it. Please move far, far away so I don't have to bump into you in dark parking lots anymore."

He purses his lips. "I guess this won't upset you, then. Last week, I proposed to my girlfriend Jessica, and she said yes. We've decided to do a simple wedding in my parents' backyard."

"Hold up." My eyes widen. "You're dating someone?"

"I didn't hide it, okay. More like, I kept it off the radar because I didn't want to hurt you. But I worried you'd hear about our engagement elsewhere and that might be a real shock."

"How long have you even known her?" I mentally tabulate when he proposed to me, a few weeks before Halloween. Last year. Fourteen months ago isn't that recent I guess.

"We met at a Fourth of July barbecue this year."

"You moved from a Christmas girl to an Fourth of July enthusiast?"

"Oh please." Foster crosses his arms. "She doesn't even like the Fourth. I doubt she could even recite the Pledge of Allegiance. She was a caterer at the party, that's all."

I'm over Foster, I really am. I loved him and he loved me, but he wanted something I couldn't give. I'm happy for him, but even so, it's hard to force the words society demands me to say out of my mouth.

I gulp once, and then say, "Congratulations. I'm happy

for you, and I'm sure you two will build a fantastic life together."

"It's all happened really fast, but it feels right and we're both delighted."

I stand up, eager to dive into work so I don't need to think about this anymore. "Well, thankfully, you won't need to worry about Sub-for-Santa. Since I'm not going anywhere, it'll stay budget neutral and you won't need to hire someone else. We can make up some stupid phase out plan and say the Mayor of Atlanta would be upset or something. You know him, don't you? Could you talk the program up to him and get a sound bite?"

Foster stands, too. "Trying to save a dying program is a mistake, and frankly, I'm not even sure I want to try."

My eyebrows fly upward. "I'm afraid you're not the judge of that. I'm the President of that program, even if I don't take the pay."

"You say you don't have time or energy for children, but you pour all your energy and money and time into this every year. These children aren't your kids, you know. And they never will be."

He stood up to emphasize his point. Well, that crap doesn't work on me. I sit back down and fold my arms. I won't leave until I'm good and ready. "You know that's a mischaracterization. I love children, but I won't have kids I can't dedicate enough of my time to, and I love my job. I won't do any children the disservice of having a mother who's never around. I won't have children, because I can't put them first in my life."

"I know, I know. Your mom chose her job and left your family. It destroyed your dad. But if you chose your career, and you're pursuing it, then when you get offered a promotion, take it. Don't hide behind excuses."

I slam my hand down on the corner of his desk. "Sub-for-Santa isn't an excuse, Foster. I have a chance to make a real difference. If even a few of these kids believe in something, if they believe that someone notices the good things they do, then I've done more than my parents ever did for me, in eighteen years."

"Well, I won't be able to help you save it, not this time. I've got too much to do with the wedding plans. You'll have to find sound bites and assemble data to present to Mr. Peters yourself."

"When is the wedding? You're probably worrying too much. The guy doesn't usually have to do much."

"It's December twenty-third."

I throw my hands up in the air. "That's only a few weeks away." Why would they get married so fast, and right before Christmas? I tilt my head. "What's the rush?"

"We want to make sure we get the tax break this year, and my parents are leaving for a transatlantic holiday cruise on Christmas Eve."

"Just a thought," I say, "but you don't need the couple of grand you'd save. So why not do it in January or February, or even go wild and wait until March."

"Jessica didn't want to wait."

"Why ever not?" It makes no sense. Foster's family would pay for everything, and help plan all the details. There's no reason to rush Christmas over a few thousand dollars. I've seen Foster drop that much on a new pair of dress shoes.

Unless.

I blurt it out without thinking it through. "Oh my gosh, she's pregnant, isn't she?"

Foster frowns. "It's a secret, Mary. Please respect that."

"Well, I'm glad you're finally getting everything I couldn't give you."

"Oh you could have. You just didn't want to."

I clench my jaw, but don't say another word.

I'm over him, but maybe I'm not entirely fine with how things went down. I swipe at an errant tear and spin around before rushing out his door.

CHAPTER 4

Foster follows me to the doorway, but my phone rings loudly down the hall, cutting him off before he can say anything. "I better take that. It's got to be a sponsor, because no one else has this number." I spin on my heel and jog around the corner to my office.

"Hello?"

"Mrs. Wiggin?" a male voice asks.

It's Miss, but close enough. "That's me. What can I help you with?"

"This is Mr. Manning. You left me a message about the Sub-for-Santa program. I've never done anything like this before, so I hope I didn't do anything wrong."

Completely unhelpful. He's never been a participant? Or a sponsor family? Ugh. "Yes," I say, "I did call you last night. We're in a bit of a confusing spot, but it might be easier to explain in person. Is there any chance I could come out and meet with you sometime this afternoon?"

"I'll be on the job until seven. Deadlines are in overdrive right now with the holidays. They're trying to finish my project and running a little over. I can meet you after that, if you don't mind coming to me."

His voice sounds vaguely familiar, but I can't think of anyone I know named Manning.

"I don't mind," I say. "What time will work for you?"

"Is eight o'clock too late?" he asks.

I scramble through the paperwork on my desk until I find the right nomination page. "That should be fine. Is your address still 236 Sunset Cove?"

"It sure is. I'll see you then."

I hang up my phone and force myself to work for the next few hours, drafting the nomination letter, updating guidelines and rules, revising the call for volunteers and call for nomination forms, and contacting churches and other clubs to ask for both nominations and sponsor families. I should've done it all in less than two hours, but glancing at the clock every two minutes slows me down.

I never should've agreed to go to lunch with this guy today. What was I thinking? At least I'm meeting him at the restaurant, so if it goes terribly, I can fake an emergency and bail. I squat down and practically crawl past Foster's office, ignoring Heather's giggling. I'd rather Heather think I'm a coward than have to interact with Mr. Perfect and listen to him highlight all my many flaws again. Once a year is more than enough for that.

I pull up in the parking lot of La Madeleine's and cut the engine. My hands still grip the steering wheel. Am I wasting my time here? Maybe I should skip this whole thing and head for my office to get ready for my three o'clock audit meeting.

Not that I need to prepare. And my stomach's growling. I force myself to let go of the steering wheel, climb out of my car, and walk into the restaurant.

Luke's sitting on a bench just inside the door in faded

jeans and a dark blue tee shirt that clings to his chest muscles, reading a book. An honest to goodness book, not something on his iPad, e-reader, or phone. Before he notices I'm here, I glance at the title. *Percy Jackson and the Lightning Thief.* I can't quite contain my giggle.

He glances up at me, his light eyes connecting with mine, and grins. Beautiful white teeth, and dimples. He tucks the book into a black bag, and stands up, slinging it over his shoulder. "You came. I might have been a little worried. I don't usually have to work so hard to convince someone to spend time with me."

I can see why.

"I hope you're hungry, because I'm starving, and it's bad first date etiquette if you eat less than me."

"I'm always hungry. Ravenous, actually, so you can eat whatever you want without fear."

"Good word," I say. "This is a modified buffet so you can get whatever a hungry wolf might want."

He mock growls. "Perfect. I have a tendency to bite whatever's close when I've waited too long to eat."

I pick a quiche, a salad, and a bowl of fruit, but he loads his plate up with pasta, fruit, a salad, and both a chicken and mushroom friand.

"I had no idea wolves liked lettuce," I say while the cashier rings us up.

"I make an exception when strawberries or poppy seed dressing are involved." He hands the cashier a credit card before I can stop him. "My treat, I insist. I know you're an impressive boss lady, but I'm kind of old fashioned like that."

"Thanks, but for future reference, I don't mind paying."

"Neither do I. How's this? As long as I'm begging you to make time for me, you let me pay. Once you realize what a catch I am and start begging me for a date, then I'll let you pick up the tab a few times."

Luke follows me to a table near the window, and we put our food down. I place my plate, my glass and my utensils on the table and put my tray above the trash cans to make room on the table. Luke's already eating when I return, so I dive in too. I alternate between a bite of quiche and a bite of salad and a bite of fruit.

"What do you do for a living?" he asks.

"I'm—"

"Wait, actually, don't tell me. I bet I can guess."

This should be good. "Sure, what do you think I do?"

"You're either a wedding planner or an accountant," he says.

My jaw drops. "You can't know that."

"You've sliced each item into perfectly even pieces, and you're switching from salad to that egg pie and then to fruit, evenly dividing all of it. That kind of precision means you're a perfectionist. Your impeccably clean slacks and button down shirt tell me you're not an artist. And you have a purse that more closely resembles a trendy briefcase."

I glare at him. "I'm an accountant."

He smirks. "What do you think I do?"

"You're fit, and you have a black bag. You're free for lunch, and you ate at a steakhouse last night, but probably not for work. You were wearing a polo shirt, and you met someone who didn't seem like a frequent flyer at the steakhouse."

He flexes his arms. "You think I'm fit, huh?"

I roll my eyes. "And confident, so I'm going with . . . You own a gym."

He pulls out a pen and draws on a napkin, first a few lines that form a hangman's post and noose. Then a head.

"You've got the body, arms, legs, and if I'm feeling generous fingers and toes, before you die." He puts his hands around his neck and pretends to choke.

"Really?"

"I didn't make up the rules, lady. You look like you need a little encouragement, and that first guess was way off."

I wrack my brain. He was reading Percy Jackson while he waited. Could he have been reading it for work? "You're in publishing?"

He shakes his head and draws a torso. "Even further away. You can do better than that."

I look at his hands. Calloused and worn. "You do something with your hands."

He draws an arm.

"That wasn't even a job," I protest. "I was just thinking out loud."

"You were fishing for information. Rules are rules."

I frown. "Carpenter? Artist?"

He draws another arm and a leg. "By traditional rules, it's one more guess until game over." He draws a line across his throat.

Oh, come on. "Fine, you're an installation artist."

He draws the last leg slowly, almost mournfully. "At least we had that one, epically good first date. Do you give up?"

I sigh. "I thought I had fingers and toes."

"Maybe I'm not feeling generous."

"You did just pay for my huge lunch."

"True. I think that tapped me out. Since I won and you lost, you owe me some kind of forfeit."

I roll my eyes. "What did you have in mind?"

"Lunch again tomorrow?" He grins.

"I'm not sure I can commit to anything like that until I

know what you do. What if you're an assassin, or a funeral home director?"

He opens his mouth in mock horror. "I *am* a funeral home director."

I shake my head. "You'd smell like formaldehyde, so obviously that's not it."

"Umm, that's my embalmer. All I do is wear drab suits and pretend to care about all the families who are grieving."

"It's an act? You don't really care?"

He shrugs. "You can't care about the whole world."

"Wow, I guess not, but the people you see just lost a loved one."

He rolls his eyes. "Oh fine, I'm not a funeral home director. I'm a beautician."

"Oh please."

"What?" He runs his hand through his hair. "Why couldn't I be a beautician?"

"I'm not even going to respond to that."

He grins. "Fine, I'm not a beautician, either."

Thank goodness. "Give me a clue, then. What's the worst part of your job?"

He taps his bottom lip, and I can't help notice how full it is. He is way, way too good looking for me.

"I get asked to help people with things around their house for free all the time."

My eyes widen. "You're a plumber?"

He shakes his head. "Warmer, though."

"You're a cable guy?"

He shakes his head. "Nope."

"An electrician?"

"Bingo." He grins and my heart drops. No one should have such a beautiful smile.

"How did an electrician afford dinner at Bentleys last night?"

"My, my," he says, "aren't you a snob? As it happens, I'm excellent at what I do. I'm the master electrician on the new Citibank building."

"Interesting."

"Is that impressive enough to justify a second date?"

"You make me sound like a gold digger. I just wanted to make sure you weren't a stripper, or something."

"You think I could be a stripper?" His eyebrows rise.

I blush. "No, I'm not saying I thought you were. I meant, I wanted to verify you weren't something embarrassing, like a con man."

He frowns. "I'm feeling like your past few first dates weren't so great. Besides, if I was a con man, I wouldn't own up to it, would I?"

I guess not. "Maybe I need to test your claim before I can agree to a second date. I've got a closet light that went out. If you're really an electrician, you can fix it. And this isn't me asking you for an annoying favor. I'm just doing my due diligence."

"Did you already try replacing the light bulb?"

"Cheeky," I say. "I'm not an absolute moron. Of course I checked that."

He grins. "I'll fix your light if you'll help me with a little something."

"What's that?"

"I haven't paid taxes in nine years, and the IRS gets more persistent every year."

I bolt upright in my chair. "Are you kidding right now? That's not good news. Nine years?"

He places his hand over mine, and my heart races even faster. "You should see your face! Mary, calm down, it was a joke. Do you really have a closet light that's not working?"

I nod my head, numbly.

He snorts. "I totally thought you were kidding, too. And I'd be happy to help you with a closet light. Wouldn't even take me half an hour. I might fix it in five minutes with a wire nut."

"So." I clear my throat while my heart decelerates. "You do pay your taxes?"

"I'm sensing this would be a deal breaker," he says.

"Uh," I sigh. "Yeah, it would, which probably makes me seem a little uptight. If you had any idea how often clients walk through my door who haven't paid in years." I shake my head.

"You must really care about your job." He takes his last bite of pasta.

I look from my empty plate to his. He ate three entrees. Holy cow. "I love my job, but each of those people's lives are in jeopardy when they let things go that far. It's nerve-wracking. I don't know how people like that even function."

"You work at a tax firm, then?" he asks.

I nod. "Yeah, filing returns. But now I've got this big wrench I have to deal with."

He tilts his head sideways. "Like what? I'm pretty handy with wrenches. Maybe I can help."

I glance around the restaurant. I don't see anyone else I know, and it's not like an electrician and I would run in the same circles anyway. "I was at Bentleys last night because my boss is moving to London to revamp things there, and they needed to talk to me about it."

He places both his hands on the table, palms down. "But you aren't moving?"

I shake my head. "My boss went to Oxford for undergrad and she's married to a Brit. She's familiar with their complicated tax code, and their culture, so she's the ideal candidate to bring our American firm's first European office up to speed."

"How does that affect you?"

I shrug. "She's been my mentor from before I even graduated from college. She brought me out for my first internship, so obviously I'll miss her. Maybe that's why they're offering me her job, now that she's leaving. They want me to head up the entire office."

"Isn't that wonderful?" he asks. "A big promotion, right?"

I nod. "It pays a lot more, that's for sure, but I don't know."

"Money isn't everything."

"A lot of people who have plenty of money say that."

He shrugs. "I'm an electrician."

"True." I nod. "More money makes things easier, but I just don't know."

"If you'd appreciate the raise, what's the problem?"

"First of all, I love what I do. I like the simple expediency of taking pieces and plugging them in, and I like helping people. The smile on someone's face when I tell them I've gotten them an extra thousand or sometimes even just an extra couple hundred dollars. The relief when someone's put off filing for years and we work through it all, and set up a payment plan they can manage. The clear-cut sense of accomplishment when I wade through a gosh awful box of receipts and notes and form them into piles, or when I hand a client their complicated business return that's tied up with a bow."

"So turn it down," he says. "It may be a tired cliché, but money really isn't everything."

"The head of the company says if I turn this down, it

won't be offered again. And I have no idea what kind of boss they might bring in instead. What if he or she is horrible? I could probably do a few returns as the Office President, plus I'd be a partner in the firm, which has a lot of benefits. I'd even get control over new offices, and policies, and I'd be the final say in recruitment. We could finally hire the same number of women as men."

"Maybe you should take it, then." He points at the dessert counter. "Would a cookie help you feel better about this terrible dilemma? Your job loves you so much they want to promote you, but you're not sure if you will like being super fancy, and getting way more money."

I lean back in the chair. "Cookies always help."

"I knew you were my kind of girl."

I tap my fingers on the table. "But I haven't even told you the hard part. I run a charity that I absolutely love, and my job right now is intense for most of the spring, and again in the early fall, but summer is low key, and I almost have the holidays off. If I take the promotion, I won't get holidays off anymore, and I can't run the charity anymore. Also, if it's not bad enough that I'd miss out on doing something I love, the head of the non-profit told me if I leave, the program ends."

He exhales. "Well, if you don't care about the money, and you like your job, and you love this charity, I think it's pretty clear you should turn it down. Pray for a good boss, and if you get a bad one, keep to your office and think bad thoughts about him or her."

"How about that dessert," I say. "Because I think you're right, and anyone who finds out what I'm going to do is going to think I'm an idiot."

He raises his eyebrows. "You just made your decision, that fast? I'm surprised you have that much confidence in the opinions of a stranger."

I stand up and point at the dessert counter. "I didn't decide because of you. I've been thinking the same thing all day. My reasons for taking the job are: money, pride, and convenience. Those don't outweigh my reasons for turning it down. Doing what I love at work and on my time off matters more than having a padded bank account. After all, I have enough money for whatever I need. I should be content with that."

We cross the room and I peer into the rows and rows of gorgeous French sweets. Éclairs, madeleine's, coconut cookies, fruit tarts of several varieties. I point at a strawberry tart, and Luke orders a blueberry muffin and a strawberry napoleon.

"For what it's worth, I think contentment's an underrated value," Luke says as he pays the cashier.

"What do you mean?" I sit down with my strawberry tart and take a bite.

"Finding joy in what you already have goes a long way toward making the world a better place. If you're always wishing you had something better, you'll never be happy with the present."

"So right now, if I was regretting my dessert choice?"

He grins. "I'd say you could trade straight across for either of mine."

"I already took a bite of this one."

Luke shrugs. "I've always lived dangerously. I'll brave your cooties."

I eye my options. A blueberry muffin with raw sugar on top, and a perfectly layered napoleon with custard, berries, pastry dough, and a sugared topping with almonds. "That strawberry napoleon looks amazing."

He jabs it with his fork, cutting off a perfect sized bite, then he passes it to me.

"You aren't going to insist on feeding me?"

"Did we fall back into 1954 and I missed it? You're capable of feeding yourself. I'd never patronize you that way."

His napoleon is way better than my tart. I slide my plate across the table, and he hands me his. "I'd just like it noted for the record, that I won."

I cough. "I'm sorry, you won what?"

"Well, first I guessed your job on the first try."

"You said wedding planner."

"Wedding planner, or accountant."

I roll my eyes.

"And, obviously I picked the best dessert."

"Wait, so you picked the best dessert, and I took it. What happens when I win?" I ask.

He takes a bite of my strawberry tart. "You can keep it."

"So lemme get this straight, in the interest of establishing clear dating rules. If I win, I keep my dessert."

He nods.

"If you win, I get to take the dessert you won with?" I raise one eyebrow.

He smiles. "That's how my parents always did it."

"Did?"

He looks down at the sad strawberry tart, one bite missing. "Mum passed away two years ago."

"I'm so sorry," I say.

"Dad's not doing so well with it, either. He's lonely. The doctors say he can't die of a broken heart, but he's doing his best to prove them wrong."

"Does he live in Australia?" I ask.

He shakes his head. "He and mum moved out here seven years ago. I wonder sometimes if that's part of the problem. They wanted to be closer to me, but they both missed their friends in Perth."

"How often do you get to see him?" I ask.

"Almost every day. He's in the assisted living off of Townsend, by the new Hilton. In fact, I'm supposed to go by and see him before I head back to work." He glances at his watch.

"What time is it?" I ask.

"One fifteen."

I take one more big bite and stand up. "I've got a meeting I need to prepare for."

"Good timing then." He motions for me to walk first, and then follows me out of the restaurant. He walks me over to my car.

He leans toward me, and time stands still. I realize he's going to kiss me, and my heart races. Until he reaches past me and opens my door.

My heart skids to a halt. Not a kiss. Just a gentlemanly gesture.

His breath puffs out in a white cloud in the brisk air. "Good luck with your meeting."

I hope he didn't notice that I turned toward him, lips parted, eyes eager. I cast my eyes down at the car door, and slide into the seat. I pull my keys out, and toss my purse on the passenger side seat. "I hope your dad's doing well. You'd think he'd be a real hit with the ladies, what with his accent and all."

"It's hard when you've lost someone. For the first few years, all you can think about it the love you lost. It becomes almost a pattern, the sorrow, the regret, the longing."

He sounds like a really good son, like he's really given a lot of thought to how his dad must feel.

"My dad never got over my mom leaving," I say, "and she didn't even die."

He shakes his head. "I don't even care if he gets over Mum. I'm okay with him never finding someone new. I just wish he'd try to make some friends, or do anything but lay in bed and watch crime shows."

"Crime shows depress me, and I didn't recently lose the love of my life. I can only imagine how depressing they'd be if my wife had died."

Luke winces, and steps back from the car.

I don't know what I said wrong, but he doesn't even wave back when I pull away.

The preparation for the Bargain Booksy meeting only takes ten minutes, thanks to Paisley's competency. I check my phone when I'm through reviewing the file and I have two texts from Luke.

THIS IS LUKE, SORRY I WAS WEIRD WHEN YOU LEFT. LONG DAY.

It's promising that he noticed he was being odd.

I HAD A GREAT TIME. CAN I SEE YOU AGAIN TOMORROW?

I type back as quickly as I can, a smile plastered on my face. SURE. TIME? PLACE?

INDIAN FOOD?

I LOVE INDIAN, YES. NOON?

I watch my phone until the dots turn into a reply. OUCH. STILL ON THE FENCE ABOUT ME?

WHY DO YOU SAY THAT? I ask.

I'VE BEEN LUNCH-ZONED.

I chortle, and I'm glad he can't hear me.

"How was lunch?" Paisley asks from behind me.

I jump and slide my phone into my top drawer. "I don't know what you mean."

"You can't fool me. We left United Way at the same time, and you took forever to get here. You met that guy from last night for lunch."

I suppress a smile.

"And you like him." She perches on the edge of my desk. "Spill."

"There's nothing to spill," I say. "I stopped for food."

Her eyebrows rise. "Oh my gosh, you really like him! Otherwise, you'd tell me."

I shake my head.

"Oh please," she says. "You can stop covering it up, because you're smiling like a loon, and you've barely listened to anything I said for the last half hour."

"I'm just happy to be working on Sub-for-Santa again."

Paisley points at my shirt. "You sure? Because you've got a little bit of strawberry tart on your lapel there, and you never eat dessert at lunch unless you're on a date."

I glance down, and she's right. I swear, and rush to the bathroom to clean it off.

Paisley's voice follows me down the hallway. "You still owe me a photo!"

When I return, it's five minutes until my meeting. "Pais, can you get a message to Shauna? Tell her I need to talk to her this afternoon and try and get fifteen minutes on my calendar after this meeting, if possible?"

Paisley nods. "Of course, but what should I tell her it's about?" She grins innocently. Which is how I know she's prying.

I promised Shauna I'd keep the whole thing a secret, which means I can't tell Paisley either. "Not everything is noteworthy," I say. "Just schedule the time."

Paisley harrumphs, but I know she'll do it.

My client shows up late, but the IRS representative is reasonable and it moves along quickly. One more meeting and we should reach an acceptable compromise. After all, it's not like my client's a huge conglomerate. I walk my clients out, and when I reach my office, a post it note's stuck to my screen. It reads: Meeting with Shauna at four-thirty.

It's four o'clock now.

I sit down at my desk and close my eyes, mentally preparing what I'll say. I appreciate her offer, and I know she's been my mentor and my champion for years. I appreciate her help and her interest in me, and I'll miss her dearly, but I don't want to run an office. I only want to prepare tax returns.

The ringing from my phone startles me, and I pick up the receiver automatically.

"I've been calling you for like two hours," my little sister Trudy says.

My cell phone was in my drawer. I slap my forehead.

"What's wrong?" I ask.

"Troy's in the hospital. It's not good, Mary. Can you come see us?"

"Of course. I'll be right there."

CHAPTER 5

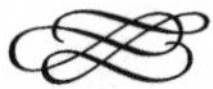

I stuff my phone in my bag and jog past the poinsettias that sit on the corner of almost every desk. I almost knock one over on my way down the hall to Shauna's office. When I poke my head inside, even though I'm half an hour early, she stands up, her eyes wide.

"Mary, you look upset. Are you okay?"

I shake my head. "My sister's little boy Troy is in the hospital."

Shauna's eyes widen. "I assume you wanted to talk to me about the job?"

I nod my head.

"We can talk about that later. Go take care of your sister."

Before I have time to turn around and go, Shauna crosses the space between us and pulls me in for a hug. She doesn't let go until I pull away.

"Thanks," I say. "I needed that. I'm sure he's fine, but he's only three and a half. She didn't give me any details, just said she needed me."

"You've always been there for her, and she'll be fine. So will Troy."

I nod, and blink away tears. I'm really going to miss having Shauna around. I hope they find a good replacement for her, someone who remembers my nephew's name, and someone who sees people and not just numbers around the office.

I don't get a ticket for speeding the entire way to the hospital, in spite of going at least twenty over the entire way. Maybe it's a good sign.

I'm winded by the time I reach the nursing station on the fourth floor of the hospital. I run five days a week. Why am I winded from jogging up some stairs? It's embarrassing.

I race down the hall until I see the name TROY written in black sharpie on a red stocking stuck to one of the large, metal hospital doors. I swing it open quietly, and creep inside. My sister's sitting on the hospital bed, rocking tiny Troy back and forth in her arms. He's whimpering quietly. I wait in the doorway until he drifts off to sleep, and Trudy transfers him into the bed. She tiptoes over to where I'm standing and pulls the curtain closed.

When she mouths the words, "Get food," I follow her out the door.

She pulls the door almost closed and then inclines her head to the right, toward the nursing station. I follow her over to it, and Trudy stops, waving to catch their attention. "Troy's finally asleep. I hope he'll stay that way, but please call my cell if I'm still downstairs when he wakes up. I'm going to try and grab something to eat."

"We can bring you a tray," a short nurse with a bob offers.

Trudy shakes her head. "I don't want him to wake up and see me eating, well you know."

Eating? What's wrong with Troy seeing her eating something? "What—"

Trudy cuts me off. "I'll explain in a minute."

A tall, black nurse with kind eyes clucks. "I understand." She writes down Trudy's cell phone. Her nametag identifies her as Patty. "I'll wait outside his door to listen for any sounds."

Trudy grabs Patty's hand and squeezes it. "Thank you."

Patty's eyes crinkle when she smiles. "I know it's scary, but it's going to be alright, honestly. This is very common."

We walk past a box of stuffed animals, the Grinch on top, the toy donation boxes, and the Make-A-Wish-Tree on the way down to the cafeteria. Trudy doesn't speak when we walk down the stairs, around the corner, or through the line. I choose things from a cafeteria lineup for the second time today, but this time with far poorer options. When we sit down and she digs into her food like a stray dog, I can't take any more silence.

"You didn't tell me anything on the phone. What's going on?" I ask.

"I'll tell you. I'm just hungry. I haven't had a bite to eat since we got here."

"How long ago was that?" I ask. "And if it's been a while, where in the world is Chris?" I may not like her husband very much, but he's like gum on the bottom of her shoe, always there to make a mess.

Trudy frowns. "Chris left us last month."

My jaw drops. "No. He couldn't have."

She swallows slowly and takes another bite without meeting my eyes.

"Why, why didn't you call me?" I ask. "Surely you were upset. Devastated."

She nods.

"Then why am I only hearing about it now?" I touch her arm. "Gertrude?"

"I couldn't say anything to you. You've been telling me all along I should make sure I'm ready to handle my life if anything goes wrong. You thought I was an idiot for marrying him."

"That's not true," I say halfheartedly. "Technically I thought he was the idiot, not you."

She sighs heavily. "You have a degree and a career, and you said loving Chris was a mistake, and you told me not to have a kid right away, to get a degree, or at least to have a job long enough to make progress with my career, but I ignored you. Love mattered more to me than security, and now Chris is gone, and all I have is Troy. My dear sweet baby, and no job, and no money, and no plan."

"You have me."

She drops her fork, and her spoon and looks at her feet. "Troy's sick, Mary. Really sick, like for the rest of his life the doctor says." She chokes up, the last words barely coming out at all. "I'm sorry to dump all this on you while you're running your program or whatever, but I didn't know what to do. I never know what to do."

I want to shake her and tell her I'll always love her no matter what. I want to tell her I'd never say 'I told you so'. But right now she doesn't need anything that feels like chastisement or judgment, even if it's about not calling me soon enough. Trudy needs support, so I let go of all my frustration and cut to the crux of the issue. "What's wrong? How exactly is Troy sick?"

"He's been thirsty all the time, and drinking cup after cup of milk, and then when we ran out, cup after cup of water. He's lost a lot of weight I guess too, and he complains that his body aches. He even has some bruising we can't explain."

"And?" I want to yell at her for not calling me, for not taking him in earlier, but I bite my tongue.

"Today he passed out, so I rushed him over here. I called Chris and he thinks I'm making all of it up."

I don't call him any of the creative names I come up with in my head. I don't call Chris on the phone and yell at him. I clench my fists under the table where Trudy can't see them, and then I let my breath out slowly. I'm proud of how calm I sound when I say, "What do the doctors say?"

She shudders. "At first they thought he had leukemia, but after running some tests, oh Mary, at least it's not leukemia, but it's going to impact every single day for the rest of his life. Troy's diabetic. Type one. He'll need insulin forever, and if I don't do a good job with his diet and his medicine, and if he doesn't act and eat responsibly, he could lose his feet and his eyesight." She bursts into tears. "It's all so horrible."

Insulin is expensive. Testing and measuring and caring for him is expensive. I shake my head. "Did they say how much it would cost to get him stabilized and buy all the equipment he needs? Your deductible portion, I mean?"

Trudy shakes her head, and whispers, "I don't have insurance."

"Wait, what? What about Medicaid or CHIP?"

A tear runs down her face. "Chris didn't want to pay for it, since we're all healthy. He makes too much to qualify for Medicaid, and since we're still married, I can't get it, either."

I close my eyes and breathe in and out once, then twice. "How much are they saying you'll need, Gertrude?"

"Well, for just this stay, it's probably going to be twe-twe-" She starts crying again, and I pat her back until she calms down. "Twenty thousand."

I nod. "That's okay. I can help. It's going to be alright."

"One of the pediatricians told us about a new protocol for children under seven who are diagnosed."

"Okay," I say. "And?"

"He said if there's any way we can afford it, we need to try to do it."

"And?" I wish she'd just spit it out.

"It's a fifty thousand dollar enrollment, with another fifty thousand in costs over the first year," she says, "but they're seeing amazing results at keeping their sugar levels consistent. Apparently what causes nerve damage and shortens his life is the inconsistency of sugar levels."

I nod my head. "You didn't tell me about Chris."

Her mouth drops open, and she shakes her head.

"And you've been here all day."

"Yeah," she says, glancing anywhere but my face.

"You didn't call me until you needed money."

Trudy twists her napkin until it begins to shred. It's not the first time she's asked me for money, but it's the first time she's asked for quite so much. "I don't want to ask you, but I don't know who else I can ask."

I lean back against my chair and groan. "I'm not upset you're asking me for money Trudy! I'm upset you didn't ask me for any help until now."

Her eyebrows draw together and her lower lip wobbles, just like it did every time my dad yelled, every time she scored poorly on a test, every time she got nothing but a new toothbrush from me for her birthday. My heart breaks all over again.

"I'm your family. I'm here for you. You should have called me the second Chris started being a butthead. The second you thought Troy was sick." I lift her chin until she's looking in my eyes. "You and Troy need a place to stay, right?"

She shakes her head.

"Of course you do. You can move in with me. I've got a three bedroom house, and I don't even use the other two bedrooms. That should save you some money in the long run. Beyond that, I may have a way to get the money you need quickly, and even if I don't, I can take out a loan or cash out a retirement fund, okay?"

Trudy leaps across the table to hug me, knocking my bland soup over and onto the floor in the process. She hasn't changed a bit in twenty years. In spite of her carelessness and her inability to plan ahead, I love her and I'll do anything for her. She collapses against my collarbone, sobbing noiselessly like always. I pet her hair slowly until she stops.

Once Trudy's calmer, and she's eaten, she heads back upstairs and I meet with the financial office. She wasn't wrong about the figures she quoted me, and it looks like the clinical trial really is the cutting edge of treatment for young children with Type One.

I guess it's a lucky break I haven't turned Shauna down yet, because money may not be everything, but it's pretty important when you need it. I guess I'm not going to turn down that promotion after all.

CHAPTER 6

When I finish filling out financial responsibility paperwork for the woman at the business office, I hike back up to the fourth floor. I'm breathing heavy again when I reach Troy's room. I make a mental note to add some stairs to my normal route.

"Did you take the stairs all the way up here?" Trudy asks me.

I nod.

"What's wrong with you?" she asks. Troy's awake now, and sitting on his mother's lap. She shifts Troy so he can see me. "Aunt Mary always does things the hard way."

Says the woman who struggled through all this alone until she monetarily absolutely had to call me. I shove aside any annoyance. With the day she's had, Trudy gets a pass.

I walk toward her, my eyes focused on Troy's angelic face. "Aunt Mary sits all day at work, so she tries to be active whenever she can."

"Aunt May May will play." Troy slips off his mom's lap and pads across the floor to where I'm standing, his short arms raised high. I lean over and pick him up under his armpits, careful not to jostle the IV port. It may not be plugged into anything right now, but I imagine a bump or tug would still hurt.

"How you doing, kiddo? You being a brave little prince?"

He nods and leans his head against my shoulder. "They been poking me all day, and I only cried a little."

"I certainly hope they brought you Jell-O.

"Nope." He shakes his head forlornly.

Nurse Patty, as if we'd paged her, knocks twice and walks in the door with a dinner tray. "We need to get you hooked up again little man, and once we're monitoring you, if you eat your dinner, you can have this blue Jell-O."

Trudy frowns. "Is that safe right now?"

Patty grins. "It's sugar free, don't you fret. We're taking care of this."

Trudy and I read Troy his choices of a variety of books the hospital had on hand, and then we tuck him into bed.

"I'd stay with you," I say, "but I've got a meeting at eight tonight."

"Sub-for-Santa?" she asks.

"Yeah, sorry. I can cancel if I need to?"

She smiles. "I'm lucky to have a sister like you. I don't tell you enough. You've done plenty. No, go to your meeting."

I put one hand on her shoulder. "You're going to be okay, and you know, Troy's lucky too, to have you for a mom."

"You'd make a wonderful mother," she says. "I've always thought so."

I shake my head. "Never. I love my job, remember?"

"Some people do both, you know."

"Not well. I've never met someone who's a truly good mother, and also manages a successful career."

"What about Shauna?" Trudy asks.

"Shauna loves her daughter, but she sees her like five hours a week. I can't do that. I won't do that."

"You aren't anything like our mom, you know. Or Dad, either."

I don't need my baby sister's psychoanalysis of my brain, thanks. Especially since she was an inch from a breakdown an hour ago.

"I'll call you tomorrow to work out the details of you moving in with me."

"We've paid for the entire month of December," Trudy says. "And Chris is stuck paying the utilities. Maybe we should wait until after Christmas. I feel like Troy's been through enough as it is."

I shrug. "Whatever you think."

By the time I reach my car, I've got less than twenty minutes to reach Mr. Manning's house. Luckily traffic has died down enough that I make it with two minutes to spare. My GPS leads me to an RV park at the edge of Decatur. It's in a surprisingly nice area, practically surrounded by mansions, or as close as it gets to mansions this close to the square. I wonder how annoyed all the neighbors are that there's an RV park smack in the middle of all their posh housing developments.

A sign on the front entrance of the park reads: The Cove. One side of the hanging mechanism has broken off, leaving the sign to dangle alarmingly.

I'm pretty sure I've identified which submission was correct. I could've saved myself a lot of time if I'd thought to check out his address on Google maps. Live and learn, I suppose. Although now that I'll be taking the new job, I won't need to manage these situations anymore. This will be my last year to manage them at all. I choke down my disappointment, because now's not the time to wallow. I drive into the RV Park and move past lot after lot until I reach the space labeled 236.

I park my car next to an old mustang sitting up on cinder blocks, and rummage around in the back seat of my sedan for an eligibility form. If I've come all the way out here, I may as well do the preliminary assessment and leave Mr. Manning the materials to finalize his family's enrollment in the program for this Christmas. I climb the steps up to the door, and knock softly in case children are sleeping. When the door opens, I look into Luke's face blankly. I can't seem to look away, and I have no idea what to say.

His light blue-green eyes look like the surf crashing over a white sand beach in this light, and his hair's slightly mussed. How can this be happening?

Luke's mouth drops and he looks over my shoulder, as though he's expecting to see someone behind me.

"Uh," I sputter. I finally ask, "What are you doing here? And where's Mr. Manning?"

"I am Mr. Manning," he says with his faint Australian accent, and suddenly it clicks. The voice on the phone I couldn't quite place, because I'd only heard it once before at the time. "Lucas Manning, but I go by Luke."

The world stops spinning, and I can't make sense of anything. The man I met in the bar at Bentleys? He's Lucas Manning, the guy who showed up on both lists for Sub-for-Santa? How?

"Mary, what are you doing here? Why are you being so weird about my name?" He steps outside, forcing me back down the steps. "I'd invite you inside, but it's a mess, and I have a meeting in a few—" he glances at his watch, "well, right now actually."

He still has no idea why I'm here. "You're Lucas Manning." I tilt my head and take in his RV. "Because you never told me your last name." I scratch my head with my free hand. "Actually, you never really told me your first name either."

"I go by Luke, usually. It's pretty common for people named Lucas." His eyes glance down at my clipboard, and it finally hits him. "Wait, your charity that you run every year. It's Sub-for-Santa?"

I nod.

His laugh fills his belly and echoes against the neighboring trailers and RVs.

"It's not that funny," I say. "And once you realize why I'm here. . ."

He snatches the clipboard out of my hands. "What's this?" He glances down at the forms and I clench my hands. He's a master electrician. He's taking me out to dinner, but he lives here? In a travel trailer in an RV park?

"You think I'm supposed to be a participant in the program?" His eyebrows rise precipitously.

"Your name was written in both categories. That's why I came out in person, to figure out where you belong." I don't mean to, but my eyes track behind him to the doorframe of his trailer.

He chuckles. "Church-going busy bodies. I suppose I should be grateful they care, but it's not helping my dating game, is it?"

I shrug. "Look, if you tell me you don't qualify, I'll remove you from the list. It's that simple."

He snorts. "I'm not quite Bill Gates, or even Jeff Bezos, but I don't qualify for a subsidized Christmas."

I smack my forehead. "Of course you don't. You don't even have kids."

He clears his throat. "I don't qualify because I make

plenty of money. We live in a trailer because it's more convenient for me since I move often from job to job. But if I were poor, I'd definitely be eligible."

We?

Luke pushes the door behind him open further, and I hear the familiar sounds of *Bubble Guppies* streaming through the doorway. And he was reading Percy Jackson earlier. Not because he's in publishing. Not because he loves fast paced mythological stories come to life. Because he has children, of course. I'm so stupid.

"Of course you have kids. I'm so sorry. I have no idea how I missed that."

"I didn't mention them. I usually wait until the second date for that. You'd be surprised how often women are put off by a man who has kids full time. But not you clearly, since you run a charity for children."

"It's pretty rare for the dad to have custody," I say. "Maybe that's the bigger surprise."

Luke frowns. "I think Dad gets custody close to one hundred percent of the time when mom dies."

My eyes bug out. "I am so, so, very sorry. I can't seem to pull my foot out of my mouth today."

"It has been a strange day," he says. "I think you get a pass. Beth's been gone for almost four years, and I still don't like to talk about it. It's probably my fault. It may also be why I wait to tell women until a second or third date. See, once they know I have kids. . ."

"You have to tell them what happened to their mother."

He nods. "And it's kind of a conversation doorstop."

"I guess so." In fact, our current conversation has effectively ground to a halt. I rock back and forth on my feet.

"Well, now that I know I don't have a stuffy case worker showing up imminently, you're welcome to come inside."

"Oh, that's funny. Because I'm the stuffy case worker."

He shrugs. “Maybe a little less stuffy than I expected.”

“What a glowing recommendation,” I say, “but I can't stay. I have a lot of paperwork I didn't finish today that I need to do tonight. But if you and your children still want to help with Sub-for-Santa by sponsoring a family, I'm delighted to make sure you remain on the appropriate list and are removed from the other.”

He grins. “That would be great.”

He waves at me when I get into my car, and then ducks back inside.

I should've told him to his face, and explained in person, but it has been a long day, and I chickened out. When I reach my own house, and pull into the garage, I whip out my phone. I close my eyes and think about Luke's dimples. His beautiful eyes, his witty banter. It's been years since I've looked forward to a date as much as I was looking forward to tomorrow's lunch.

When I open my eyes again, I've already gotten a text message from Luke, before even sending him one. It's a photo of Luke’s grinning face next to a little boy who looks just like him, sticking out his tongue. On the left, a dark blonde girl in pigtails is making a duck face, her lips pursed, her eyes sassy.

I wish he hadn't sent me a photo. It makes it so much harder for me to do what I have to do. But those beautiful children deserve a good mother. Luke deserves a wife who can take his first wife's place, not someone who wants to be chained to a desk. Not someone who will miss out on math competitions, and have no time to help with the science fair. Those kids need a mom who will give them fresh cookies and milk when they come home from school.

My mom left us for her job, and I will never, ever do that to a child of mine. If I didn't love my job so much, this wouldn't be so hard. But I won't ever abandon my child, because I'll never have one.

I should wait until tomorrow so it's not so painfully obvious. I should come up with a better excuse, but I don't have the energy or the patience.

I text Luke back. SOMETHING CAME UP AT WORK. CAN'T MAKE LUNCH ANYMORE. SO SORRY.

My phone rings in my hand, and caller ID tells me it's Luke. I'm so surprised that I drop it between the seat and the center console in my car. I couldn't answer it now even if I wanted to, which I don't. I slide my seat back and feel around underneath my seat for a few minutes before my fingers finally close over it. My voicemail chimes, telling me I have a new message.

No thanks.

I'm in my kitchen when the text notification chimes. CALL ME BACK.

I don't respond. A bear never wanders off if you keep feeding it.

YOU DON'T HAVE A MEETING. COME TO LUNCH WITH ME TMW.

When I don't reply, he sends another.

AT LEAST TALK TO ME ABOUT IT.

I hold firm.

IT'S MY ACCENT, ISN'T IT?

I suppress a smile, put my phone on silent, and stick it in the top drawer of my nightstand. Then I grab a pint of ice cream out of the freezer and flop onto the sofa. Today has been a rollercoaster, which means tomorrow must be better. I light a balsam and pine candle, and turn on one of my favorite episodes of Gilmore Girls, when Lorelai and Luke finally become a proper couple. I fast forward through the mess with Rory and Dean, and by the end, I can almost smile again. I'd feel a lot better if Lorelai wasn't in love with someone named Luke. But at the end of the day, I'm way better off than she is. It's not like I'm secretly in love with anyone for years without being able to admit it to myself or to him.

I simply know myself, and I don't want to cause any more damage for Luke or for me by pursuing a relationship that can't go anywhere.

I brush my teeth and climb into bed, checking my phone one last time before turning out my lamp. I don't want this to be any harder than it needs to be, but for some reason I'm disappointed that he hasn't sent me any more texts.

CHAPTER 7

I'm brushing my teeth the next morning when Luke finally texts me again. WHAT'S THE MEETING ABOUT?

I roll my eyes, but a smile creeps onto my face anyway. I'M MEETING WITH RETAILERS ABOUT DONATIONS FOR THE SFS PROGRAM.

WHEN WILL IT END?

He's tenacious; I'll give him that. NO IDEA.

I'M WILLING TO GRACIOUSLY POSTPONE TO TOMORROW, BUT I WANT AN UPGRADE. DINNER.

My heart flutters, and I want to dance around my bathroom, preen in the mirror and maybe even text Paisley with delight. I'm obviously attracted to him, and he's funny, and it's exciting. But I can't keep stressing over something I know can never be. I close my eyes and imagine myself turning into my mother. Spending all my time combing hair and doing laundry and starting to resent being a mom. I don't want to give up my career, and I don't want to resent my kids.

I don't want to abandon my own children like she did, or implode like my dad did.

My hands are stiff and I keep having to delete and retype, but I finally force the words out. My index finger hovers over send button, shaking. I swallow hard and hit send.

LUKE, THIS ISN'T GOING TO WORK. I'M SORRY.

THERE'S CHEMISTRY BETWEEN US. I KNOW YOU FEEL IT TOO. WHAT HAPPENED? IT CAN'T BE MY KIDS. THEY'RE ADORABLE.

The photo was cute, and I sound like a monster if I tell him it's the kids. I stick the phone face down on the counter. Until it buzzes again.

YOU DO NOT LIKE GREEN EGGS AND HAM, I GET IT. BUT TRY THEM TRY THEM AND YOU MAY...

Oh good grief. He's only reinforcing the fact that he's a father to two young children. No one else would jump right to a Dr. Seuss themed text. I only recognize the reference because Troy loves that book so much.

YES, I MAY. EXCEPT I DON'T WANT TO TRY THEM, NOT IN A BOAT OR A HOUSE OR WITH A MOUSE.

I watch my phone for a full twenty minutes, before deciding to stop fretting and get ready for work. He doesn't text me back on the drive into the office, or while I slink past Heather and Foster's office and into my own.

I congratulate myself on doing that without being spotted, and breathe a big sigh of relief. I begin the exhausting phone call and follow up email and letter process for each of our nominees, glancing at my phone after each one. I shouldn't care, because I told him I'm done. I can't date him.

I glance at my phone again. What's wrong with me? I try to forget about Luke through inundating myself in explaining the details of what aspects of the tax return I need to see. This is something I can handle, and it's something I know. It's one of the reasons I'm so good at running this charity.

I'm hunched over a pile of papers when I hear the tap on my door. I glance at my phone one more time before looking up. Nothing.

Because Luke is standing in my doorway, holding a bouquet of roses. Gorgeous roses—white with frilly pink edges.

"I don't know what I did wrong, and you said you didn't like green eggs and ham, so I thought I'd bring flowers instead. If you're just not that into me, I'll leave you alone." His fingers form an x over his heart. "Cross my heart. But I haven't been as excited about anyone in, well." He runs his free hand through his hair. "In years, if I'm being honest. And you seemed to like me almost as much as I like you before you saw where I live. I just want to reassure you, I'm not a charity case or a con man. I even brought a birth certificate, and social security card and a driver's license for verification." He gestures at his back pocket with a half a grin.

I drop my face into my hands. "It's not that at all. It's more complicated than that, and has nothing to do with your address or the fact that your home is on wheels."

"What is it, then?" He takes a step into my office and sets the roses gently on the edge of my desk.

"Look, the thing is—"

Foster appears in the doorway. "Uh, who's this?" He looks so smug, and I think about how he's got everything he wanted from me from someone new, like a year after I turned him down.

Fury flares in my chest. Foster thinks I'm a loser, he thinks I'm broken. He thinks no one will want me, since I won't grow and pop out a baby. I stand up and pick up the flowers, bringing them to my face and inhaling their light, sweet, fragrance. "Isn't my boyfriend the sweetest?"

Luke frowns at first, but he must see something in my face, because he winks, and turns toward Foster. "Luke Manning, boyfriend extraordinaire. Nice to meet you. You must be the man who's planning to dismantle Mary's amazing Sub-for-Santa program."

Foster frowns and shifts, narrowing his eyes at Luke.

I'm impressed that Luke stares him right in the eyes, completely unintimidated. Since Luke's wearing a polo shirt with cargo pants and work boots, and Foster's wearing one of his many designer suits, it's even more impressive that Luke doesn't bend under the Bradshaw glare.

"Foster Bradshaw. I'm the President of the United Way chapter here in Atlanta, but my family has been in oil for years and years. And I'm not dismantling anything. I'm merely handing down a mandate passed down to me."

"Surely the buck stops with the President?" Luke leans against the doorframe comfortably, like he owns my office.

"My family may carry great weight," Foster says smugly, "but I try not to throw my weight around."

Luke glances my way with wide eyes, and a half smile. He turns back to face Foster slowly. "I forgot my pedigree chart when I left the house today, sadly. Running the entire chapter of United Way sure sounds like a lot of work. I'm not nearly as industrious. In fact, I'm borderline lazy. I've been independently wealthy ever since I discovered the key component to the creation of LED light bulbs."

I laugh and shake my head, because otherwise Foster's going to feel threatened and tear into poor Luke.

"Luke's a stand up comedian in his free time," I say. "But seriously, he's the master electrician for the Citibank building downtown. Which means he's pretty good with his hands."

Foster's nostrils flare. "That building is an eyesore. I signed the petition against tearing down the old Stonefield building."

Luke shrugs. "I came in long after all those decisions had been made. I'm not the architect, or anything fancy. I'm just there to make sure the lights all work when it opens in two weeks."

Foster looks down his nose at Luke. "In any case, I walked down to see whether Mary would have time to run a projection for me, now that my gorgeous fiancé and I will be married before the end of the year."

I know, I should not still be doing taxes for my ex. Ugh. "Maybe you should find a new preparer?"

Foster's jaw drops. "Why?" He turns to Luke. "Does it upset you that Mary does my taxes? Because it's really a compliment. She's the best, that's all."

Luke holds Foster's gaze. "This is the first I've heard about it."

I sigh. This is getting tedious. "Oh fine, but next year, you need someone new. When do you need it by?"

Foster exhales heavily. "Thank goodness. I didn't think I could find anyone in the next week or two, and I know quarterly payments aren't due until January, but I'd love a feel for what mine will be before the end of the year. Then I can make some charitable donations if I need to."

I suppress the urge to roll my eyes. "Sure, email me the stuff."

"Or if you'd prefer I can print it off and we can look over it at dinner. We should touch bases on some last minute Sub-for-Santa details, too."

Absolutely no way I'm going to sit through a dinner with Foster. I'd rather die slowly of . . . leprosy. Plus, he's only asking me because Luke's here. I've never met someone more inclined to pee all over anything he perceives as his. Which makes Foster a dog. I'm still okay with the analogy.

I shake my head. "I can't. Luke and I already have plans."

Luke sucks air noisily through his teeth. "Sorry man. Dibs."

"Dibs?" Foster asks, every aspect of his face reflecting his total disgust. "What is Mary in this scenario? The last blueberry muffin?"

Luke grins. "If I lick her, will you go away and leave us alone?"

I chortle in a very un-lady-like way.

Luke's smiling, but Foster's unimpressed. "You two are perfect for each other." He storms back down the hall, but for the first time, someone else got the upper hand with Foster.

My smile can't be contained.

"Where did you want to go for lunch?" Luke asks. "I hear Georgia Brown's has great ham. I bet they'd be willing to dye it green."

"There's no Georgia Brown's here. It's only in Washington D.C."

His eyes glance skyward. "Hazard of moving so often."

"Sit down, Luke."

He sits.

"I'm sorry you got stuck in the middle of that, but I appreciate you were willing to roll with it for me. Things got a little nasty with Foster and I after we broke up, and he just told me he's getting married."

Luke shrugs. "I'm happy to be your fake boyfriend. In fact, I might even make a decent real boyfriend, if you'd ever answer my calls, or you know, agree to let me buy you food. Green or otherwise."

"The thing about that." I moan. "There's no way to say this without sounding like a troll. But I can't date you because you have kids. Adorable kids, but kids. I don't date anyone who has children, or who wants children."

"Wait." He glances pointedly at a photo of me with Troy on my desk, both of us sticking our tongues out. He raises his eyebrows. "You don't like kids?"

I shake my head. "It's not that. I like them; actually, usually I love them. But I adore my career, and I can't be a mediocre mom. So I'd either hate myself for failing them if I ever had any, or I'd resent them for costing me my career."

Luke scratches his head. "I could swear I heard once or twice that women can actually do both. But maybe I'm just making that one up."

"Try to understand what I'm saying, Luke. I'm sure your children are absolutely lovely, but this isn't a new thing for me. My parents were beyond awful and I won't ever allow myself to follow in their footsteps. Can you understand?"

He shrugs. "Not really, but maybe this'll make you feel better. I'm only here until January. So even if we hit it off big time, my Citibank work will be done and I'll be moving to the next big job."

I narrow my eyes at him. "You're saying any relationship between us was doomed from the start? Why bother dating me at all, then?"

Luke leans back in his chair. "Have you ever been single at the holidays?"

I have. Parties, gatherings, cheer. And you're alone for all of it while couple after couple smiles and leans on each other and smooches.

It sucks.

He shrugs. "Look, you don't wanna date someone with kids, and I get it. It's pretty common actually. For all their big talk, most women don't love other people's children. That's fine. But mine aren't monsters, and it might be nice to have a date to your office party. I'd like a hot date to mine." He winks.

I sigh. "Fine, so we go out for a few weeks, have a fun time, and then you take your kids and leave. That's what you're proposing?"

He nods. "And I don't feel bad that you'll be devastated and you don't worry you'll get attached to me and be stuck raising my demon spawn."

"I don't think they're spawn." I tap my lip with my pen. The problem is that I get too attached, but if I know they're leaving. . . "What if I like you too much? I might be depressed when you move."

He laughs. "If someone told you that the container of ice cream at the store was the last one that would ever be made, like your president has banned this particular kind of ice cream for being too good. Would you eat it? Or walk away because you knew you'd be sad to never have it again?"

I roll my eyes. "Of course I'd eat it."

He points at me. "I'd love to spend the next few weeks with you, and since you won't ever be a parent to my kids you don't need to worry. We can just enjoy our last bites of ice cream together."

The corners of my mouth tug upward. "Dinner later, then?"

He grins so big I can almost see his molars. "Lunch today, dinner tonight. The sky's the limit, baby."

My heart flutters again and this time, I don't shut it down.

"I can't do lunch right now. I've cut it too close and I need to rush over to my real job. But dinner I can do."

"You pick the place," he says, "but you let me pay. Deal?"

"Sure, but only as long as you promise me one thing."

He stands up. "What's that?"

"No green eggs or ham."

He barks a laugh. "I promise." Text me your address and I'll pick you up at seven-thirty."

I should have told him no. I should have been smart. I shouldn't eat a vat of ice cream, no matter how good it is. But the thought of eating it has me smiling like an idiot for the rest of the day.

CHAPTER 8

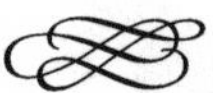

I want to talk to Shauna as soon as I reach my office, but she's out for several days, apparently, probably preparing for her big move. I think about calling or texting her, because I need to tell her I'll take the job before they find another, probably better option. I need that money. Or, more accurately, Troy does.

I knock off work early, which is no big deal because technically I don't even have to work the last few weeks of the year, at least, until I take the big promotion. I send Paisley home on my way out the door, and she beams at the news.

"I have so much holiday shopping to do. I better get started."

I groan. "Don't mention shopping to me."

She grins. "Lots of families?"

I shake my head. "Nah, I'm only doing one this year." I don't add that it's because I'm spending all my money and then some on Troy.

"Wow, that's unlike you. Didn't you do five last year?"

"I might end up taking more if we don't get enough

sponsors, but for now we have more sponsors than nominations by three."

"That's good. It means word is getting out."

I nod my head. "My shopping woes are because I haven't even started on my friends and family yet."

"I like Nordstrom's," Paisley says. "Or Christmas cookies."

I roll my eyes. "I may as well just hand you a fistful of cash."

"Yes!" She tosses her hands up in the air. "Why didn't I think of that?"

"You're shameless."

"Hey, what are you getting for your soon-to-be-fiancé?" She shimmies.

"Cute, but Pais." I lower my voice. "He has two kids."

Her face falls. "You're kidding."

My lips compress and I cross my arms. "Nope, and get this. He's Lucas Manning."

Her jaw drops. "Wait, the guy who's poor and rich?"

I laugh. "He's neither. But he does live in a trailer since he travels a lot for work, and so the women from church—"

Paisley jumps up. "They didn't."

I nod. "They assumed he was poor."

"Oh em gee. Well. So he's hot. He has kids, and he's charitable minded." She holds her hands out and lifts them up and down like scales. "What are you going to do?"

I blush. "I told him I couldn't date him, obviously."

"Then why are your cheeks the magenta of humiliation that brings out that nearly Easter egg green color in your eyes?" Paisley leans toward me and puts her hands on her desk. "I think you're waffling on this stupid no kids rule."

"It's not stupid," I say. "It's sensible, and it keeps me from becoming my mother."

"So you're not seeing him again?" Paisley asks.

I look down. "We're going to dinner tonight."

"What?!"

I shush her. "Keep your voice down. Geez. He's leaving in a few weeks, okay? For a new job. So, I figured, what's the harm in having someone to date for the holiday season?"

Paisley's smile can only be described as sly.

"Stop it." I frown. "That smile is annoying."

Her smile grows. "This one is much smarter than Foster ever was."

"Foster went to Yale," I say automatically. "He's very smart."

"Yeah, yeah." Paisley waves her hand around. "So smart he can't tell his nose from his elbow. But, sure. Foster's smart. I'm just saying, Lucas Manning is smarter."

"Duly noted." I grab my purse and walk toward the door.

Paisley follows me out, a spring in her step and a glint in her eye. When I climb into my car, my phone buzzes.

I STILL NEED A PHOTO.

I copy the one Luke sent me and forward it to her.

OMG. YES. MARY, YOU SHOULD SEND OUT HOLIDAY CARDS WITH THIS GUY.

I send her an eye roll emoji.

FINE IF YOU AREN'T, THEN CAN I BORROW HIM?

Paisley is absurd.

ARE YOU TAKING HIM TO FOSTER'S WEDDING? PLEASE SAY YES. I WANT FOSTER TO MEET HIM SO BAD.

I sigh. She's never going to give up. I'M NOT GOING TO FOSTER'S WEDDING. NO WAY I'LL GET AN INVITE. BUT THEY'VE MET.

Paisley sends me the screaming blue and yellow person

emoji. DID FOSTER'S HEAD EXPLODE? TELL ME HIS HEAD EXPLODED.

I CAN'T SPEND ALL DAY TEXTING YOU, YOU KNOW. I'M GOING TO SEE TROY, AND I HAVE A DATE WITH LUKE TONIGHT.

Paisley sends me a gif of a baby throwing a tantrum. I swear, she is ridiculous. FINE. WEAR THE BLACK STRAPPY HEELS AND I'LL LEAVE YOU ALONE.

I shake my head, and start my drive to the hospital. Thankfully, I've left early enough to avoid traffic, and I slide my car into a spot outside the hospital by four-thirty. I make a quick stop in the gift shop to buy a stuffed animal. To my delight, they have a fluffy green frog with dots on its back. I hope Troy still loves frogs. Kids can be more fickle than men, their obsessions changing in the blink of an eye.

When the elevator doors open on Troy's floor, the sounds of a happy toddler fill the hallway. Troy and Trudy are both singing a ridiculous song, his favorite, about five speckled frogs. It probably began as ten frogs, but it's hard to handle any more repetitions than are strictly necessary.

I push the door open and shake the green frog at Troy.

The squeals reassure me that he can see it.

"Aunt May May! Is that for me?"

I walk around the door so he can see me, too. "How'd you know it was me?"

He shrugs. "No one else brings me presents. And I love frogs."

He's such a smart little guy. "You're going to be an accountant one day, aren't you. Just like me?"

His green eyes widen. "You count things, right? I'm learning. One, two, fwee, foh, five six."

"How'd you learn that?" I ask.

He frowns. "They poke me with a needle and it hurts.

They do it a lot. So I'm counting each time they do it. Six times today."

"I'm lucky to have such a brave nephew," I say. "I'm glad you're learning to count so well, but I'm sorry they're poking you."

He bobs his head, and I hand him the frog. "This frog isn't just any frog. He begged me to buy him at the gift shop. I told him no at first, but then he said that if I bought him, he'd tell me his name."

"What is it?" Troy asks, eyes as round as an owl's.

I whisper. "He said his name's Hoppy."

Troy nods and repeats the word.

"He also needs a kiss every day. If you'll do that, and remember his name, he'll be there for you to hug every time you're scared, or sad or lonely. And hugging him will also help you feel better when they poke you."

Troy hugs Hoppy to his chest.

"Trudy, have you given any thought to the timeframe on my offer?" I ask. "Because I have. You're going to be so much better off getting things settled sooner, rather than later."

She folds her arms. "I'm not going to uproot anything before Christmas."

"But my house is much bigger, and nicer, and I'd help you with it. It's always better to do things now, than to wait."

She shakes her head. "I'll think about it in January."

"By which point you'll have paid another month's rent!"

"I won't have to pay the rent, because Chris is paying that."

Finally, the thing that's been bugging me all day has been answered. She won't leave because she's still hoping the functioning alcoholic who left her will come back. He's very unlikely to do that with a scowly older sister on the scene making him feel like the loser he really is. I want to scream at her, but I can't do it in front of Troy, and it probably wouldn't help anyway.

"I just wanted to come see how you were doing, Troy. And tell your mom that I think the thing we discussed will be just fine. So you can move ahead with the clinical trial."

She nods her head, and a tear slides down her cheek. "I know you want what's best for me, I'm not sure you're right about what that is."

"Your happiness is all I ever want," I say. "But you get to choose for yourself. My support has no strings attached. When you decide you need me, I'm here."

She crosses the room and pulls me close for a tight hug, which warms my heart. But the little arms that wrap around the backs of my knees are almost too much to take. I reach over and pick up Troy, still clutching Hoppy. I kiss him on the forehead. "I'm very proud of you for being super duper brave."

"Thanks Aunt May May. You come tomorrow?" he asks.

"I've got a big meeting tomorrow night with volunteers, but I'll come before that if I can."

It's a fifteen-minute drive from the hospital to my house. I pull over four times and start a text to Luke begging off each time. After all, we aren't ice cream and that analogy makes no sense. What we're doing is stupid. He's leaving, and I'm never going to have kids of my own, much less marry someone who has them. Ironically, if he was divorced, I might be fine with it, because I would never be their mom. That burden would fall on someone else's shoulders. But it's not like I can tell him that if his wife hadn't died, and he'd just left her, I'd be okay with it.

The hot water of the shower eases some of my anxiety over the work drama, Troy being sick, and the upcoming date. Even though I stand under the boiling stream for too long, I'm still ready for my date with half an hour to spare. I decide to sit in the formal living room of my house and read until he arrives. Of course, I'd read a lot faster if I wasn't glancing up every single time a car drove past.

I wonder what Luke drives. It can't be the mustang that's up on blocks, and I didn't see anything else. I hope it's not a motorcycle. That would be a complete nightmare. I've seen the numbers on motorcycle accidents, and no matter how you skew them, they're bad news.

I glance at my watch. Luke's six minutes late. Which isn't a big deal to most people, I remind myself. Plenty of people I know operate under the assumption that they're on time for any specified event as long as they arrive within the fifteen minutes following the stated time. My dad and my sister both feel like anything under half an hour should be commended.

I still hate it.

I'm probably more wound up than usual, thinking about little Troy and whether he's adjusting to his new circumstances, and whether my sister's okay. How can I convince her to let go of the Chris shaped anvil around her neck so she can move on?

A red Ford Raptor drives past my house, stops and reverses, and backs into the driveway. Where in the world was he hiding that? I glance at my watch. Eleven minutes late, which means it's likely he's one of those fifteen minute grace period, inconsiderate, selfish jerks.

Or maybe he had some issues with the tiny people I've been trying to pretend he doesn't have.

I slide my hands down my sweater to smooth it, and glance in the mirror quickly to make sure my makeup hasn't smudged. I almost never wear red lipstick, but with this particular moss green sweater, the combination turns my eyes a unique olive color. Or that's what Foster used to tell me. Not that his opinions matter anymore.

He jogs up the steps in nice slacks and a cream-colored polo shirt, covered with a brown leather jacket. Before he even has a chance to knock, I open the door.

"Whoa," he jumps. "That scared me."

"Sorry about that," I say. "I saw you coming, and figured I'd spare your knuckles."

He raises his eyebrows. "Your last pansy boyfriend may have had porcelain knuckles," He holds up his hands and slaps his right hand with his left. "But these babies are tough."

After I lock the front door, he takes my hand in his, and I follow him to his car, grinning like an idiot. I'm glad it's dark enough he probably can't see.

He opens the passenger side door for me. "So. You were acting like you didn't even want to go, but you were watching for me by the window?"

I blush.

He walks around to the driver side, and when he slides in, he glances at my face. "Hey, I was only teasing. I didn't mean to upset you."

"It's been a rough few days." I buckle my seatbelt. "I'm fine, though."

"Me and my knuckles can handle rough. What's going on?"

"Everything." I'm embarrassed when my voice wobbles. "After lunch with you the other day, I decided to turn down the promotion."

"Actually," Luke says, "tell me where we're going and then keep going."

"Oh, right. I pick the place. Do you still want Indian?"

"I haven't been living here for very long, and I'm not

used to your neighborhood. Maybe you've got a restaurant suggestion?"

"Sure. I love the place on Bleaker." I give him some basic instructions to leave my neighborhood, but after a few turns we reach the parkway. "You stay on here until Bleaker, then it's on your right."

"Perfect. Now back to how your boss reacted when you told her to take her job and stuff it."

I chuckle. "Yeah, I didn't ever get that far."

"No?" he asks. "Why not? Cold feet? Late onset greed?"

"Late onset greed? You're so weird."

"You love it." He takes my hand in his, and my heart flutters in a way I could get used to.

I lean back in the seat and exhale. "I didn't get greedy. The opposite, actually. I got a call from my sister right before I was going to turn it down."

"And?"

"My nephew was recently diagnosed as a type one diabetic. He's not even four for another few weeks, and the doctors say it's way, way rare to be diagnosed so early. The poor guy is struggling. He hates getting poked all the time, of course, and he doesn't understand why he can't eat non-stop goldfish like he used to. Like every three-year-old in America."

He squeezes my hand. "I'm so sorry. That's terrible."

"Plus, my sister Trudy didn't tell me until yesterday, but her loser husband left them. She won't even move in with me, because she's stupidly still hoping the jerk will come back home."

"Wow," Luke says. "Just wow, that's a lot to take in at once."

"It's a good thing I didn't tell my boss I was turning the promotion down, because Trudy's gonna need a lot of help."

Luke raises one eyebrow. "Your sister's name is Trudy?"

"Gertrude, actually. I know, it's a terrible name for a young person. My mom named my sister after her grandma and then Mom bails on the whole family. If she's going to saddle a kid with an awful name, she could at least have the decency to stick around and help defend her when the other kids start making jokes."

"Your mom bailed on you guys? When?"

"Trudy was a baby. I was about to start school."

"Do you still see her?"

I shake my head. "She calls every few years. I haven't seen her in a decade."

"I'm sorry."

"I don't even care anymore." Which is a lie. I'll always care.

"I can't understand any mother ever leaving her kids on purpose."

"Mom got pregnant with me when she was in high school. She married my dad, but she didn't want to. She wanted to see the world, and we tied her down. Working as a trucker was the only thing she ever liked, the freedom, the control, and her own place where no one could bother her." I shrug. "A trucker. She left me to be a trucker. I sound like someone from Jerry Springer."

His thumb brushes against the inside of my palm. "You couldn't be on Jerry Springer."

"No?"

He shakes his head. "Too many teeth, and you don't have roots in your hair. Also, it's been washed this week."

"You keep those compliments coming like that, and you never know where tonight might lead." I suck my teeth and smile lopsided and crazy.

He laughs.

"Anyway, my point was that my sister needs money,

and I have the means to get it for her, which I should do. So now I'll have to take the new job. Which should be fine, except my awful ex, who you met today, is going to axe the Sub-for-Santa program if I'm not there to run it anymore."

"Maybe that's a blessing in disguise," Luke says.

"Don't you start, too."

"Hold on," Luke says. "Start what?"

"My dad, and sister, and Foster and everyone else I know except my secretary Paisley thinks my obsession with the whole thing is unhealthy. They've been after me to quit for a while."

Luke pulls into a parking place right in front of Bombay Palace. He shuts his truck off and turns to face me directly. "You aren't obsessed. That's when you can't think of anything else. You're dedicated and that's an admirable quality. What I meant was, instead of reporting to the United Way, why not start your own charity that only does Sub-for-Santa? Then you don't need a boss, or anyone else to tell you what to do, really."

"Oh no, I couldn't do that."

As I say the words, I realize they might not be true. United Way provides me a copier and office space, but I do everything else. Pushing the word out to the community for nominations, vetting the nominees, finding the volunteers, coordinating the efforts, creating the rules and checking that they're followed. Why do I need United Way?

"I disagree. You could call it whatever you want, but obviously this entire thing is already run by you."

What if he's right?

"One small problem. With this new job, I can't spend more than a few hours a week during the holidays on this. Unless I found another volunteer to do everything I do, which would be a tall order, there's no way this would get done. It's too much work, and not enough excitement in the community for it."

Before Luke can open my door, I pull the handle open and climb out, noticing as I do that he has two booster seats in the back of his car. He really is a cute dad. Which would be amazing if I wanted kids.

When we walk in, there's not a single other customer in the restaurant. It's never busy, but it seems especially sad on Wednesday nights for some reason. Honestly that's one of the reasons I go so often in the middle of the week. I hate crowds, and if this place ever goes under, I might cry. Okay, I would cry.

I sit down at an empty table, knowing Jay will be over with menus shortly. "Since you've never been here, let me tell you. Their chicken pakora is amazing. Like I might slice off your finger if you reach for the last piece. And the korma is great if you like mild things. It's all my nephew Troy will eat. The naan is to die for, and my favorite is just a little different than the usual tikka masala, called chicken makhani. The chicken's shredded and simmered and oh my word. It's transformational."

Luke's grinning like an idiot.

"What?"

"You are so cute when you like something."

"Mary!" Jay shouts. "You brought a friend this time, and a handsome one, too." Jay holds out his hand to Luke, who takes it and they shake vigorously. Once the he-man handshakes finally end, Jay hands us each a menu. "This girl is a gem, you know. You should hang on to her with both hands."

For the first time since I met him, Luke actually looks uncomfortable.

"We're both starving," I say. "Can you take our drink orders and food at the same time?"

"Of course I can." Jay whips out his notepad. "What do you want?"

"I think we need a little bit of everything." Luke glances at the menu. "Two orders of the pakora, since I don't want to get stabbed."

Jay laughs. "Mary loves her pakora. She likes it spicy though. Think you can keep up?"

Luke meets my eye. "I aim to try."

"Other than the pakora, what else?" Jay points at the menu.

"Since we're on Mary's turf, maybe she should pick three things for the table and we can share?"

"Good idea," Jay says.

I choose kheema samosas, which is a lamb appetizer wrapped in dough, chicken makhani, saagwala, and korma, plus a few orders of naan. The food takes forever, like always, but the company is good and the weight of the last few days slides off my shoulders.

I've barely finished my pakora, and ladled rice and makhani on my plate when Luke's phone rings. "Hello?"

His brow furrows.

"No, he was fine earlier."

Pause.

"How many times?"

Pause.

"I'll be right there. Thanks for calling me. You did the right thing."

I motion for Jay to come over. "We need to go boxes for all this. Luke's got a family emergency."

"Yes, I'm so sorry," Luke says to me, "but Chase is throwing up. Like a lot. I need to make sure he's okay."

I place one hand over his and his eyes widen softly and then he sighs.

"It's going to be okay," I say. "All kids get the stomach flu. It's not fun, but he'll be fine."

Jay brings us our boxes, Luke hands him a card, and I start filling the boxes with the food we haven't even touched.

"Any chance I can run by the house and check on him before I take you home?" he asks.

I shake my head. "No, just go. I can get an Uber from here. It's really no big deal."

He frowns. "Do you hate the idea of being around my kids that much?"

My jaw drops. "Of course not, that's not it at all. How selfish would I be to say, hey Chase, your dad's here but now he has to leave again with me. I'm trying to be considerate, not a high maintenance mess."

He shakes his head. "My cousin-in-law will be there so once he's fine I can drive you home. Besides, it's a second date rule for me that I need to fix something for you to prove I'm manly. I was thinking maybe a closet light might be on the blink or something." He winks.

"What an awful pun," I say. "But it would be great to actually see what I'm wearing. It's been sort of a guessing game for the past few weeks."

"Your sweater matches well enough," he says.

"I'm kidding, Luke. I have flashlights."

"Right, of course. As an added bonus, you'll get to meet Amy, my daughter. After you came by the other day, she's been asking to meet you."

I should protest. I don't want to be involved in his kids' lives. It's a slippery slope, and I avoid those at all times. But he looks so earnest, and there's a sick kid involved, and I don't think he'll budge on me taking an Uber. Which means if I turn him down, I'm basically making his poor son wait to see his dad.

"Fine," I say. "I'll go with you, but only if you promise I can take an Uber from your house if he gets upset and doesn't want you to leave. I won't ruin a baby's night so you can give me a ride."

"It's a deal," Luke says.

CHAPTER 9

Luke doesn't sound anxious on the way home, but his hands grip the steering wheel of his Raptor a little too tightly, and he sits ramrod straight.

"I'm sorry to spoil our date," he says. "I think Chase should be fine in a few days. I'd love to make it up to you on Saturday night. Any chance you're free?"

"I usually save Saturdays for my boyfriend," I say. "He's pretty flexible otherwise, but he likes Saturday nights to himself."

Luke's head whips around and he stares at me. Then he laughs. "You almost had me there. So is that a yes, or a no?"

"Sure, a redo on Saturday."

"Phew. I was worried I botched my shot by bailing for a stomach bug."

"Good parents always put their kids first. It's your job to do that." I have firsthand experience it's not what all parents do. "Please don't apologize for being a good dad, not to me."

"Thanks."

I ought to distract him before Luke crushes that poor

steering wheel into dust. "How's the Citibank job coming along? Almost done?"

He rolls his eyes heavenward. "Let's just say that not everyone the contractor hired to work electrical could change a light bulb, much less repair your closet light."

"On a job that big, if your people can't do the work, what do you do?"

He shrugs. "It's a nightmare, but it's not the first time I've dealt with this problem. It's pretty common actually. Licensed electricians are expensive, and subs usually bid out as low as they can to get the job. If they can use unskilled labor instead of skilled, their profit margin goes up."

"Is your reputation on the line if it goes wrong?"

"That's the downside to being the project manager for electrical. I've been spending half my day every day showing these guys how to do their own job without being electrocuted or overloading the circuits. It's a frustrating mess. We should have been done two weeks ago, but instead I've got a day crew and a night crew fixing the stuff they screwed up initially."

"I never gave much thought to the work that went into any of my lights, or outlets, or anything at either of my offices. Or my home, for that matter."

"You shouldn't. If your crew did its job during construction, you never will, other than the occasional malfunctioning light."

"I guess you'll make sure no one at Citibank ever has to think about it?"

"That's the plan. I've gotten pretty good at identifying which men I can trust to help me quality check and which men need to be supervised heavily. At least we're down to punch list items at this point."

My eyebrows rise. "I didn't realize it was so close."

"Ribbon cutting is coming up fast."

"Wait, does that mean you'll be leaving sooner? Before January?"

"Worried about me leaving? Weren't you trying to brush me off yesterday?" He grins.

I stiffen. "Not at all, but if you won't be here for Christmas, I'll need to reassign the family I lined up for you."

"You've already assigned me a family?"

I nod. "Three children. Two boys and one girl. Twelve, seven and three years old. The three-year-old boy loves rockets, and the twelve year old wants board games. It was a refreshing request after sifting through more than a dozen tweens, all asking for cell phones or iPads."

"What about the seven year old?"

I sigh. "Her mom wrote, 'anything.' I hate when they do that, but it's fairly common. I never know whether the mom's lazy and doesn't know her kid, or whether they have so little that absolutely anything will make them happy. Either way, it's sad."

"Don't worry. We'll do some research and come up with great stuff for all three."

"Unless you leave earlier," I say.

He shakes his head. "Nah, my next job starts January 15. I like to leave myself a few weeks between jobs in case one of them gets delayed. Even if it's not my fault, sometimes things go wrong."

"Plus, it's New Years. And you mentioned your dad's here. Won't you and your kids miss him? And the cousin you mentioned?"

Luke shrugs. "I always try to find an autumn job back in Atlanta, or take a few weeks off so we can come here to visit. My brother's here too, but he's always working. Family's important, and my kids miss their cousins and my pops, and their uncle, but they love the adventure, too.

When my job lasts longer than six months, sometimes I take Dad with me. I hate bouncing him around for a few months here or there, though, and my brother gets all upset."

"What about school? Doesn't that throw things off for your kids?"

"Nah, not yet anyway. Chase is four, and Amy's five. I did enroll her in a pre-school and she loves it. St. Paul's Catholic Church has a decent program. But she's a free spirit and I line up a full time caretaker for them while I'm working, someone qualified and engaged."

"But when the time comes, you're going to enroll them in school? And stay somewhere for the school year, at least?"

He shrugs. "Probably. They can both read fairly well already, so I know they won't be behind. I've got nine months before Amy's due to start school. I may look for a longer gig, or I may find a homeschool program. Haven't decided yet."

He turns into the Cove.

My palms are clammy, and my heart's racing. Why am I so nervous to meet his kids? It's not like they'll ever be my kids. I'm only hanging out with Luke for the few weeks he has left here in Atlanta. Calm down, Mary. Everything's okay. My head knows it's fine, but my heart isn't listening very well.

Luke parks around the back of the large trailer, which explains why I didn't see his truck when I came by last time. He opens my door again and offers his hand when I climb out, which is helpful since the Raptor cab sits pretty high above the ground. When my feet both touch dirt, he doesn't let go. He interlaces our hands, and pulls me along behind him on the fifteen-foot walk to the trailer's back door as if he knows I need the little nudge.

Luke releases my hand to climb the steps to the entry, which are fairly narrow. He had to do it, but somehow without his hand in mine, I'm untethered, drifting, and nervous. I might like Luke a little too much already. It's the only reason I'd be stressed out like this about seeing the inside of his home, and meeting his kids.

They're four and five, I remind myself. They like anyone who can do a Yoda impression, or who can snort milk out of their nose. I've got this.

He pauses in the doorway and waves me up. "Come on in. It's freezing outside."

My feet override my brain and I hop up to the open doorway. I take a deep breath, and step inside. The inside of the trailer is much nicer than I expected. It's a small space, but with the pop outs on either side, it doesn't feel oppressive like I expected. There's an island in the kitchen with a sink, and against the walls, there's a love seat and two large movie theater chairs that both face a generous sized television. A small table and two chairs nestled against the wall complete the room, and everything's trimmed in dark wood and looks pretty solidly made.

"I hear them back in my bedroom." Luke points at the brown leather loveseat. "If you want to wait here, you're welcome to."

I sit and pull out my phone. I wonder what people did to kill time before phones. Stare at the wall, maybe? I'm almost finished with an email updating a local restaurant chain about the details of the offer in compromise our favorite law firm is hammering out when I hear a tiny shuffling sound.

I stand up and turn toward the noise, which is coming from the kitchen cabinets. Oh, no, please oh please let him not have mice. I shudder.

"Do you like fruit loops?" a tiny, muffled voice asks.

I startle and look around. I don't see anyone, but the sound is definitely not coming from a mouse, thank goodness.

"I do like Fruit Loops, but I think Golden Grahams are a little better, personally." The question had to have come from his daughter Amy. "I'd love to know who's asking?"

A cabinet door opens under the kitchen counter and a small girl with dark blonde pigtails unfolds herself and climbs out. Her two braids are fuzzy, like they were done this morning and need to be combed out. She's sucking on her thumb. Didn't Luke say she was five? I'm no expert, but I don't think five year olds should still be doing that.

"Can I have some fruit loops?" she asks.

"I don't know," I say. "You probably need to ask your dad about that."

She frowns, her deep blue eyes narrowing at me. "He says they're for breakfast, but we haven't had any for almost a week. Aunt Becca finally bought some today, but not early enough for breakfast."

This poor little girl. Her brother's sucking up all the time and energy and all she wants is a few cups of her favorite breakfast cereal. I'd be nervous about stepping on Luke's toes if I thought this was going somewhere, but I don't need to worry. So he doesn't like how I deal with his kids? Oh well.

I stand up and walk into the kitchen. "You'd make an excellent lawyer someday, you know that?"

She shrugs. "My dad says I should be a shoe salesman."

I chuckle. "Why is that?"

She sticks out her bottom lip. "I love shoes, and I'm good at talking him into buying more than I need."

I hide my smile by turning toward the living room. Once I have my face schooled into neutrality again, I turn back. "Little Amy, maybe you can help me. Where are these contraband Fruit Loops?"

She points to the cabinet above the fridge. "What's contramand?"

I stifle a laugh. "Contraband. It means something you aren't supposed to have."

Her eyebrows rise. "Oh I can have them, just not when I didn't eat dinner."

My bottom lip drops open. "Well, well, well. You didn't eat your dinner?"

She looks at the ground. "No, I mean, I can't have them after dinner."

I giggle. She's hilarious. "It appears someone who lives here knows you pretty well. They obviously stuck those Fruit Loops up high enough that you can't reach them, huh?"

She nods her head, her eyes mournful, her tone resigned. "And all the chairs in this stupid house-on-wheels are stuck to the floor, so I can't even push one over to climb up."

I drop my jaw and widen my eyes in mock horror. "Next time I come, I'm bringing a screwdriver. You've gotta have some way to be a little naughty, don't you think?"

Her eyes sparkle. "Are you really?"

I grin. "Sure. But for now, I can reach them for you. Why don't you grab a bowl and I'll pour it before your dad comes back."

"Okay." Amy scrambles around me and flings a drawer open. I wasn't expecting bowls in a drawer, but I guess she can't reach the cabinets without climbing. Kid friendly house here, even if it is on wheels.

Amy bolts her cereal, and is slurping the milk when I hear steps coming from the back of the trailer. I toss her bowl into the sink and turn to face Luke with what I hope is an innocent smile.

"What are you two up to in here?" he asks.

I shrug and Amy watches me. A split second later, her shoulders rise and fall in the exact same way. On a whim, I cross my arms, and she does, too. I can't quite keep the smirk off my lips.

Luke lifts one eyebrow and stares at me, and then turns to stare at Amy. After five seconds she breaks down into a fit of giggles.

"What is so very funny, young lady?" Luke walks into the small kitchen, filling the entire space. He glances at the sink and Amy turns to me and bites her lip.

"Your pretty friend gave me Fruit Loops!" Amy turns to me and whispers. "It's always better to confess than be caught. Especially with my dad."

I whisper back. "I can't believe you threw me under the bus like that."

"The bus?" She shrugs. "I'm five."

Luke laughs. "Alright Amy, I appreciate you entertaining my beautiful friend while I checked on Chase. He's feeling a little better, so Aunt Becca said I can take my friend home. Can you be patient until I get back?"

Amy lifts her chin. "Will you read to me when you get home?"

He smiles. "I will."

"Five books?"

Luke's eyebrows rise. "We just finished Percy Jackson."

"And now you're only reading me baby books." She scowls.

He shakes his head. "Not baby books, age appropriate ones. I'll read two Dr. Seuss ones."

"Three," Amy counters.

Luke sighs heavily. "I'll read three, but no bonuses or

extras or wheedling."

Amy's eyes dart sideways to my face. "I'm five. I'm not making any promises about wheedling."

She's cracking me up.

Luke walks toward the door. "You ready to go, Mary?"

I cross the room as well. "Yeah, thanks."

Luke walks down the steps, but before I can follow him, Amy's tiny hand grabs mine. "You'll come back, right?"

My heart constricts. How can I tell her no? But if I say yes, she'll ask me again and again. Nothing is ever enough for a small child. "Well, your dad has a lot of work, and so do I. I'm sure I'll see you again, but I'm not sure precisely when."

Her precious face falls, her mouth turning down, her shoulders slumping.

I kneel in front of her. "Amy, you and your dad are going to be helping some kids this year, kids whose parents can't buy them much for Christmas. I'm in charge of setting everything up for that program."

She bobs her head, but doesn't meet my eye.

"What's wrong?" I ask.

"Nothing."

I let go of her hand, and reach under her chin to lift it until she's looking me in the eye. "You can tell me if something's upsetting you."

"My school's Christmas pageant is tomorrow. I get to play the angel, and I'm going to do a really good job, even though my dumb wings are made of cardboard, and Collins hogged all the glitter for the wise man crowns." The animation in her face has returned, thankfully.

"Cardboard? Angels can't fly with cardboard wings unless they're sparkly," I say.

"That's what I told Mrs. Hassan!"

I tsk. "I had an angel costume a long time ago, and it

had real wings made with white feathers."

She gasps and claps. "Do you still have it?"

"I'm not sure," I say. "I can check. But even if I kept them, if your program's tomorrow night, I'm not sure how I'd get them to you in time. Maybe they can flap their way over."

"All my friends will have their dads *and* their moms there. Even the ones whose parents don't like each other anymore still come. They just sit further apart, and sometimes they yell."

"I'm so sorry your mom can't be there," I say. "I'm sure she's equally sad."

"Up in heaven?" she asks.

I nod my head. "Do you believe in heaven?"

"Well, that's where angels live. And my mom had to go somewhere and she was a really good mom. So yeah, I think she's probably in heaven. That's why I picked to be an angel."

I smile. "I've got to go now, but I'll see you around."

Amy grabs my hand with both of hers this time. "Wait, please."

Luke climbs the steps and shakes his head. "Amy, you have to let Mary go, or she'll never want to come back."

Amy drops my hands like they burned her. I can barely hear her next words. "Could you come to my play tomorrow night, Mary? It's late, so you can do it after work maybe. It doesn't even start until seven. You can even come if you don't find the wings. Mine stink, but I have a really neat halo made of gold pipe cleaners, and I know my lines, like really, really, super, duper well."

Luke's leaving in less than a month. It won't be my fault things end when it's time to go. Maybe it'll be good for her to have someone there, even if it's not someone permanent.

"I suppose I can go, if it's okay with your dad."

Luke nods his head. "Fine by me. I hear the pageant is wonderful. You'd really be missing out if you didn't come. And of course, Amy clearly needs your wings."

The drive to my house only takes ten minutes.

"Where's your new job?" I ask.

"Louisville."

"Oh man, if I were you, I'd have picked somewhere that's warm for the winter."

He smacks his forehead. "You couldn't have mentioned that two months ago?"

A few minutes from my neighborhood, we pass a big, white, colonial style home. The entire outline of the house is lit up with sparkly white lights. Enormous oak trees line the circular drive, shading it during spring and summer when they're covered in leaves.

"I've loved that house for twenty years."

Luke glances at it sideways. "Why?"

"This family used to live there with three kids and a dog. They had shiny hair, and pretty white teeth, and they'd rake leaves into piles and leap into them. They always seemed so happy. I used to pretend they were my family, and it was my house. It doesn't hurt that the house is perfect and has like everything a house should have."

Luke looks at me sideways. "How would you know?"

I blush. "It went on the market a few years ago, and I might have gone to look at it. There's a big pool with a diving board, a cupola covered in flowering vines, and a huge custom built swing set. The whole downstairs has these gorgeous hardwood floors, and the kitchen and all the bathrooms have matching mica-flecked countertops. I know everyone loves white now, but I never moved on from the dark, hardwood cabinets, and these were custom made." I sigh. "It's stupid, I know, and out dated, and it's still my dream house. I guess dreams when you're a little kid die hard."

"You love it that much?"

"There are even windows in every room to keep it from looking like a cave with all the dark wood. I couldn't quite afford it then, and I doubt it'll go up for sale again anytime soon. Which is really for the best, because why would I need a mansion with a pool?"

Luke laughs. "Not much of a swimmer?"

I shake my head. "Stupid, right?"

"The heart wants what the heart wants."

He's right. And I'm terribly afraid my heart's gearing up to be broken in a few weeks when Luke and his kids leave for Louisville. When we stop in front of my current, modest but snug home, I fling his truck door open and race up to the front porch. Luke's eyes widen, but he doesn't chase me up to the top step.

Why did I sabotage what could have been a great first kiss? A defense mechanism, I think. The same instinct is screaming for me to shut this whole thing down. After waving at Luke, I close and lock the door and lean against it with my eyes closed. I should text or call him and tell him that I'd put the ice cream back in the freezer. Or that I'm not interested in his green eggs and ham.

I should cut my losses right now.

I should, but I don't. I pull out the photo he sent me and stare at his smiling face. Then I glance at Amy's, too. I can see Luke in her eyes.

Instead of texting Luke to dump him, I spend the next two hours rummaging around in my storage closet and upending every box I have. After two and a half hours, I find them. Somewhat discolored from years of sitting in storage, but still fluffy and mostly white.

My old angel wings.

CHAPTER 10

Paisley doesn't make it to the United Way office Thursday morning, since Shauna's back and she insisted our audit case files be prepared by the end of the week for an office review. So when I walk in the door on Thursday afternoon, she's perched like a hawk on the edge of my desk.

"And?" Her eyebrows waggle like those of an unhinged villain on an Acme cartoon.

"Good afternoon, Paisley. How are you today?"

She stands up. "Oh come on. You didn't text me last night, or this morning. I deserve some details. My dress got this whole thing off the ground, and you still haven't returned that, by the way."

I sigh. "Sorry. It's been a crazy week."

"A crazy *good* week?"

"I sprinted from his truck up to my house so he couldn't even think about kissing me goodnight."

Her jaw drops. "What in the world is wrong with you? I've been drooling over his photo for twenty-four hours and you *run away*?"

"He's got kids, and one of them was puking last night, and it cut our date short. Not my fault."

Paisley puts a hand on her hip. "And what? You were worried you'd get sick?"

"I've got so much to do for Sub-for-Santa right now that I cannot handle a stomach virus."

Paisley slumps into a chair. "You're a real downer, you know that?"

"Yes, I know. But I met his daughter, and she wants me to go to her Christmas pageant tonight."

Paisley stands up and walks into her cubicle, returning with a brown box full of files. She whomps them on my desk. "That's the best news I've heard all day. I bet she's cute."

"She's adorable," I say. "And she wants to borrow my wings, so she can be an angel in the play, which she picked because her mother's an angel."

Paisley's face falls and she says, "Oooooh, if that isn't the cutest thing you ever heard, your heart is made of stone."

I nod. "I know, I know."

"So you're going?"

"I told her I'd try."

"But?"

I gesture at the boxes. "But I've got a lot of work and I can't always do what I want to do."

I spend all afternoon reviewing case files for audits scheduled next month. I'll have to review them again the week of the meeting, so this is a complete and total waste of time. Why am I dragging my feet? Why don't I march into Shauna's office and tell her I'll take the promotion?

If this offer came in the spring, or even the summer, I might not be struggling as much to accept it. But now, in early December, I'm spending every single morning working on Sub-for-Santa. I'm meeting and talking on the phone with families who are excited to help. I'm holding families' hands so they can provide the necessary paperwork to be included. I'm reading about their children, their darling, precious, little children, and imagining the magic they'll feel on Christmas morning when the impossible happens.

Deep down in my gut, I resent having to let this go even though I know it's not Trudy's fault.

My phone rings and instead of waiting for Paisley to answer it, I pick up. Anything to give me a reason to delay telling Shauna my plan.

"Hello?"

"Mary?" Trudy asks. "It's me."

I giggle. "Hey me, how are you?" Trudy always says it's 'me' and I always pretend I don't know who she is. After so many years, it's not even funny anymore, but it's just what we do.

Trudy forces a laugh. "Ha ha. But seriously. I've finished all the paperwork for Troy's clinical trial. They'll notify us tomorrow for sure, but they think he could start with the continuous insulin monitor, toddler edition, as soon as next week."

"That's amazing," I say.

"Well, kind of. The thing is, to start we need—"

"You need the money. How much exactly?"

"Sixty thousand dollars."

I pinch the bridge of my nose, and briefly consider telling her I'll give her the money only if she stops waiting on her idiotic husband to return. If she moves in with me, the money is hers. Terrorist tactics may not be my best call, so I don't push it. "I've got a meeting with my boss today. I'll see if I can get an advance from her that will hopefully clear that, after tax. I'll call you back tonight or tomorrow."

"Thank you, Mary. You have no idea what this means to me."

I hang up, but I disagree. I know exactly what it means. Sixty-thousand dollars is what it means to her, same as it means to me. Even if my boss can't give me an advance on my bonus, I can pull it out of my retirement account. I'll just have to take a tremendously large penalty for doing it. I regularly chastise clients for acting so imprudently. Maybe this will give me a little more compassion for their idiocy.

I walk down the hall and tap on Shauna's door.

"Come in," she says.

I poke my head inside, and Shauna's head lifts up from a hefty stack of paperwork I'm pretty sure is the quarterly and end of year preliminary reports.

"What do you need?" she asks.

"I've been giving it a lot of thought," I say.

"Wait." Shauna walks across her room and closes the door. "Okay, you've been thinking, and please, please tell me you're going to take the job."

"Actually, I meant to come and tell you I wasn't."

Shauna puts her hand on her hip. "You aren't being smart about this. You're being emotional."

I hold out my hand to stop her. "But my sister's son is really sick, and frankly I need the money. So I'm going to take it, if it's still on the table."

She beams. "Of course. We said you had weeks to decide. I'm so glad it will be you taking my place. I know you love tax returns, but you can still do them, a handful anyway, and you get to review the complex ones to make sure they're accurate, which is more fun than the grunt work ones anyhow."

I like the grunt work. I'm helping people with their lives. "I guess so."

"You can also keep a few of your clients, but you get out of here at a regular time every single day, instead of drowning under piles of paper and millions of forms in the months before tax deadlines."

"I know that too. I hate to seem so ungrateful. I really do appreciate your recommendation."

"You're still upset about your charity thing." Her voice is flat.

"I am. But I'll be okay with it, I swear."

She leans against her desk. "You're going to be the best boss this office has ever had."

"Not better than you," I say loyally.

She snorts. "You're way better at taxes, and you'll do great."

"There is one other thing," I say.

Shauna walks around to sit at her desk chair again, and gestures for me to sit down. "What's that?"

"I know this is a horrible thing to be asking, but my nephew is eligible for a clinical trial that might help eliminate a lot of the terrible side effects type one diabetics suffer from down the road. It's super rare for a kid to be diagnosed this early, and he's struggling. This trial is specific to very young children."

Shauna taps her fingers on the desk. "That all sounds like good news. Why do I sense a 'but'?"

"Because you're smart. The but is that clinical trials cost a lot of money. More money than I have on hand." Or in savings, thanks to my floating the Sub-for-Santa program last time it floundered. I don't mention that, knowing how she feels about it already. "I was hoping I might get an advance on my bonus this year."

Shauna exhales heavily. "Well, the only reason it might be possible is that Frank & Meacham is a small firm, relatively speaking. I'm supposed to review these reports with Peter tonight before he flies back to New York. If you joined us again, and accepted his offer, he'd be delighted. It would be a great time to lay out the news about your nephew and explain why you'd like an advance."

I nod my head. "If he refuses, how sure are we that I'll get a big chunk of money in a month or so?"

"You're thinking of a short term, unsecured loan?"

I nod. "If I can't get an advance, interest on that would be preferable to penalties on my retirement account."

"You better head home and change. Peter only eats at the best of the best. Tonight he's insisting on Uchi."

"I love Uchi. What time are you meeting him there?" Please be early, please be early.

"Six o'clock."

Not great, but it could be worse. If I have to, I can duck out early and channel my inner Nascar to make it to St. Paul's Catholic church for Amy's show. I drive home and change into a pine-green cocktail dress and patent leather, black, high heels. It's only 4:45.

I look up the location for the new Citibank building. It's not too far from Uchi, and I take that as a sign of sorts. I should go by and try and drop off these wings, just in case my dinner goes long. Also, I kind of want to see Luke in his element. I pull into a metered lot a block away, and with my old wings under my arm, I hike down to the construction site. Thinking about him in a hard hat with a utility belt makes me a little swoony.

I walk up the front steps and across the threshold before a barrel chested man with a full beard stops me. "Ma'am you can't walk in here. It's a work zone."

"Uh, I'm looking for Luke Manning." I speak clearly and enunciate each word so he'll understand. "He's head of electrical for the site."

"I speak English, lady." The man spits brown juice on the ground a few inches from my feet. "But he ain't here."

Whether he really speaks English may be debatable, but I don't push the issue. This man's face tells me I shouldn't be here, and I reluctantly agree. But I can't quite help myself asking, "As in, he isn't here right now? Or he doesn't work here?"

The barrel chested man wipes his hand over his mouth. "He's in charge of the electrical crap. Yeah, he works here, a few hours a week, at least." He laughs, and a few other men join in.

"Well, thanks. It was nice to meet you all."

A man standing on scaffolding above the door, where the word Citibank stands out in blue and red, says, "Pretty Boy never talks about anybody. You his girlfriend?"

"You mean he doesn't join in for your reindeer games?" I ask, my eyes wide with feigned innocence. "That's such a shame. I'm sure you boys are delightful to work with, but to answer your question, no, Luke's just a friend."

Whistles and hoots start from all around. The man on the scaffolding swings to the ground. "Luke may be dumb enough to get friend-zoned, but I'd love to ask you out. Name's Xander. What's your name?"

"It's so nice to meet you Xander. My name's Notta."

"Nice to meet you, Notta."

"I forgot to tell you my last name," I say. "It's Chance." I spin around a hundred and eighty degrees and march back toward my car. The sound of laughter, followed by catcalls and hooting follows me, but I don't slow down and I don't look back.

In spite of my ill-advised detour, I reach Uchi with ten minutes to spare. I wait at the bar, and this time no handsome men make eye contact, much less approach me to talk or buy me a drink. I'm ready to start pacing when

Shauna arrives five minutes late. She waves me over and tells the hostess, "Please seat us now, and I'll order some sushi for the table while we wait."

I relax a little. It seems like Shauna's motivated to move this thing along. She and I walk through the year-end reports while we wait for Peter to show up. He finally arrives, thirty-five minutes after six.

I should be leaving right now for Amy's play. Except Trudy and Troy need me, too. If I can't get this advance, I'll have to dump out my retirement accounts, which I vowed never to do, or procure some kind of high interest, short-term loan. I'm a Kleenex being pulled in two directions, about to be ripped in half.

As soon as we finish the quarterly reports, our food arrives and Shauna and Peter both gush about how beautifully presented it is. I can't think of a single good thing to say about my food. It's ten til seven, and I have to get out of here.

"Mr. Meacham," I say, "Shauna hasn't told you the good news yet, but I've been thinking and thinking about it and—"

Shauna says, "Mary doesn't really want the job because she loves tax returns and she loves her end of the year vacation. However, she has in investment opportunity she's keen to try her hand at. I think we can persuade her to take the job if we can somehow give her an advance before the holidays, so she can get in on this deal."

My jaw drops. What's she doing?

Peter's laugh begins in his gut and pours out of his mouth. I almost cover my ears, it's so loud. "I like initiative, you know. Hard line negotiations right out of the gate."

He pats his stomach. "You even waited until I had food in my belly to spring this one on me, huh?"

"Actually," I say, "I am interested in the job but—"

"She was worried you'd think her investment wasn't a wise one, but I assured her you don't get involved in the specifics." Shauna glares at me. The message is clear: let me handle this.

I lean back and cross my arms. "What do you think, sir?"

He smiles. "I think I'd like you to explain the yearly reports to me. Let's see how ready you are for this big promotion. Dazzle me, would you?"

I'm lucky Shauna and I reviewed these earlier, or I'd fall flat on my face right now. "Well, I'm not sure about the dazzling, but I think I can muddle my way through."

I don't impress Peter Meacham, but he doesn't seem to want to take the offer back either. Unfortunately, the annual report is long, like Dead Sea Scrolls long. By the time we're done, I glance at my watch. Seven forty-two. I groan inwardly. Even if I left now, I'd never make it in time. I imagine Amy's face. The poor kid is gonna be devastated, and it's all my fault.

Finally, the dinner wraps up around eight-fifteen. No mention has been made of my advance. "Any chance of that advance, sir?"

Peter grins. "You want the job, and I'm glad. But you're gonna have to wait for the bonus like the rest of us. Trust me, amazing investments come around often. Very often. You'll find plenty of things after the money is in hand, and you'll probably thank me for stopping you from dumping your money into this one."

"The thing is," I say, "it wasn't—"

Shauna touches my arm. "I tried to tell her, it wasn't that great an opportunity to begin with. But if she's really insistent, she can always empty out her retirement account, or take out an equity line of credit."

I keep things together until I reach my car, but then I

break down and sob on the steering wheel. I could have skipped this entire dinner and gone to Amy's play. But work is my priority and I've kept it that way. Amy's not my kid and her dad's not my boyfriend, so why do I feel so awful about missing it?

This is exactly why I should never have gone out with a dad in the first place. At least after tonight, Luke won't push me anymore, I can virtually guarantee. I doubt he'll even be speaking to me.

I should drive straight home, but when my tears dry up, I glance behind me at the feathery wings spread across half of the backseat. The stupid wings I never should have mentioned, much less spent hours hunting for. Or driven by Luke's place of work with. I really hope none of those contractors mention that I dropped by. I've lost my mind since meeting him, and it's time to get things back on track.

I point my car toward home, but somehow I end up halfway to Luke's house before I realize what I'm doing. It may be irrational, but I want to apologize. Not to Luke, but to Amy. The precocious little girl who loves Fruit Loops and will advocate for why she should get them. The tiny little thing who hides in cabinets, and negotiated with her dad for more bedtime stories. The little girl who mournfully and plainly told me that no mother comes to her performances, and she picked an angel because that's what her mom is.

The worst part is that I was that little girl. Only, my mom didn't have a good excuse like being dead. No mother came to my science fair. No mother came to my math competitions. No mother came to my graduation from high school, or from college. I vowed I would never be anything like my own mother.

Now it's my fault Amy's disappointed.

When I reach the Cove, I drive past Luke's RV and notice his Raptor parked behind it. I park my car a few spaces down and put my hand on the handle. Except I can't bring myself to open it. I want to apologize, to explain what I was doing. But when I really think about what I was doing...

I was trying to make my sacrifice for my sister easier for me. I wanted to avoid the necessity of tax penalties or high interest. And it didn't even work.

What's wrong with me lately? I'm a CPA, but somehow that made me lose sight of what matters, and it's not money. It's not making sure my retirement's on track either. It's making sure my sister and her son are taken care of. After all, that's why I'm not ever having kids myself. So that I can have the security I always longed for.

I grab a post-it and write a brief message: Tell Amy I'm sorry, M. I stick it to the wings and leave them on the steps to the RV.

I don't know what I was thinking. I'm not the kind of girl who can enjoy ice cream knowing it's my last bowl. I'm the kid who winds up filling the melty bowl of ice cream with her own tears.

CHAPTER 11

Luke sends me two messages on Friday. A photo of Amy with cardboard wings, and a big old cheesy smile, and a second photo of Amy wearing pajamas, and my white feathery wings. She's waving in the second one. I type fifteen responses, and delete them all without sending.

Obviously he's pissed. He has a right to be. I watch Gilmore Girls until midnight on Friday and fall asleep on the sofa without brushing my teeth.

I always wake up on Saturday and run eight miles in the park around the corner from my little blue house. I don't have a dog to run with, and I don't have a jogging partner, but that's never bothered me. Until today.

On the first mile, I count three dog joggers, and two couple runners. Single joggers? Me and a lady who's seventy if she's a day. I want to stop counting, but I can't seem to help myself. I run faster and faster, running ten miles instead of my usual eight. When I finally walk back to my house and bend over double, the numbers stream like a litany through my head. Eight people on a run with their dogs. Nine couples jogging together. Three singles, counting myself.

I'm drinking a glass of orange juice and waiting to stop sweating before I shower when my phone lights up. Eight-thirty a.m. on a Saturday, and Luke's calling me. He's such a dad.

I want to answer and tell him how sorry I am. I want to ask him if Amy was devastated, or whether she even noticed I wasn't there. I want to pick up, and beg him not to leave in a few weeks. Which is precisely why I don't answer the phone at all.

Instead, I group text Paisley, Trudy, and my oldest friend from school, Addy. GIRLS NIGHT OUT? I COULD REALLY USE ONE.

Addy texts back right away. I'M IN.

Paisley texts next. HECK TO THE YEAH.

I smile. She's so young.

Trudy calls me instead of texting.

"Hello?"

"Hey it's me."

"I'm sorry, I don't know any mes."

"It's your baby sister! It's Ger-trude." She pronounces each syllable slowly. "You know, we had the same crappy parents. Dad passed out on the sofa every day? We ate ramen every day but Friday, when we splurged on hotdogs?"

"Oh," I say. "That me. I vaguely remember you. Okay, what do you want?"

She sighs. "I'd love to go out, but I don't think I can find a sitter for Troy."

I smack my head. Of course she can't. I'm such a jerk.

"We've only been home from the hospital for one night," she says. "I don't want to freak him out."

I should apologize. I should tell her of course she can't

go anywhere. But I can't help the words that pop out next. "What about Chris? Surely he could take a night, since you've dealt with all this alone." I'm so angry at him for being a complete waste of space. Who doesn't even come to the hospital when his son is sick?

"Chris doesn't know yet."

My head almost spins off. I breathe in and out a few times before I speak to avoid yelling at her. "I don't care what your relationship's like right now, he has a right to know what's going on with his son, Trudy."

"He has a girlfriend, Mary. When I asked him why he cheated on me, he said ever since we had Troy, I've been such a drag that he just needed to be with someone fun again. I can't save my family unless I figure out how to be fun again, and monitoring sugar levels and making a three year old take insulin isn't fun."

I swear. Of course Trudy isn't fun. Chris abdicates his responsibilities, leaving her to do everything for their family. It makes it impossible for her to be fun. I don't waste my time explaining that right now.

"He's a loser Trudy. He's lucky if all I do is hunt him down and castrate him. When you call and tell me your son's sick, I don't get to say, 'oh that's inconvenient for me, maybe hit me up next time something bad goes down. Maybe I'll be less annoyed then.' That's not how it works, because family isn't about some kind of twenty-four seven party. It's being there when the crap hits the fan."

And now, for my second act, I've made my sister cry.

"You're better off without him Trudy, and he's a complete idiot in my book, but he deserves to know what's going on. You can't hide the parts of your life involving Troy from him, because those things aren't about you and your insecurities, or your relationship, or even his girlfriend. Your job is to make sure Troy has the support he needs. Swallow your fear and call your husband right now. Not so he can watch his son for what I'm sure is a much needed girls' night out for you, but so that he has a chance to do the right thing."

Trudy whispers, "What if he doesn't?"

"We can only control our own actions. If he doesn't, well you won't need to worry about him having a girlfriend when I'm through with him."

Trudy barks a laugh, and it's far from her normal bubbling joy, but I'll take it. "And hey, I know it's later than you wanted, but I should be able to get the money you need by Wednesday or Thursday of next week." A home equity line of credit will take too long, months it turns out, but if I empty out my retirement account, even with the withholdings, it should be enough.

"Thanks Mary. You'll never know how grateful I am. I'll call Chris today, I swear."

"You better. I'll check in tomorrow, and if you haven't told him by then, I'll call him myself. I'm joking about the castration, because I like not being in jail, but I doubt there will be a realm further from fun than any conversation he and I might have."

Once I've showered, I head over to the Sub-for-Santa office where I know Paisley is waiting for me to meet with nominees. It's one of my favorite things to do, so when Luke calls again, I pretend it didn't happen. He doesn't leave a message or text me, so it's relatively easy to ignore.

Paisley makes it a little harder. "Your phone's lighting up like a roman candle on New Year's. What's up?"

I blush.

"Luke, huh? Why aren't you hunched over it, fingers frantically sending witty banter back to the big guy?"

I roll my eyes.

"If you aren't careful, your eyes will get stuck that way."

"Oh please. That's just something moms say."

"Well," Paisley says, "since your mom bailed like a loser, I figured you might not have heard. But seriously, why aren't you replying?"

"He's not texting," I say. "He's *calling*."

Paisley's jaw drops. "What is he, sixty?"

I nod. "I know, right? People don't call, not anymore. And I missed his daughter's play, and I have no idea how to tell him sorry. Actually, I don't even want to say sorry. I'm mad I'm in this situation, and I think I ought to just break things off. We were supposed to have a date tonight, but obviously that's off now that I ruined everything. He hasn't brought it up at all, not even to talk about where or what or when."

"Hence the girls night?"

I nod.

Paisley bites her lip and doesn't bring it up again, and that's when I know I'm probably right. I've irredeemably screwed this up, and it shouldn't even matter, but for some reason it does.

Around five, Paisley and I have worked through sixteen families, adding eleven to our list for this year. Paisley leaves to get ready for our girls' night, but I stick around to compile a list of match emails I'll need to send to sponsoring families. By the time I finish, I feel calmer about everything.

I am not my mother. The only duty I owe is to my sister and her son. I'm fulfilling that, even if it sets my retirement back a little. Or a lot.

My phone bings, and it's a message from Addy. BEN IS SICK AND WANTS ME HOME. CAN WE DO TOMORROW?

Addy's high maintenance husband would drive me nuts. He's sick, so she has to stay home and what? Ladle chicken noodle soup into his mouth? I roll my eyes, but before I can reply, Paisley does.

BEN CAN SUCK A LEMON.

I smirk. TMW. FINE BY ME.

Paisley sends a variety of colorful emoticons, which I take to mean she's okay with moving it to tomorrow.

On the drive home, I'm almost relieved. After my long run, and my long Saturday in my secondary office, I'm ready to unwind, not go dancing. I pull into my garage and walk through the door into my kitchen. I take my boots off and leave them by the door. Then I unzip my skirt and lay it over the back of a chair. I toss my blouse on top of my end table, and once I reach my bedroom, I pull on a Metallica t-shirt, big flannel pajama pants I stole from Foster, and fluffy pink bunny slippers Paisley gave me last Christmas.

No one loves Christmas like Pais. I'm actually surprised she didn't give me a full pink bunny suit. *The Christmas Story* is her favorite movie.

So far today, I've only consumed one ham sandwich, and one bowl of multigrain cheerios. After running ten miles, I need food. I mentally scan the inside of my fridge to see what I might make. Scrambled eggs. Toast with jam. A salad with boiled eggs. I open the freezer and I realize why none of that sounded great when I see a pint of double chocolate Blue Bell ice cream. I usually eat quite clean, and I'm over Foster, and I barely know Luke, and money is only money. But still, it's been a long week.

I grab the pint and consider a bowl, but since I love the environment, I really ought to eat it straight from the container. I plop down on my sofa and turn on an episode of Gilmore Girls. The one where Jess finally kisses Rory, one of my favorites. Dopey Dean's upset, but it's totally worth it. I've only eaten a few bites when there's a knock at the door. I pause my show just as Jess is about to kiss her. I'm cranky about the timing on this person, whoever it is.

Ice cream in hand, I stroll toward the door. Who would be here at six p.m. on a Saturday? It's probably Paisley in platform heels wearing a light-up Christmas tree sweater. That girl loves her eggnog. It would be just like her to try to convince me to go out both nights, and feel like she's doing me a favor.

I swing the door open while saying, "I'm too tired, Pai—"

Luke's arm is raised as though he was about to knock again. He's not wearing a Christmas tree sweater, but the sweater he is wearing is a festive color of cranberry. His eyes travel from my face, down to my toes and then back up again.

"Uh, hey there Mary. I couldn't get you on the phone to confirm, but I thought we had a date."

I force a smile and hope my mouth isn't too chocolate-y. As if that's my problem right now.

CHAPTER 12

He frowns. "I guess I know in the future that if you don't answer when I call, our plans are off."

"I left the wings for Amy when I missed the pageant. I thought. . ." I trail off, because what was I thinking? We had a date planned, but then I raced into the house so fast last time, I wasn't sure whether it was on or not. Then after I completely flaked on Amy's performance and didn't answer his calls, he thought everything was fine?

"Why yes," Luke says, "I would love to come inside to talk about this where it's warm."

"Uh, sure." I open the door wider and tilt myself sideways so he can push past me and into my living room. He's carrying some kind of box, and I'm wondering what it is until I notice my skirt and blouse and boots are strewn all over the room. I haven't done dishes in days, and I badly need to sweep. My face flushes and want to run and hide, or yell at Luke, or maybe both.

"You really didn't think we had a date tonight, did you?"

I shake my head. "Not after I missed Amy's performance, no."

"You said you'd try to come. You're working two jobs, and you did bring the wings by, which was a kind gesture. Amy's been alternating between pretending to be a bird and an angel all day long. Chase is pretending to be a cat whenever she's a bird, so there's been a lot of shrieking, but all in all, I'd say bringing those over was a good idea."

"I'm glad she's enjoying them." My fingers itch to clean up the dishes. My feet itch to walk into my closet, to hide or at least change out of these absurd pajamas. Luke's presence locks me into place.

"Did you come by the job site Thursday?" he asks.

I nod. "Yeah. I had a work meeting sprung on me late Thursday night to prepare for my new promotion, and I was worried I'd miss Amy's performance. I thought maybe I could drop off her wings to you there since it was on my way to the meeting."

Luke beams. "That was considerate. I'm sorry I missed you. I'd just left. You made quite an impression on the boys. I'm sorry they were so awful."

I raise one eyebrow. "How did you know they were gross?"

He grins, both dimples showing and I melt a little bit. "Safe guess, because they're always gross around women when they're in a group for some reason. It's like they lose their collective minds. I'm sorry for that."

"Should I go change clothes?" I ask.

Luke shrugs out of his coat. "You said you were tired when you answered the door. Why don't we order pizza and hang out here. Unless you want me to leave?"

I shake my head. "No, it's fine. I just thought you'd be upset, and Amy too."

He frowns. "Amy was sad, but you told her you'd try, and you explained you had a lot of work. It was a pretty last minute invite."

"Maybe I should change clothes."

"If you're uncomfortable you should, but don't change for me. I think you look great."

I sputter. "Nothing about this twenty year old t-shirt and hand me down pajama pants ensemble is great."

He shrugs. "It works for you. You look as beautiful as the first night I saw you in that red dress."

"That better not be true."

"It's my truth." Luke pulls out his phone. "What pizza place do you like?"

"Sorrento's is good and they're close. Since we're at my house, it can be my treat." I grab my phone and dial the number, turning toward the kitchen so he can't object. "Yes, this is Mary Wiggin. I'd like a large pizza, half with pineapple and bacon and. . ." I turn to ask Luke what he wants, but he's moved.

He's standing just behind me. He lifts the phone from my hand, and says, "One large with pineapple and bacon for the entire pizza. Also, breadsticks and cinnastix. And I'd like to pay with a credit card."

I shake my head and try to grab the phone back, but he blocks me easily.

"It's my house," I squeak. "It's my phone. It's my pizza place!"

He moves quickly for such a big guy. Every time I get close to my phone, he turns and slips away.

"What were you?" I ask. "A quarterback?"

He rattles off a sequence of numbers and an expiration date, and hits end call. He tosses my phone to the sofa and holds up both hands. "Truce! I call a truce."

I put my hand on my hip. "You can't call a truce once the bomb's already gone off. Besides, you started it."

"No, I didn't," he says. "Besides, I have a score to settle.

You think I'm poor. You tried to sign me and my kids up to get a free Christmas."

I sigh.

"Look, I'm just trying to be gentlemanly. I know it's not popular anymore, but I'm old fashioned. I can't club a baby seal and drag it home for dinner, but I can pay for pizza when you need a night in."

My heart twinges when I think about how we can only call dinner in for another few weeks before he'll be gone. Which, I remind myself, is the only reason I'll even date someone like him.

"What are you watching?" Luke asks.

I blush again like an idiot. "It's an old show about a mom and daughter." A way better mom than I got, and a daughter who almost always does everything right. I'm watching parent porn, I suppose. I walk into the living room and grab the remote so I can shut it off, regrettably right before the best part. "I've seen it way too many times."

Luke raises one eyebrow. "Wait, you thought our date was cancelled. Is this your breakup movie?"

"We didn't break up," I say.

He raises his eyebrows. "Well, I know that. But you didn't."

I shake my head. "You and I weren't even going out."

He brings one hand to his chest in feigned horror. "And only a few days ago, you proclaimed I was your boyfriend to your ex."

"This isn't my breakup movie anyway," I say. "That's *While You Were Sleeping*. Or *Someone Like You*." I exhale noisily. "Gilmore Girls as a breakup movie? It's not even a movie."

"Well, as long as it's not signaling the doom of our love, I'd be happy to watch it with you," he says.

"Uh, I really doubt you'd enjoy it. It resides squarely in the chick-flick-rom-com zip code."

He sits down on the couch. "I like chick flicks, or at least I like some of them. The funny ones, the smart ones. *You've Got Mail,* and *Kate and Leopold,* for example."

I sit down next to him and clutch a pillow to my chest. "Well, you can't watch this episode. It'll ruin the whole show. You've gotta start from the beginning." I queue it up on Netflix and hit play, but sitting a foot away from him on my couch, my eye's drawn to our clothing. My ratty pajamas versus his beautiful red sweater and dark jeans. "I'm going to run change clothes. I'll be right back."

Luke bobs his head, which I take as agreement.

Once I'm standing in my room, I'm crippled by indecision. Pants, or a skirt? Blouse, or a fitted t-shirt? Or should I wear a dress? That's probably going to look like I'm trying too hard.

I finally choose a dove grey cashmere sweater and pull it over my head. I've just poured myself into a pair of black jeggings when I realize that I'll melt to death in this. I pull both things off and toss them into a pile. I try a skirt and red blouse next, but it's too 'look at me look at me'. I can't go from pajamas to a girl's night out ensemble. Too pathetic. I toss that into the corner, too. I try on another handful of outfits before settling on a white fitted t-shirt and lightweight, black, cargo pants. I'm not in pajamas, but it doesn't scream that I'm trying too hard.

When I open my door, I realize Luke's washing my dishes. By the looks of the pile, he's been at it for a while. I walk closer and realize he's almost done. And the floor has obviously been swept. I don't even have time to object to his menial labor before the doorbell rings.

Luke jogs to the door and signs for the bill, as I take the pizza from the delivery guy.

"Merry Christmas, Dave."

Dave grins at me. "Nice to see you ordering a large."

I roll my eyes and carry the pizza over to a kitchen counter that now shines like a new penny. By the time I'm pulling plates out of the cabinet, Luke has shut and locked the door and he's drying the last bowl.

"Luke. You can't clean my house."

"Why not?"

"It's embarrassing. Maybe even worse than the pajamas."

"Why?" he asks, looking genuinely puzzled. "You've got a full time job and a full time charitable gig, and you said you were exhausted. I figured you'd be happy for a little help. Unless . . . did I wash something wrong?"

I shake my head. "You did everything right."

He smiles.

"But we're missing Gilmore Girls, and that's an unforgivable sin."

"I was watching while I cleaned," Luke protests.

I groan. "You're one of those people."

Luke puts four slices on his plate and carries it across the room. "What does that mean?"

"You can't really relax," I say. "You watch and clean. You watch and cook. You watch and work."

"I prefer to think of myself as efficient."

"But it makes me feel guilty." I grab a piece for myself. "You want anything to drink, Mister Efficiency?"

"I'm guessing you don't have any beer, since you said you don't drink?"

I shake my head. "Sorry."

"It's fine. Root beer?"

I grab two sodas and carry them to the sofa, along with my pizza and the box of breadsticks.

"Whoa there girl, you're gonna drop that." Luke springs up and takes the breadsticks and sodas from me.

"Watch the show," I say.

Luke sets everything on the coffee table and grabs his plate. The amount of food he eats is impressive, even to me. And I have twelve hundred extra calories today thanks to my run.

"How do you stay so fit?" I ask.

"You think I'm fit?" His big blue eyes widen. "I'll be honest. I got winded walking up your front porch step."

I roll my eyes. "Oh fine, don't answer."

"I'm pretty active at work, and with my kiddos at home. I do lift a few times a week at the Y. Mostly, I think I got pretty lucky, genetically speaking."

I'll say.

He finishes his pizza and grabs the dishes, hauling them all into the kitchen. I pause the show.

"Why'd you stop it?" he asks.

I shrug. "It's disrespectful not to pay attention."

He whistles. "You are serious about this show. Well, since you've got it stopped anyway, maybe this is a good time for you to show me that closet light that doesn't work." He crosses to the entry and grabs his box. Why didn't I realize he'd be planning to fix my dumb light?

Uh, the light in my master, where there are piles of clothes everywhere? He'll either think I'm a slob or he'll know I completely freaked out when I went to my room to change. I'm not sure which is worse.

"Mary?"

"No, yeah, I mean, sure. Lemme show you where it is." I walk slowly toward my bedroom, trying to figure out how I can stall him and go tidy it up first.

"Wait." I stop and turn toward him, placing one hand on

his chest. My fingers curl against the hard muscle and I want to grab his sweater and pull him close to me. "Is this just a ploy so I'll owe you and you can get your taxes done for free?"

Luke grins, but there's something weird about his smile. I can't figure out what.

"Because if so, I have to tell you, I'm the best accountant at my firm, and it's a good firm. One of the nation's best. It'll cost you more than one closet light repair for me to do your taxes. Especially if you're self-employed."

His eyes travel down to my mouth, and a shiver runs through me. He leans toward me slowly, so slowly that part of me wants to run and part of me wants to grab him and pull him closer. Kiss me already!

"Trust me," he whispers the words an inch away from my lips. "If I ever ask you to do my taxes, I'll pay you much more than a simple closet repair."

If he asks me? Like I'm not good enough? I put one hand on my hip and back up until I bump into the door. "I'm an awesome CPA. You'd be lucky to have me do your taxes."

He throws his head back and laughs. "I believe you, absolutely. I'll just say, my taxes are extremely complex and thinking about them gives me a horrible headache. I don't want to associate you with a headache."

"Oh," I say, suddenly wishing I hadn't put so much space between us.

Luke closes the space and presses his mouth to mine so fast I don't have any time to fret. A thrill runs from my toes up to the top of my head and I shiver. He wraps his arms around me then, as if he wants to warm me up. He has no idea that he's the one causing the tremor. I collapse against him, my hand winding up around his neck and into his hair, but far too soon he pulls back and clears his throat.

"Not that I couldn't do that all day gladly, but this box is kind of heavy." He hefts it up and down. "Maybe we focus on the closet for now and circle back to this later."

The blood rushes to my face, and I spin around to open the door. I don't walk through though, because I forgot what a mess things are in here. Ugh. If I ask to run in and clean up, that's weird. Since I already told him he can fix my light, I'll just have to hope he's not too judgmental. He's already washed a sink full of dishes for me. How much worse could this be?

As I walk through my room, I see it anew through the eyes of a stranger. My bed isn't made. My dresser's covered with page after page of lists from United Way, and files from work. Lotion, tissues, a lamp, jewelry, and an assortment of oddball things clutter up the top of my nightstand. I cringe. Even without those things, there's a huge pile of pillows on the floor near my bed, and several smaller heaps of clothes lying haphazardly all over. On my dresser, on the floor by the door, and near the foot of my bed.

I groan. "It's not usually this messy. Like I said, it's been a long week."

"I'm a guy," Luke says. "Nothing bothers me. But do you have a stool, by chance? Or a short ladder?"

"Yes, of course. I'll go grab one, but that's the light that's not working." I point through the master bath, which is pretty clean, thank goodness, and toward the closet door.

I fetch him a stool, and then work on tidying up my room while he climbs up on the stool and starts fiddling with the light in the closet. He comes out to ask where the breaker is, and I show him the garage, which is immaculate at least. Less than eight minutes later, I know because I watch the clock, my closet light blinks on.

"Good job." I clap. "That was so fast."

He walks out with his box. "Now cinnastix, and Gilmore Girls."

Once we're both sitting on the sofa again, I un-pause the show. He watches it dutifully, while I mostly watch him. His high cheekbones, and his square jaw, which is stubbly this late at night, make my heart flutter. Once we're done with the cinnastix, I turn out the lights and settle back down on the sofa, but I don't want to be obvious, so I sit on the far end, leaning on the armrest on the left side.

He laughs when Lorelai and her mother start fighting in the kitchen. "You like this movie because the grandmother's a nightmare?"

I can't really tell him it's because the mother has no reason to fight for her daughter, but she does anyway. It sounds too pathetic.

Just before the first episode ends, he shifts to stretch his legs. "I'm freezing over here. What's your thermostat set at?"

"I can get you a blanket," I say.

He sighs. "That line didn't work at all. I'll have to throw it out of the rotation." He pats the sofa next to him. "I'd rather you come over here and warm me up."

My heartbeat picks up and adrenaline shoots through my body. I slide over, and his left arm wraps around me and draws my head up against his chest. His breath ruffles my hair and I curl a little closer. The first episode ends, and I turn my face toward Luke to ask whether he wants to watch another, but his eyes aren't on the TV.

They stare into mine, as his head comes down slowly. I could pull away, and maybe I should, but I don't. His full, beautiful, half smiling lips lower and lower, and I move up toward him until our mouths finally meet. I close my eyes then, and give over to the feeling of a man's mouth on mine.

His lips press lightly at first, and then pull back. My ragged breathing fills the room for one beat, and then another, but before I open my eyes, his mouth covers mine again, this time harder, more insistent. When I bring my left arm up to his right shoulder and pull him closer, he moans against my lips.

Something inside my chest tingles, and when his arms wrap around my waist and pull me closer still, I reach both hands up to his face. It's been a long time since I kissed anyone. So long that I forgot how much I missed it.

Luke knows exactly what he's doing, kissing me lightly, and then pulling back enough that I whimper before pressing his advantage. His hand skims the bare skin between my shirt and my pants, and I melt inside. I place his hand on the bottom of my shirt, ready for more.

Until Luke stiffens. I don't know why until some of the fog clears out of my brain and I realize his phone is playing The Eye of the Tiger. His strong hands shift me upright, and reach into his pocket. He fishes it out and says, "Yes?"

Why wouldn't he ignore his phone? I doubt I'd have noticed if an entire First Baptist Choir started singing carols on my front porch.

"No, the doctor said he only needed that the first day. He's fine to have crackers if he wants, and Seven-up, too. But he's probably okay to have spaghetti or cereal at this point. He hasn't thrown up in more than twenty-four hours."

His kids. Of course, but what a buzz kill. My head clears quickly and I scoot back over to the far side of the sofa. I skip Gilmore Girls episode two back to the beginning, and then pause it.

Luke hangs up his phone. "Sorry about that. My cousin wasn't completely clear on what to do with Chase."

"Oh, it's fine. I totally understand," I lie. I know nothing about puking kids, thank goodness. He's a good dad, which is great for the world. It's just not great for me.

"Why'd you run off?" He smiles at me and pats the sofa cushion.

"I'm kind of tired. Maybe we ought to call it a night. Plus, it sounds like Chase needs you."

Luke grins even wider, and scoots closer to me. "You're jealous."

"That's ridiculous."

He smiles so big there's a little gap on either side of his teeth. "You're jealous of my kids."

I smash myself as far back against the armrest as I can. "I'm not. That would be idiotic."

"You are."

"Are you calling me dumb?"

He snorts and shakes his head. "Not at all. But I saw your face, and I may be pretty rusty, but I recognize that look."

I roll my eyes, and when he scoots toward me again, I stand up. "I'm not jealous, but I am a pragmatist. I meant to tell you this Monday." I take a big breath in and let it out. "This isn't going to work."

Luke tilts his head. "For something that doesn't work, that kiss felt pretty good to me."

I shake my head vehemently. "No, what I mean is, you've got kids and I can't deal with that. Also, you're moving."

"I am moving. Soon."

I nod. "Right. As I said, this whole thing," I gesture from him to myself and back again, "is doomed. You'll just have to wait to look for a booty call until you've gotten to Kentucky."

Luke rocks back on the sofa, eyes wide. "That's not at all what this is. Is that what it feels like to you? I was hoping you'd come to my daughter's Christmas pageant, for heaven's sake. If that's what you do with someone you're only using then. . ."

"No, no, that's not what I mean. Look, all I'm saying is." I sit on the sofa. Everything's a jumble in my head. Foster's getting married to someone who wants kids. I'm getting a promotion I don't want since I said I'd take it, but it's not like that's going to help me, since I have to dump out my retirement for sweet little Troy. I'm going to have to work forever.

Then it hits me, and I'm embarrassed I didn't think of this before. I'm a CPA for heaven's sake. But it's been a long week, and I've had a lot on my mind. I can take it out as a rollover. Use that money, and as long as the same amount goes into another retirement fund within thirty days, I won't owe penalties. I beam.

"Now you're super happy? I'm a little confused right now."

I perch on the edge of the sofa, a foot away from Luke. I want him to take my hand in his. I want him to pull me close and kiss me until I forget my own name again. But that's not going to help, and it'll make things way worse tomorrow. "What I meant was, you're moving, and I'm not. It'll only hurt you and your kids and me if we keep seeing each other. So this needs to be goodbye."

His eyebrows shoot up. "You used me for a closet repair, didn't you? This happens to me all the time."

"I'm serious." I swat his forearm, and he grabs my hand. Electricity zings up my arm and I shiver. I yank my hand back.

"So am I. I don't know what we're doing, and I know you don't want to marry me, okay? I'm okay with that, because I'm leaving soon."

"Then we're on the same page."

"No." He shakes his head. "We aren't. Because you're

trying to break up with me every twenty minutes, and I'm thinking about you, every day, from the moment I wake up until the minute I go to sleep. I don't even comprehend how you want to pretend we never met. I can't do that. I'd rather eat a donut while I live across from the bakery than pretend it doesn't exist because I'm moving."

I pull my hand free of his big, callused, manly hand, and fold my arms. "I'm tired of being baked goods or ice cream. And we're at an impasse, because I can't date you. It'll hurt too much. Sticking with your analogy, I don't want to deal with the miserable, gut wrenching diet later."

Luke runs his hand through his hair. "Fine. We won't date. But Amy's been badgering me to invite you over. I know you don't want to be a stand-in-mom, but would you at least come to dinner tomorrow?"

This is exactly what's wrong with kids. You give them an inch and they ask for more, more, more. It's never enough because kids need everything. And I can't give them everything, so it's better if I give them nothing at all.

I need to tell Luke that I won't go to dinner. I won't further complicate this mess we've made. I won't become more embroiled in his life. I don't have the time or the energy, which is why my house is falling apart and everything is such an embarrassing mess. That's what I need to say. It seems sort of harsh, so I try a more tactful method.

"I'm shopping for Christmas presents," I say, "for my own family and friends, and for my assigned family tomorrow. I'm not sure how long it will take."

Luke tosses his hands in the air, and grins. "Perfect. We were doing the same thing. We could shop together, and then go back to my place and I'll grill."

He's like gum on my shoe. Really hot, really sexy gum that I don't actually want to scrape off even though I know that I should.

"Oh fine." I give in, but I hold up one finger and wave it in his face. "But it's not a date!" And after this, I'm definitely phasing them out. It'll be easy to do, because with my new job, Troy's medical stuff and Sub-for-Santa, it's about to get super crazy.

CHAPTER 13

My hands shake when I reach up to knock on the door to the trailer where Luke and his two kids live, and not because it's cold. The light snowfall brought a smile to my face this morning. I love the snow, and my coat is plenty warm. My hands are shaking because I should have cancelled. I shouldn't be spending any more time with Luke, or his daughter Amy.

I breathe in and out slowly and lift my fist again, but before I can knock, the door opens.

My mouth drops.

Amy grins up at me, her thick, russet hair plaited in pristine braids, not a single fuzzy spot or hair out of place. "Hey Mary! I saw you through the window and I've been waiting for you to knock, but you never did. I got tired of waiting."

I glance behind Amy to where her dad's standing with a bemused expression on his classically handsome face. "She was probably answering a text or something, honey. It's not polite to tell people you were staring at them or that you thought they were moving slowly."

Amy frowns. “She had to know I saw her, or why'd I open the door, Dad?”

He shakes his head. “Come on in, Mary. If we can ever find Chase's shoe, we'll be ready to go. Recovery from lunch took a little longer than I thought, since Chase dumped his entire bowl of SpaghettiOs on the floor.”

“It was an accident,” a voice I presume belongs to Chase whines from the other room.

Luke rolls his eyes heavenward and ducks back behind me into the door he called his bedroom last time. My pulse picks up a little thinking about what his bedroom looks like. His bed. I shake my head to clear my thoughts.

“Where did you see it last?” I ask Amy.

She puts one hand on her hip and tilts her head just like her dad does. “If we remembered that, I wouldn't be looking.”

I smirk. “Well, where have you looked?”

“Why don't you come with me,” Amy says. “You can help me check my room.”

“You have your own room?” I follow her through the living room and out a door, into a small room with bunk beds built into the wall.

She scrunches her nose. “Ever since he got out of a crib, me and Chase have to share.”

I laugh. “It does make sense. Your dad probably wants his space.”

She sighs like a teenager. “What about me? I want my own space, and now I have to share these tiny drawers with him.”

She points at the five drawers directly across from the bunk beds.

“They don't look so tiny to me.” I crouch down and look under the bunk bed. No shoe immediately obvious, but a blue rabbit, a green Christmas stocking and a red fire truck sort of block my line of vision. I pull them out and notice a red Stride Rite sneaker jammed into the back corner. I flatten down and shimmy toward the back, my coat rubbing against the bed frame. All the shimmying and whatnot has left me sweating in my coat. I should've taken it off.

I shove one more inch, and finally my fingers close over the shoe. I inchworm back out and straighten up to my knees, holding it aloft triumphantly.

Amy's mouth forms a little "o", and she and I walk out into the family room.

"I think I found it," I say loudly, and maybe a little too proudly.

Luke clears his throat, and I notice he's sitting on the floor near the front door, shoving a little boy's foot into a scuffed brown shoe. "We just found it. But hey, you did find *a* shoe."

I glance from the small red shoe in my hand to the brown one being shoved on Chase's foot. The one I found is obviously far too small.

Chase, shoes on both feet, leaps up and grins at me. One second later, he chucks a small, blue, rubber ball and it beans me in the nose.

"Catch," he belatedly says.

Stars burst across my field of vision and I bring my hand up to my nose. No blood drips from it, so that's something.

"Chase, no! We don't throw balls at anyone, much less a guest." Luke runs across to where I'm standing and touches my hand. "Are you alright?"

I nod, feeling silly for keeping my hand over my face, but it still smarts. "It's fine. It startled me, is all." I force my hand down to my side, but my right eye waters so badly that I have to reach back up and wipe the tears away.

"You're crying," Amy yells. "Chase you need to apologize."

Chase's chubby cheeked face falls, and he turns toward the corner of the room and starts to cry himself.

Amy yells at Chase, which makes him cry more.

Instead of screaming, Luke laughs. He crouches down by Amy. "That's not helping, sweetheart. Please stop screaming at him."

Amy balls her hands into fists and stomps her foot, but she stops hollering.

"Chase, come see Dad. I know you're embarrassed now, but little men always say sorry when they've done something wrong. My friend Miss Mary, came to go shopping with us, and she's not going to stay if we're rude and throw balls at her face."

Chase shakes his head, but won't leave the corner.

Luke whispers to me, "I'm sorry. I know this is annoying, but I can't let it go. That's how kids end up spoiled and not listening. He'll come around in a minute and once he apologizes, we can go. It'll be fine."

I've been around Troy enough to know he's embarrassed. Trudy insists on Troy apologizing before we can move on, too.

I walk over to where Chase is facing the corner and crouch down. "Hi, Chase. My name is Mary. I'm not upset about the ball. I have a nephew who's close to your age, and he loves balls, too. I'm usually faster at blocking them."

He angles his head a bit. "Your nephew throws balls a lot? In the house?"

Chase's dark, dark hair and almost black brows frame eyes that are practically golden. He must take after his mother. "How old are you, Chase?"

He turns back toward the wall, and I can barely hear his mumbled words. "Four."

"My nephew is named Troy, and he's only three for two more months, so he's not as wise and well behaved as you. His mother's always telling him not to throw balls, but sometimes he forgets."

Chase nods. "Me too."

"I forget things, sometimes."

He turns around and peers into my face. "You do? Like what?"

I shrug. "I have a lot of things to do at work. A lot of numbers to look at, and a lot of forms to fill out. Sometimes I forget one. In fact, during tax season, I have another person whose entire job it is to go behind me checking what I do to make sure I don't forget things."

Chase's eyes widen. "Is it your mom?"

I shake my head. "No, actually, I haven't seen my mother in more than twenty years."

Chase's mouth drops open. "Why not?"

I realize his mother died around the time he was born and wish I could bite my own tongue off. "My mom didn't like being a mom," I say awkwardly. "It made her really sad, and after a while, she left our family."

He nods his head. "My mom didn't want to leave, but she had to go back to heaven. God needed her."

My heart cracks a little bit. "I'm sorry to hear that, and I'm sure she misses you a lot."

"I'm sorry your mom left on purpose."

No one has said anything like that to me, maybe ever. My eyes well with tears and I blink them back before I scare this tiny human. "Me too, buddy. But it was a long time ago, and I'm okay now."

He reaches out a hand and puts it on my shoulder. "Are you sure?"

I nod my head. "I'm sure."

"I'm sorry I hit you in the face with my ball," Chase says. "You're pretty nice."

I force my mouth into a smile. "That was a very nice apology." I stand up. "I bet your dad will let us go to the store now. Are you excited to do some shopping?"

Chase shrugs. "Not really. Dad says we're not buying anything for me, not even the dollar stuff."

I glance at Luke and he nods. "We have very limited space, and we already have everything we need, right?"

Amy smirks. "Not everything."

Luke bundles Chase and Amy into coats, and I can't help myself. "What is it you don't have, Amy?"

"Not this again." Luke rolls his eyes heavenward.

"A puppy," Amy says. "We don't even have a single pet. Not even a boring old fish. Dad says the water would slosh too much when we move. But a dog wouldn't slosh at all."

Luke's voice sounds weary when he says, "You can't have a dog—"

"In a trailer." Amy stomps her foot. "Dad, I know. You've only said that a gazillion times." Amy pulls a pair of mittens out of her pocket, and I notice one is blue, and the other is green. "But we could have a cat, maybe. No one would hardly even notice a cat."

Luke picks up Chase and opens the door. "Maybe one day, okay? When you're older, and you can take care of it, but not yet."

Amy trudges out to her dad's truck and waits patiently while he buckles Chase into a booster seat. Once Chase is buckled in, she scrambles under and climbs into her booster, buckling herself in.

"You're still in a five point harness?" I ask.

She rolls her eyes. "Don't ask. Dad's a little bit paranoid."

I turn toward Luke and widen my eyes. "Paranoid, huh?"

He shrugs. "She's like a sponge. Don't even get me started on the technical electrical words she uses. I swear, if I could take her on a job with me, I could let about half my guys go."

I climb into the passenger side and buckle a beaming Amy. "When I grow up, I'm going to work with my dad. He already said he'll hire me."

I nod. "It's great you know what you want to do. I had no idea at your age. I thought I would be a famous ballerina."

Amy's eyes widen. "Can you dance?"

I shake my head. "Not even a little bit. I couldn't even do the Macarena."

"The whadda?"

I laugh. "It's an old song that you wouldn't know. I'm so bad they'd have laughed me off the stage if I ever auditioned."

Luke clucks. "I doubt that." He turns the truck on, and then reaches over and takes my gloved hand in his before pulling out onto the main road. My heart flip flops and I close my eyes. I've always loved the holidays more than the rest of the year combined, but between a new job that I don't want starting in January, and Luke leaving, this New Years is gonna suck.

We've driven half a mile from the RV Park when Chase says, "We've been in the truck forever. How far are we going?"

Luke chortles. "Target. It's another mile and a half away. Think you'll possibly survive that long?"

Chase whines. "I don't know ke-cause I'm starving."

Luke smiles. "Because. And how can you be hungry? You ate lunch an hour ago."

I've been around Troy enough to know that it doesn't matter how recently Chase ate, not to a kid. In fact, once Troy started complaining of hunger as we were driving away from the IHOP parking lot.

I'm pretty proud of myself when I pull two bags of Fruit Loops out of my purse. "If it's okay with your dad, I brought you guys some snacks."

If Amy were an emoji, her face would've had hearts for eyeballs. Once I get the nod from Luke, I hand the baggies back.

Not two seconds after they started eating, Chase chimes in again. "I'm thirsty."

I pull two sippy cups out of my purse and pass those back without asking. Every dad allows water, right?

"Umm, Mary Poppins, what did you bring for me?" Luke asks. "I'm starting to feel a little left out over here."

"My bag is kind of magical. It may only be a knock off Prada from Mexico, but my sister Trudy calls it my magical Aunt bag."

"Your sister's name is Trudy?" Amy's nose scrunches and her eyes squint up.

I nod and stifle a laugh. "Yeah, it wasn't my mom's best decision."

"I would be so mad at my mom if she named me that." Amy smiles. "I like Amy. And I like Mary, too."

I bob my head. "Well, my dad named me after his mother, so my mom got to name their next child."

"You're lucky you were born first." Amy crunches on a Fruit Loop loudly.

"You're not wrong kid. You're not wrong." For more reasons than she knows.

Once we reach Target, both kids have emptied their bags. "Thanks," Amy tells me when she hands me the empty Ziploc. She glares at Chase, but he drops his baggie on the floor and jumps into his dad's arms. She sighs and shakes her head. "It's like he has no manners at all."

I laugh this time, and Luke does too. "Chase, tell Miss Mary thank you."

"Thanks," he says. "I like cereal."

Chase holds Luke's hand across the wet sidewalk, but instead of walking over to take Luke's other hand, Amy looks up at me. "Can I hold your hand, Miss Mary?"

My heart cracks a little bit inside, and I can barely speak through the frog that crawled into my throat. "Sure."

Neither of us stumble or slip on the way inside, but when we reach the front of the store and the doors slide open, I don't want to let go. I do though, so that I can pull my list out of my coat pocket and reach for a cart.

"What are you looking for?" Amy asks me.

"I have a family with two girls." I don't admit that every year I choose at least one family with two girls. Just like my family. "I figure that's easier, because I have no idea what to buy for boys."

"Can I help you shop, then? Dad said we have one girl who's seven and I'm really grown up for my age. You and me can pick that stuff and we can let the boys go get dumb Legos and stuff."

"You don't like Legos?" I ask.

Amy shakes her head. "Chase left his out once, and I stepped on one. I threw them all away before he woke up from his nap, and no one's ever noticed."

Luke's jaw drops. "You threw them out? I didn't know where they went."

Amy's eyes dart from side to side, and then she looks at her feet.

"If something cut my finger, I'd toss it too," I say. "I think that was sensible."

"Legos cost an arm and a leg," Luke says. "Besides. You can't go around throwing away other people's things."

Amy's bottom lip sticks out. "You threw out my Barbie."

"You cut off the bottom of her feet," Luke says. "She was broken."

"She got sick of wearing heels all the time," Amy says. "She wasn't broken. She was improved."

Luke grins in spite of himself. "The point is, no more throwing things away without asking me. Okay?"

Amy nods. "Sorry. But can Mary and I go shop and you get the boring boy stuff?"

Luke glances up at me, clearly nervous about cutting me loose with one of his kids. This was supposed to be time with him, not babysitting hour. I glance down at Amy's eager face. Her eyes shine up at me, her teeth catching her bottom lip.

I nod at Luke. "It's fine with me. I'd like her help picking out something for my sister. With a name like Gertrude, she really needs a good Christmas present this year."

Luke snorts. "Meet back here near the carts in an hour?"

I shake my head. "We can't meet here, goof. It's past the register." I narrow my eyes at him. "Are you trying to make me buy your family's stuff?"

"Maybe we should meet by the little dog," Amy says, a glint in her eye.

Luke groans. "You just want an excuse to beg for another pair of shoes. We already have enough shoes for an army of five-year-old girls."

"I need red ones," she whines. "To go with my Christmas dress."

Luke throws both hands in the air. "Mary, maybe you can help. She has black church shoes, and brown ones, white ones, and a pair of sparkly gold ones. Do you think she needs another pair?"

"You were just inside my closet. I can't believe you'd ask me this." I tilt my head sideways. "Did you not see the rows of shoes, Luke? Of course she needs red ones."

Amy smiles and holds her hand up for a high five.

Luke mutters. "I should've known this was a terrible idea. Amy already runs the show. The last thing she needs is an accomplice."

"I don't need a nacumpliss." Amy glances up at me. "I need a teacher."

"I think you mean a mentor," I say. "And I'm happy to show you the way to shoe bliss."

I push the cart up the aisle before Luke can argue with us.

"You do not understand girls," Amy says over her shoulder. Then to me, she whispers, "What's bliss?"

"I know what you're doing." Luke winks. "You can't run away from me forever, you know."

Except I don't need to run forever. Only until January. The thought makes me profoundly sad.

CHAPTER 14

Amy and I spend quite a bit of time looking at stuffed animals. She loves dogs. Fluffy dogs, small dogs, big dogs, puppies, speckled and black and white. She loves them all, at least in toy form.

"What about cats? This one's kind of cute." I squeeze a fluffy, calico, kitten plush and shake it at her.

She frowns. "Cats don't play fetch. Cats don't do tricks. I don't need a rude pet. I already have a brother."

I laugh then. "I never had a brother."

Amy lifts one eyebrow. "You aren't missing much."

"Not a fan of Chase?"

Amy shrugs. "I love him. He's just messy and kind of smelly and always throwing things. And I wish I had a sister instead."

I bob my head. "I love my sister a lot, but when we were young, she was messy, and smelly and threw things a lot. Once she got older, she'd borrow my things and break, stain or lose them."

"Did you yell at her?"

I shake my head. "My dad did enough of that."

"My dad yells sometimes."

"Often? Or just sometimes?"

Amy pets the calico cat on its head. "Not a lot, but sometimes he gets really mad when we don't listen, or won't eat, or break things."

I smile. "Does he yell more, or hug you more?"

She squeezes the cat. "Definitely hugs more."

"Then it sounds like a pretty decent balance. My dad didn't hug us enough, so my sister got most of her hugs from me. Which was alright, because I needed some, too."

"You sound like a good big sister."

I lift both eyebrows. "How do you know I'm the big sister?"

Amy scrunches her nose. "I think you said. But even if you didn't, I can tell. Big sisters learn stuff like bringing snacks in their purses."

She has a point. Amy carefully selects a stuffed animal for each girl. A crab with a baby for the five-year-old.

"Little kids like to play with baby stuff," she says.

I don't laugh at her, since she isn't kidding. For the seven-year-old, she chooses a stuffed horse.

"Why a horse?" I ask.

She shakes her head. "I don't know, I just have a good feeling about it. I think I'll really like horses when I'm older."

And for the thirteen-year-old, she insists on a huge white bunny with a bow.

"She's a teenager," I point out. "She might not want a stuffed rabbit."

Amy hugs the rabbit close. "Anyone that has parents who can't get her something will want to hug something soft. Even if she's older. She'll like it, I just know it."

I toss it in the cart. I pick a few additional items for the teenager. Scarves, sunglasses, headphones, a purse, some simple cosmetics, like lip-gloss and nail polish. Amy chooses toy items, and we choose a few other things together. Soft, fleecy blankets, slippers, and bathrobes. Eventually we wind up on the jewelry aisle.

Amy pores over the necklaces and selects one for the five-year-old with a dolphin pendant and a crystal. I help her choose a package of chokers for the seven-year-old, but she can't seem to settle on anything for the teenager.

"What's wrong?" I ask.

She sighs and looks through the glass case forlornly. "I don't know anything about jewelry for old people."

I grin. "I'm not sure thirteen qualifies as old, but maybe we should play it safe. I bet she'd like a watch."

"If we're getting her a watch, we should get her sister a watch."

Amy's pretty astute for a five-year-old. We put the dolphin pendant back and pick watches for both of the sisters, and then one for the brother, too.

"So you want a puppy, but if your dad says no," I say, "what else will you ask Santa for?"

Amy taps her lip with one finger. "I don't really want anything else."

"What about one of the robotic dogs? I've heard they're nice."

Amy rolls her eyes at me. "They aren't. I want something that can lick my hand."

My lip curls. "I don't like when dogs lick me. Who knows where else that tongue has been?" I push the cart over to the rendezvous point for Luke and Chase. "There has to be something you'd like, other than a puppy."

Amy looks at her shoes and I realize we never found her the sparkly red shoes she wanted.

"Oh no, we need to find your shoes, and we better be really quick."

Her eyes light up and we race together over to the shoe section. I sit down next to her on the ground and help her try some on. We find the perfect pair, but they're too small, so I flag down an employee. "Can you get these in a larger size from the back?"

"I can try," the woman says.

"We really need to find this pair," I say, "because they're a perfect match for her Christmas dress."

The woman smiles. "I'll do the best I can. I'm sure you hear this all the time ma'am, but your daughter has the most beautiful eyes."

I freeze, unsure whether to correct her, but when I glance at Amy, she's beaming. "Thank you," she says.

"Sorry about that," I say. "She obviously didn't know."

"I know, wasn't that great?" she asks.

"Uh, sure." I suppose for someone who never has a mom around, it might be nice to feel like you're doing something normal. I'd know. I never had a mom, either. Not that I ever went shopping for sparkly shoes or anything.

Amy claps her hands together. "And, I know what I want for Christmas now."

"What's that?" I ask.

She reaches over and takes my hand in hers. "I want you to stay and be my mom. Mine was super nice, but she died when Chase was born, and I've been so patient about getting a new one, but I'm really tired of waiting. And that lady thought you looked like my mom, and you know to bring Fruit Loops when we're going somewhere, and water." She looks up at me earnestly, her beautiful eyes gazing into mine.

And I have no idea what to say.

CHAPTER 15

My eyes widen and I can't seem to blink. "Well, I'm not sure that's something Santa can bring."

She looks down at the ground and her tiny shoulders slump. "If I can't have a new mom, I guess maybe I'll ask for a house that doesn't move. I'm sick of making great friends and then I can never keep any of them."

I reach over and take her hand. "I can understand that."

She looks up at me. "You'd be my friend if I stayed here, right? Even if you don't want to be my mom?"

It's not that I don't want to be her mom. I want to tell her that I'd like to be her mom, but I can't say that. It's not my place, and I can't have kids. But a little girl who wants a friend? My heart swells. "Even if you don't stay, I'll always be your friend, Amy."

"What do you want for Christmas?" Her mouth drops open, and her eyes light up. "Do you want a puppy? I can come play with it, and even walk it for you, if you want."

I laugh. "Uh, no. But that reminds me. We need to meet your dad and Luke at the big plastic dog."

"But my shoes!"

As if on cue, the woman comes walking up from the back, a small box in hand.

Amy thanks her, and so do I. When Amy tries on the new shoes, they fit her perfectly.

"Oh, I love them," I say.

"You may not want to be my mom," Amy says. "But you'd be a really good one for someone, because you've had so much practice with your sister."

My lungs stop working, and my hands shake. I'd be a terrible mom, because like my own mother, I'd always miss things for work. I can't speak or even look Amy in the eyes, so I toss her shoes in the cart and start walking. She follows along after me, blessedly quiet for a moment.

We're only ten feet from the dog, and Luke's not there yet.

My vocal chords finally work again. "You deserve the best mom in the world."

Amy frowns. "I don't need the best mom, just a good one would be fine. Aunt Linda says no mom is perfect, and they all have to learn as they go. I promise I'll be super patient."

I crouch down right in front of her and tuck a stray hair behind her ear. "You are a lovely little girl, and there's no doubt you'd be a perfect daughter. I'm sure your dad will find you a mother very soon."

"What about a puppy for you?" Amy asks. "My dad won't get me one, but maybe he'd let me get one for you. You're an adult, and Dad says your house doesn't have wheels under it."

I stand up again and brush my pants off. "It's not always easy to be a grown up. I work a lot, and a dog would be hard for me to care for alone. Besides, puppies pee everywhere and chew on everything. If I got one, it would eat my shoes and ruin my carpet."

She nods. "How about a hamster, then? I hear they're easy to take care of. And they can't chew on anything that's not in their cage."

I shake my head. "It's a good idea, but I don't need a pet. In fact, I can't think of a single thing I want for Christmas this year. I have everything I could possibly ask for. I think that's why Santa doesn't come to adults as much. They already have almost everything they want."

Amy narrows her eyes at me. "I think Santa doesn't come to adults because they won't admit what they really want."

Luke walks up then, pushing the cart with Chase sitting in the front. Luke's coat is slung over the side of the cart, and his blue polo shirt clings to his chest. I bite my lip, remembering how his pecs felt under my hand. She might be right. What I really want is for Luke not to be moving. And not to have kids. Although when I think about Amy and Chase, I can't really wish he didn't have them. That feels wrong. They're such cute, sweet children.

"You ladies have any luck?"

Amy shows him the things we found, one at a time. Luke oohs and aahs appropriately, but Chase starts throwing things out of the cart, and we end up rushing toward the register. "It's okay, buddy, we're going now, okay?"

I start pulling things out of the cart for my girls, but Luke stops me. "I'll get it. If you insist, you can tally up what you owe me back at my place." Several people have stacked us in line behind us.

"Please let me pay," he repeats.

I cringe a little, but I don't want to make a big deal about it at the register. "You've got two kids and I'm sure—"

Luke shakes his head. "It's fine, I promise."

I let it go, but after we've got the kids buckled into car seats, and the gifts stowed under the truck's bed cover in the back, I notice a big sign a few blocks down the road. I whisper to Luke. "Do you have time for Chuck-e-Cheese?" I incline my head toward the sign. "My treat, since you paid in there."

He lifts one eyebrow. "Have you been to Chuck-e-Cheese in the last two decades? You'd probably be getting the bad end of this deal."

I tilt my head to the side. "How bad can it be?"

He turns around to check behind him before backing out and while he's looking at the kids, says, "Hey guys, Miss Mary wants to know if you two like Chuck-e-Cheese. She said she's never been, and wants to know if it's any fun."

Their animated whoops and hollers fill the car, and I close my eyes briefly, pondering whether I can cover my ears without offending them. Once it's quiet enough we can hear again, I say, "I think that's a yes."

Luke laughs. "I'd say so."

Chase is so excited once we park in the lot outside, that he squirms out of Luke's arms and insists on running across the sloshy parking lot. Luke races after him, glancing back at me apologetically. Amy stands on a dry patch and holds out her hand for mine after she climbs down.

"Thanks for bringing us," she says.

I take her hand. "You're doing me the favor. I didn't get any Fruit Loops earlier, so I'm about to perish with hunger."

Amy tilts her head. "Yeah right. Dad never brings us here. He hates Chuck-e-Cheese, so I know it was your idea."

Luke glances back at me, grinning ear to ear as Chase

drags him toward the entrance. He's so handsome, with his big dimples, and his perfect hair that I almost can't stand it.

"We better hurry," I say.

Amy shivers. "It is cold."

We rush inside, where they stamp our hands, and I learn that Luke's right. It's not a cheap place to hang out, and it's a madhouse. We elbow another couple out of the way to secure a table where we can wait for what I'm assuming will be truly amazing pizza, or probably not. I lay our coats on the booth benches so no one gets any funny ideas while we get drinks.

I'm walking toward the fountain drink station, Amy on my heels, when Luke comes over and crouches down by Amy. "How about you and Chase go play and let me talk to my friend Mary for a little while?"

Amy frowns. "She's my friend, too. She promised."

Luke nods. "She is your friend, and you've kind of taken up all her time today. I think it's my turn for a few minutes. Can you go play with Chase?" He bops her on the nose with a card.

She huffs, but she takes the card. She doesn't run off, though. She turns toward me instead. "Are you going home right after this?"

I glance at Luke. We hadn't even discussed dinner, and now that we're eating here, I'm not sure what I'm doing.

He reaches over and takes my hand in his. He held my hand in the truck earlier, but it's different with gloves off. His fingers are warm and my heart races when our fingers interlace. "Can you stay a little longer?"

"Yeah," I say, "I guess so."

Amy beams at me, and then bounds off to find Chase. They both start throwing small, squishy, brown footballs over a touchdown pole.

Luke lets go of my hand to fill up our drinks, but once

we've gotten the sodas to the table, he reaches over the laminate tabletop and interlaces the fingers of both his hands with mine. "Thanks for suggesting a kid friendly place. I know you aren't a fan, but you've been pretty understanding."

I look down at where our fingers join. My small hands and his large calloused ones. I trace the callouses on the sides of his fingers. "I like kids actually. Remember?"

His lips compress. "I thought you said you wouldn't date anyone with kids."

I bite my lip. "I did, but it's not because I don't like them."

"So you don't mind?"

I roll my eyes. "Well, I would be breaking all my rules if I were actually dating you, right? But this doesn't count, because you're leaving soon."

He grins. "I don't want you to run screaming out of here, although I'm not sure anyone working in this madhouse would blame you, but it feels sort of like we're actually dating. To me anyway."

My heart flip flops. "My parents did such a bad job with us, Luke. You have no idea."

Luke squeezes my hands. "Which is why you know how to get things right."

I shake my head. "My mom only cared about work. She left us because she couldn't do both, or maybe she didn't want to do both. And when she left, it completely broke my dad. He started drinking and Trudy and I, we just had to kind of fend for ourselves. I won't risk the chance that I'm like that at my core. I can't. Do you understand?"

He lowers his head, his eyes on me until I meet them. "Not really, because I see you, Mary. I haven't known you long, but you're nothing like the woman you're describing."

I shake my head. "You don't get it. My dad always told

me I'm just like her. My mom might have left for an unpopular career, but she loved driving trucks. She loved seeing the world, and the feeling of accomplishment when she dropped off her load. She told me and I remember it. My dad's right. I am like her, and even though I didn't mean to become a career woman, I did. I love my job, and I want to work, and I'll always want to work. I always thought I'd be more like my baby sister—she has a little boy, and she stays home with him. I love Troy, and she loves staying home with him, but that's not me. I'm not like her, I'm like, well, I'm like my mom was."

Luke clears his throat. "I don't want to upset you, and I'm not trying to be argumentative, honestly, but are you really saying the only way to be a good mom is to stay home with your kids?" His eyebrows rise.

I pull my hands back and lean back in the booth. "I'm not saying that, not precisely. But I would want to be involved if I had kids. And I spend so much time right now at work, and the rest of my time either running, or volunteering. I don't want to give any of that up. There isn't enough time left over in my life for me to bake a cake twice a month, much less have kids, not the way I'd want to take care of them."

The pizza comes before Luke can reply, and the kids notice it's arrived. They shoot toward our table like heat seeking arrows, darting in and out of groups of people. Chase even shoots underneath a tall dad's legs and I suppress a laugh when the man almost topples over.

Once they arrive, Amy stares defiantly at her dad as she slides in next to me in the booth. Luke grins at her, and places a slice of pizza on her plate. He doesn't bring up kids, or jobs or anything else. We talk, we laugh, and once the pizza's gone, I even ride a plastic horse while Amy watches and claps.

"What did you think of Chuck-e-Cheese?" Amy asks. "As fun as you thought it would be?"

"It was a lot of fun."

Amy narrows her eyes at me. "You didn't even do anything. You just sat here talking the whole time." She grabs my hand and drags me over to the Chuck-e-Cheese booth, where a machine draws our picture. Next we're off to ride on a train car that my bum barely fits into. I'm laughing about it when Luke snaps a photo.

I throw my hand up. "Really?"

"Yeah Dad, you didn't even warn us." Amy hops off the train and stands right next to me, mouth in the biggest smile possible. Luke snaps a few more photos.

Amy holds out her hand. "Now I'll take one of you."

Before I can object, Luke tosses Amy the phone and sweeps me up, his arms under my armpits and my knees.

I squeal, and Amy snaps photos. I'm completely shocked when Luke kisses me, but I kiss him back briefly, before pushing against his chest until he puts me down.

When I glance at Amy, she's giggling. "I didn't know my Dad loved you."

"Oh no—" I start to say, but Luke's eyes find mine, and the words die on my mouth.

"I can't believe you never got to come here when you were little." Amy sighs. "I feel so sorry for you as a kid. But at least you can come whenever you want now." Amy's eyes are wide, certain that my heart is breaking over the lost memories of Chuck-e-Cheese.

Luke takes my hand in his, and something swells inside my chest. If I didn't know better, I'd say it was my heart, growing three sizes like the Grinch's did. My dad never cared enough to bring us here instead of getting himself more beer, but Luke cares about his kids, and I care about them. I don't want to, but I do.

Luke and I spend the next few minutes using up the rest of the credits. I clearly over estimated what we'd need. Rookie mistake. Luke throws basketballs into a basket with Chase, over and over, and I go where my skills will be recognized. When the points are finally gone from the cards, and our pockets are full of tickets, we head for the ticket muncher. After the kids have traded in their tickets for a handful of sticky candy, we head out to the car.

"How can you do the spider bot so good?" Chase asks me. I won fistful after fistful of tickets for the two of them, once they realized I was amazing at nailing the bull's eye. "You must come here all the time."

Amy rolls her eyes. "She'd never been here before, dummy."

"Don't call your brother dummy." Luke says it like he's said the same thing a million times.

Chase seems unperturbed. "You've never been here? How can you do that, then?"

I chuckle. "We didn't come to Chuck-e-Cheese," I say, "but my neighbor had an old video game called a play station, and you're looking at the neighborhood champion of Call of Duty for like five years in a row."

Chase's eyebrows rise. "Really?"

I nod. "I've never held a real gun, but boy can I shoot fake ones."

"Cool," he says. "Dad won't even let me have a bb gun."

"You'd probably shoot your eye out," I say.

Amy claps. "I love that movie. Can we watch it?"

I glance at the sun, just beginning to set, and watch as Luke clips Chase into his booster. "I don't know, guys. I'll have to talk to your dad about that. I've kind of taken over your whole day."

"You weren't even here for breakfast," Amy says.

"Or lunch," Chase says.

"Oh," Amy says, "maybe you can stay for breakfast tomorrow. Dad makes the best pancakes."

The first time I'm invited to spend the night at Luke's house, it's by a five year old. I glance at Luke's face, which is stricken, and giggle. "Maybe I can come over for breakfast another time."

"If you kids get your pajamas on super fast, maybe we can watch *A Christmas Story*, but I don't know whether Miss Mary can stay or not. She and I only talked about shopping today, and she may have plans for later."

"Plans for what?" Amy asks. "Because it's a really funny movie. This kid writes and writes all these letters and stuff asking for a gun, and everyone tells him he can't have it, because—"

"And then," Chase says loudly, "he has to dress up as a pink bunny!"

I turn to look at Luke's face and he shrugs at me. "You're welcome to stay, but I understand if you can't."

"How could I miss seeing a kid dress up in a pink bunny costume?" I ask.

Amy claps her hands. "Yay! You can help me get my pajamas on. Can you brush my teeth?"

First, Luke and I move all the gifts for my girls into my trunk. But afterward, I do help Amy brush her teeth, and I help her button up her fleecy pink jammies, too. "I think I need a pair of these," I say.

She opens her mouth and coos. "That's so great. Now I know what you want for Christmas."

"I guess you do," I tell her. "But you don't need to give me anything. I'm just glad to have you as a friend."

"Can I tell you a secret?" she asks.

I nod.

She leans toward me and whispers in my ear. "I wish we weren't moving."

I press my lips together to keep from saying, "Me too."

When Amy and I reach the family room, Luke's got the movie queued up on the television. Two large, brown leather, movie theater style seats sit directly in front of the TV. The brown leather loveseat perpendicular to the TV is open, and Luke and Chase are sitting in the large seats.

Luke picks Chase up and gives him a little shove. "You two have to share the loveseat. Adults get the big seats."

Amy whines a little. "Why can't I sit on Mary's lap?"

Luke shakes his head. "You're lucky to be staying up late at all. Don't push it."

Her bottom lip juts out, but she lets it go. She climbs up onto the loveseat and Chase does the same, a blue blanket in one chubby hand. I notice he's biting on it when Luke hits play. A few minutes into the movie, Luke pulls a blanket over our lap, and takes my hand in his again. It's like we're in high school, hiding our PDA from his kids. I giggle a little and he glances at me sideways.

A few minutes in, my eyes begin to droop, and Luke puts his arm around me. I snuggle my head against his chest. My eyes drift closed and I doze off.

Until Luke shakes me awake.

I sit up, a little dazed. "Is everything okay?"

He holds up my phone. "I'm sorry I pulled this out of your purse, but it was ringing and ringing. I thought maybe something was wrong."

I blink a few times to clear my eyes and take my phone. Trudy called twice. Paisley called three times. When I realize Addy called too, I smack my forehead. "I had plans tonight. Oh my gosh, I completely forgot we moved girls night to tonight."

I sit up straight and the blanket slides off my knees and onto the floor. "My sister and my two best friends were meeting at my house so we could go dancing."

I almost swear, until I realize Amy and Chase are both watching me curiously. I bite my tongue and look down at my clothes. Jeans and a grey sweater. I absolutely cannot go out dancing in this. I'll die of heat stroke.

I stand up. "I'm so sorry, but I need to run."

Amy jogs across the room and grabs my leg. "Don't go. Please don't go."

I crouch down at the same time as Luke, and Amy releases my leg to keep from getting her hand squashed between my calf and my thigh.

"Sweetheart," he says, "Mary has to leave. She stayed much longer than we intended, and we need to be grateful for the time we got."

Amy's bottom lip wobbles. Chase bites on his blanket one step behind her. "Can you come back tomorrow?"

I shake my head. "I don't know. I've got some things I need to catch up on."

Chase drops his blanket. "Why do you work a lot?"

I stand up. That's my cue. "Well," I say. "I like what I do at work." And now after one day with these cute kiddos, I already feel guilty for it.

"Please come tomorrow." Amy takes my hand. "My dad's making us move soon, and I want to see you as much as I can before then."

I squeeze her hand. "I had so much fun today, but I've got some more shopping to do for my sister and her son and some friends tomorrow. Between that and some work, I doubt I'll make it back over."

Her face falls and so do my spirits, but I pull on my coat anyhow. "You have so much to look forward to, though. Christmas is just around the corner."

"Can you please come with us when we drop off the gifts for our family?" Amy begs. "You helped me pick everything. You have to come."

I bob my head. "I'll really try to do that, okay? I'd like to. That's the best part of being Santa's helper."

Amy beams at me, but when I walk toward the door, she releases my hand without a fight. "Have a fun time with your sister."

I smile at her. "If she forgives me for being so late, I'm sure I will."

"If she stays mad, you can come back," Chase says. "I won't throw any more balls at your head. I promise."

I pat his head and reach for the doorknob. "Thanks for being so nice to me today, guys. I had a great time."

I hear the movie resume as I step out the door. Luke slips through and jogs down the steps after me, and reaches for my hand before I can escape.

"Where are you going?" His husky voice washes over me.

"The girls are not going to be pleased," I say.

He tugs me back toward him, and my hands come up to splay across his chest. He must be freezing out here without a coat. His head lowers slowly toward mine, his eyes large and expressive, and his lips open just a bit.

His lips close over mine, heat and pressure amidst the icy, Christmas air. I cling to him and my arms wrap around his neck.

Then, too quickly, he releases me. "I don't want to make you late."

My head feels fuzzy. "You don't?"

He grins. "Fine, I do. I'd like to keep you here and never let you go, but I don't want your friends to hate me before they've even met me." He swats my backside when I turn toward the car. "Drive safely, and have fun. But not too much fun."

I glance back over my shoulder, and when I look into his eyes, I'm almost ready to ditch my friends. But I'll never hear the end of it as it is, so I slide into my liquid nitrogen front seat and turn my car on. Once my engine roars to life, Luke waves and ducks back inside.

My fingers touch my lips and I sit in the car for a moment. I tell myself it's so the heater will warm up a little, but really, it's just kind of hard to drive away.

CHAPTER 16

Sunset Cove isn't too far from my house, but it's seven-thirty already. I call Paisley the second I leave. I could've called Trudy or Addy, but Paisley's going to be the most understanding.

She picks up before the first ring has ended. "Girl. We've been waiting for you for like twenty minutes. Where are you?"

"Waiting where?" I ask.

She huffs. "At your house. When you didn't confirm a time or anything, we decided to come here. Figured you'd be the designated driver."

As always. Sometimes I wonder if that's the only thing my friends love about me. I never drink, so I can always bring them all home safely.

"I'm sorry," I say. "I forgot we moved it to tonight, and I was over at Luke's place."

"Oooh, I was worried you were going to cut Luke off. Well, we're all ready when you are, but you'll have to pay us back for making us wait with lots of details. I haven't had a decent date in months."

I hear Addy in the background. "Who's Luke? How come I haven't heard about him?"

"Because you're always busy," Trudy says. "But I'm her sister and we've been together a ton in the last two weeks. Why haven't I heard anything?"

I sigh. "Paisley, catch them up and I'll give you details when I get there."

I'm just around the corner from my house, driving past the local Pet Smart when I see the sign. "SPCA Event 8 a.m. until 8 p.m."

My car clock says 7:40 pm, and the girls are already annoyed, but my hands turn the wheel on their own. I'm sliding into a spot, and running into the front of the store before I realize what I'm doing. I don't want a dog. I've never had one, but I hate when they jump up on me and lick me. If I wanted a pet, which I don't, I'd totally be a cat person.

And yet, here I am, staring at a plastic playpen where eight or nine bouncy puppies are frolicking. A woman with a dark bob streaks toward me as eagerly as a car salesman. "What brings you in tonight?" Her big, white, teeth gleam when she smiles and I wish I could turn down the wattage.

"Uh, I don't know really. My boyfriend's daughter wants a puppy so badly." My boyfriend? Why'd I say that? I want to clamp one hand over my mouth.

"Well, is your boyfriend coming inside? Usually couples pick this sort of thing out together."

"Oh, he doesn't want a dog," I say. "But I was thinking of getting one she could play with at my house."

Her beatific smile wilts. "Umm, but do you want a dog? Because it's a big commitment, and we don't really support people getting one and bringing it back when the relationship falters."

"Why would the relationship falter?"

The woman's mouth opens and she says, "Uhh," and then closes her mouth.

I close my eyes. I'm such an idiot. What am I doing here? I take a step back from the puppy pen and glance around wildly, looking for anything I could use as an excuse to leave.

My eyes lock onto the beautiful brown eyes of an enormous, fluffy, mostly white dog. I have no desire for a cute, bouncy, puppy, and even less desire for a huge, hairy, full grown dog. But when our eyes meet, this fluff ball lifts its head and its ears perk up. I realize the white mixes with biscuit and grey along its ears and darkens on its face to a dark grey muzzle. There's grey and tan all along its back, too.

It's the prettiest dog I've ever seen, even if it looks like it hasn't eaten in a year.

I completely forget about the judge-y woman with the bob, and cross the entry way to where this dog rests calmly, ignoring the indignity of its leash being clipped to a wire rack. Once I'm within arm's reach of it, it sits up all the way, its gargantuan haunches resting on the ground, but its huge front legs entirely straight. Its face continues to stare into mine, eyes pleading with me silently.

"Don't leave me here," it seems to say. Now that I'm close, its matted coat and ragged claws stand out, and it smells like vomit. I scrunch my nose.

"Stand," I say.

It stands up.

"Sit," I say.

It sits.

"Down," I say.

It lays down and places it's big, beautiful head on its dirty front paws.

"What about this dog?" I ask loudly, so Mrs. Hundred Watt Smile will be sure to hear me.

"Oh, she's not part of our puppy event. In fact, someone surrendered her today without even obtaining the proper permissions. Dogs are only supposed to be surrendered at the main location. She's a stray, but we aren't taking adult animals right now. We would have refused her entirely, except that she's a Pyrenees."

"Excuse me?" I ask.

The woman shakes her head in annoyance. "When an animal turns up that's purebred, like this one appears to be, we don't check them into the SPCA where they have seven days before being gassed. We call the various rescues, and usually find someone for them. A woman's coming by to pick her up shortly."

"So she's going to a home that loves Peerobees?"

"The full name is actually 'Great' Pyrenees, with the word great first and then pronounced Peer, uh, knees."

"Oh, sorry. Pyrenees. Great Pyrenees."

"Better. But no, she's not going to a new home. The woman who's coming for her likes and is familiar with this breed, and probably has several already. She'll foster her until she's evaluated and they can find another home."

"It's a girl?" I ask.

She nods. "But if she can't be placed within a reasonable amount of time, she'll come back to us."

"What's reasonable?"

Mrs. Hundred Watt Smile shrugs. "A month? Maybe a little longer with the holidays."

"That's terrible," I say. "In a month, they'll send her to you, and you'll kill her?"

The woman says, "We kill a lot of dogs. I'm sorry you find it upsetting, but it's the reality that keeps your streets clean and orderly."

"Can I get the phone number for this woman?" I ask. "I might want her."

She raises one eyebrow. "You said your boyfriend's daughter wants a puppy."

"I did, and then you said I should only get a dog that *I* want, and I like this one."

She presses her lips together. "We don't give dogs to people on a whim. We want a solid commitment. It's not good for these dogs to be bouncing around. She's been through enough trauma."

I pull a business card out of my purse. "Here's my info. Give it to the rescue lady. Maybe she'll feel differently."

The woman hands me a piece of paper with a number scrawled on it. "If you don't hear from her, and you feel confident you want a dog and you're prepared to care for one, give her a call."

"Thanks."

I crouch down in front of the beautiful dog again and whisper to her. "I work a lot, and I've never had a dog. You might hate my house. But I left my information, and maybe your foster mom will call me."

I stand up and practically jog back out the door to my car.

When I finally reach my house, Trudy, Paisley, and Addy, my best friend since high school, pounce on me the second I walk in the door.

"What took you so long?" Trudy asks.

"Yeah, where does he live?" Paisley asks. "Macon?"

"And how could you forget we're doing a girls' night?" Addy puts one hand on her hip.

I drop my purse on the kitchen counter. "Merry Christmas to all of you! It's so good to see you. Sorry you had to wait for me."

I walk across the kitchen and into the family room,

where I plop onto the sofa. Trudy trails behind me, Paisley bounces, and Addy practically stalks, but they all reach the family room and sit down next to me. Trudy takes the other end of the couch, and Addy and Paisley each claim a chair.

"If we're going dancing," I say, "there's not much of a rush. It never picks up before nine-thirty or ten."

"Not on a Sunday. It starts earlier, because it ends earlier. People have work to go to. Which isn't the point," Trudy says. "I lined up one of the nurses from the hospital to be my sitter so I could see you, not so I could sit at your house and tap my feet."

Paisley rolls her eyes. "No one cares about waiting a little while. And we ate some of your frozen sugar cookies while we waited, so thanks for that."

I chuckle. "Of course you did."

Addy taps her fingers on the arm of the chair impatiently. "Now, details. Who's this Luke and how did you meet? And when? Paisley wasn't very forthcoming." She scowls and I realize she's jealous that Paisley knew about someone she didn't. A jealous Addy is a crabby Abby. I smile at my rhyme.

"I met Luke at Bentleys the other night while I was waiting for Shauna."

"Wait, why were you waiting at Bentleys?" Trudy asks. "I didn't know that."

"Shauna offered me a promotion, for her job actually. She's moving back to London."

Trudy's eyebrows rise. "Wow, will you take it?"

She knows I love my job; I love running numbers and doing returns. I don't want her to realize why I'm taking it, so this needs to be convincing.

"Yep," I say. "I'm taking it. Because it's the chance I've

been waiting for. It's more hours, but they're evenly spread, not just focused on tax season."

Paisley glances from Trudy to me and back again, but she doesn't say anything about my reasons. I practically cry with relief.

"Congrats on the promotion," Addy says. "I really have been out of the loop."

I shrug. "It's not a big deal, honestly."

"Um," Trudy says, "you just said it's the chance you've been waiting for."

"Is it more money?" Addy asks.

I nod.

"Why didn't you group text us and like shout and gush and brag?" Addy asks. "That's why you have friends. So we can celebrate."

I shrug my shoulders. "I guess I didn't want to annoy you guys."

Addy shakes her head. "Well that backfired. Now I'm annoyed you didn't tell me."

I roll my eyes. "Well, get over it, because I met a guy named Luke that night, while I was waiting on Shauna. He was funny, and pretty persistent. I finally gave him my number."

Paisley grins. "And he's super hot."

"Wait," Trudy says. "You've *met* him?"

Paisley smiles and tosses her hair. "I loaned her my dress the night they met. Then I've been texting her about it non-stop, and she showed me a photo he sent. He's blue eyed, and he has the most beautiful smile I've ever seen. Oh, and he's tall. Did I mention Mary says he's tall?"

I roll my eyes. "The point is, between work stuff and Sub-for-Santa, which Foster's shutting down for good this time, I haven't had time to update anyone. Plus, Trudy, you've been busy with your stuff."

"How's Troy?" Paisley asks. "I've been praying for the little guy."

Addy throws her hands in the air. "What's wrong with Troy?"

I glare at Trudy. "You've got to tell people. About all of it, or no one can help you, goofball."

Trudy looks down at her black boots and mumbles something even I can't hear.

"I can't understand you," Addy says. "What's going on?"

I take pity on poor Trudy. "Chris left, and shortly after she found out he had a girlfriend, she discovered Troy's got type one diabetes. It's been a rough few weeks."

A tear runs down Trudy's face. "I don't wanna talk about any of it, though. I'm sick of thinking about it, and crying about it, and wallowing. Tonight I need to have a little fun."

I stand up and brush my hands on my jeans. "Speaking of, I'll go change. You guys can psychoanalyze me on the way to Flare, okay?"

"Oh, we will analyze," Paisley says. "You're not getting out of this conversation. I want to know what you were doing over at his house all day. I thought this was casual and not long for the earth."

"Wait," Trudy says. "What?"

Paisley's jaw drops. "Oh em gee, did you stay the night at his place last night? Is that why you were over there?"

I pull up short and pivot on my heel to refute that. "Of course not. We've only been out a few times."

"Well, then what did you do?" Paisley calls. "A day date is odd."

Paisley, Trudy and Addy follow me back to my room and start expressing opinions on every outfit I pull out of my closet.

"Not the black dress," Addy says. "It's too dark for your complexion."

"Thanks for that." I toss the dress in the corner. Goodwill bound, apparently.

"Not the yellow," Paisley says. "You look like a banana."

"Oh my gosh," I say. "Where were you guys when I was buying this stuff?"

Addy shrugs. "We're here now."

Finally no one objects when I slide into brown pants and a bright, emerald green tank top with an ivory, chunky, off the shoulder, knit sweater flung over the top.

"Perfect," Trudy says. "Not trying too hard, not too hot or cold, and lots of texture. I love it." She tosses a long, black leather necklace with a huge silver heart pendant at the bottom over my head. "Let's go."

Once they're all loaded into my car, Trudy in the front seat, Pais and Addy in the back, Paisley picks up again. "Enough deflecting. What were you doing today over at Luke's house?"

My fingers grip the steering wheel so tightly, my knuckles turn white. "We were shopping."

"Shopping? For what?" Paisley asks. "Wedding rings?"

"Oh my gosh, Pais," Addy says. "Knock it off."

Paisley glares at Addy, which I can see through my rear view mirror.

"We were shopping for our Sub-for-Santa families."

"You roped him into that?" Addy asks.

I shake my head. "He signed up for it himself, before he ever met me. In fact, we went on a date before I realized he was even on the list. It was a little awkward when I did. That's one of the reasons Paisley knows all about him. Someone signed him up to be sponsored, actually, and he signed up to take a family."

"It was obviously a mistake," Paisley says. "He didn't need to be sponsored."

"Wait a second." Addy's eyes widen. "If someone thought he needed to be sponsored... Does he have kids?"

They all know that's a deal breaker for me.

I sigh melodramatically. "He's a master electrician and runs big jobs, like the Citibank building construction downtown that's just finishing up. But he travels for work, so he and, yes, his two kids, live in a travel trailer, which is why a well- intentioned lady from his church thought he needed some help."

I brace myself, ready for the barrage of criticism. I know they mean well, so I'll deal with it.

No one says a word.

I was ready for jokes, good-natured criticism, or even chastising. But silence? Do they think he sounds that awful?

"His kids are actually kind of cute," I say.

"You think everyone's kids are cute," Trudy says. "Even Troy, and he's a nightmare."

I pat her hand. "Troy's not a nightmare. He's high spirited." And probably not disciplined quite as much as he should be, but that doesn't seem helpful to say.

"You don't want kids. Ever," Addy says, unhelpfully.

"No, I know that," I say, "but the thing is—"

"Wow, if you're considering him even though he has kids?" Paisley smiles smugly. "You're smitten. Like a little baby cat. You're a smitten kitten."

I shake my head. "No, it's not like that Pais. I already told you, he's moving in like three weeks or something. So it doesn't matter. I can like him, and interact with his kids, and it can't go anywhere."

Trudy's fingers grip my free hand hard. "Where's he moving to next? Because you can't leave." Panic floods her voice and her eyes stare at me wildly. "I need you. Troy and me, we both need you."

I squeeze her hand back. "I'm not leaving, Trudy. I promise. He's leaving for Kentucky, and I won't be going with him. I'll be here for you no matter what. I always will."

"Today you went shopping with him and his kids?" Addy asks. "Like all day long?"

"Nah, only part of the day. I went over after lunch, and we did Sub-for-Santa shopping, and then we got dinner."

"Where'd you go?" Paisley asks. "Somewhere good?"

I toss my hair. "We had the two kids with us, so we went to Chuck-e-Cheese."

Addy laughs. "Oh man, you must really like him."

I suppress my grin, because she's right. I do, probably way, way too much.

"All his daughter wants for Christmas is a puppy," I say, "and she can't have one because they live in a trailer. It's too hard to have a dog when you travel so much, and they just don't have the space. And you guys, I saw some kind of puppy adoption event on my way back home today. I actually stopped in and looked at the puppies. I know it sounds crazy, but when I saw the SPCA sign, it felt like, I don't know, like maybe it was some kind of divine message or something."

Silence again.

"Okay, guys, say something."

Trudy shakes her head slowly. "Girl, I don't know what to say. We've wanted you to find someone for forever, but."

"This all sounds pretty crazy to me, too." Trudy's eyes won't meet mine.

I pull into the parking lot behind our favorite nightclub. Flare's music is always good, and they don't allow cigarettes anywhere on premises. Which is kind of funny, since the name sounds like a place that would be all about flames.

"We're here," I say.

"Yep," Trudy says. "We are."

They all pile out and practically run away from the car. Or maybe they're running from me. I walk slowly to make sure there's no ice, past the garland around the handrail that flows up the ramp to the front entrance. The sparkly lights, fake holly and music blaring from inside should make me happy. But I keep thinking about how I can't get a dog just because Amy wants one, because that's crazy. But maybe I could get a dog for me. And that emaciated, fluffy, white one might be the perfect one. I didn't realize I was lonely until I started thinking about Luke moving.

I slide through the front doors and head for the dance floor. My friends always make a beeline right for it. Except they aren't there. I squint in the semi-dark until I finally find them, huddled around a standing table in the back corner. I approach them cautiously, dodging the stumbling and slurring bachelorette party one table over.

"What's going on?" I ask. "Too tired to dance?"

Addy frowns. "We've been thinking about this whole thing with Luke, and you know we love you, so this is coming from a good place."

I scowl. "If you're prefacing it, it can't be good."

Paisley raises her hand, like we're in first grade. "Uh, for the record, 'we' doesn't include me. I don't agree with them."

Addy arches one brow and rolls her eyes. "Fine, me and Trudy. We think you need to dump Luke."

I toss my hands in the air. "You've been badgering me to date ever since Foster and I broke up."

Trudy shakes her head. "True, but not like this. Not a

guy who has *kids*, which you don't want, and *is leaving in a few weeks*."

Addy nods. "Exactly. You're forgetting about girls' nights, you're going to Chuck-e-Cheese, and you're looking for dogs to adopt? None of those things are 'Mary' in the slightest. This guy's changing you, and the last time I saw something like that it was—"

Trudy pokes Addy and she gasps. "What was that for?"

Trudy slaps her forehead. "Don't say Foster, don't go there. Remember? We agreed."

My jaw drops. "Luke is nothing like Foster."

My sister raises one eyebrow. "Well, he's not rich, and he's not from Atlanta. And he's living in a trailer, so yeah, they seem different in all the wrong ways. But your reaction to Luke is kind of the same. With Foster you gave up running and started cycling. You gave up coffee in favor of tea. You started brunching every Sunday."

Addy scrunches her nose. "You stopped being *you* so you could be Foster's version of you."

I stomp my foot. "Listen up. None of that crap makes me who I am. I can try something new with the guy I'm dating and actually like it, you know. But at the end of the day, I was still me. We didn't fit, so we broke up."

"It shattered you," Paisley says in a voice so quiet I can barely hear her. Of course, the bachelorette party behind me isn't helping. The bride-to-be, presumably, has a sash and is downing what is already one too many glasses of wine. Between their raucous laughter, and the ghastly *Santa Claus is Coming to Town* dance remix, I can barely hear myself think, much less come up with a coherent argument.

"This music is wrong," I say. "Play dance music, or Christmas music. But Christmas dance music?" I feign puking.

"You're right," Addy says, "but you're trying to change the subject."

I lean against the table, until I realize it's sticky, but by then it's too late. My sweater now sports an elbow stain of unknown origin. Gross. "Look, Foster tried to change me. He begged, and pleaded, and cajoled me to agree to have kids. But I didn't want any, and I didn't cave."

"Luke has two kids," Trudy says. "And you're looking at getting a dog?" She closes her eyes and shakes her head slowly. "We're worried about this. He's not good for you."

"What about you, Trudy? Have you told Chris that you're done with him yet?"

Her eyebrows draw together and her lips compress.

"You can't tell me that I have to dump a perfectly wonderful guy, when you haven't even given up on your cheating, worthless husband."

"I'm trying to help you avoid the exact same misery I'm dealing with," Trudy says. "And you don't get to pressure me about Chris, because we have a child together. It's different."

Kids complicate everything. I already know this too well.

Addy touches my hand. "We're your friends, Mary. We love you. We're trying to help you here, so don't take this wrong."

"It doesn't matter," I say slowly. "I appreciate your input, but Luke's moving. Why can't I date someone for a few weeks and then go back to normal? I've got a holiday party next week, and then it's Christmas. Why bother breaking up with him, when it's going to end by default a few weeks after that?"

"Because you're taking control," Trudy says. "Exactly like you keep telling me to do with Chris."

"What about you?" I ask Paisley. "You haven't said a word."

Paisley meets my eyes. "I don't agree you should dump Luke just because he's making you go to Chuck-e-Cheese, or because he has kids. But I've kept my mouth shut, because . . . Well, you like him so much, Mary. I was so excited to see it, but now we know he's leaving? I do think you need to end it on your terms. Otherwise, he'll re-engage with you every time he comes into town to visit family or friends, and in between jobs. If this can't go anywhere, and you seem adamant it can't, you should dump him now, before he wrecks you even worse."

"If I had to go back in time," I say loudly, competing with the giggling bridesmaids and terrible Christmas music, "I'd still date my ex, even knowing how it would turn out. Even though it all turned out badly, I don't regret —" the music cuts off and it's suddenly silent. My voice fills the entire area around me when I finish my sentence, "a single minute I spent with Foster."

The bridal party turns slowly toward us, and their seven faces all locking strangely on mine.

"Oh. My. Gosh." The bride's words slur. "You're Mary effing Wiggin."

I've entered the twilight zone. How does this girl know my name? The music picks up again, with a dance mix of Silent Night. I couldn't describe the horror of it if I tried. "Umm, I am Mary Wiggin," I yell. "And who are you?"

The bride to be has a crown with flashy pink stones, tilted askew on a hugely puffy bun of blonde curls. Her dark brown eyes flash, while some of her lipstick holds on for dear life to her two front teeth. "I'm Jessica Hansen. I'm marrying Foster Bradshaw."

My jaw drops and I speak without thinking. "But you can't be. You've been drinking!"

She swaggers toward me, her friends stumbling behind her, their heels clicking loudly enough on the tile dance floor that I can hear them over the music. "I can drink whatever I want. I turned twenty-three this year."

I look her over, head to toe. She's wearing a bubble gum pink sheath dress that shows off her figure, and she's either courting a future replete with skin cancer, or she spends a good chunk on spray tanning. Either way, I see why Foster's enamored. But she's so different from me, I wonder whether I knew Foster at all.

"Hello?" She snaps in my face. "Where do you get off telling me what to do?"

The scattered "Yeahs," and "Word," and "You go girl," from her posse irritate me.

"Because you're pregnant," I say. "You'll give your baby fetal alcohol syndrome if you drink while pregnant, you idiot. You're so young that maybe you haven't yet had sex-ed class in high school, but that's like the number two rule, right after using two forms of birth control. It seems like you didn't pay much attention to that one, either."

Instead of panicking, like I'd expect, or turning bright red, she actually doubles down on the scowling. "Not that it's any of your business, but I'm not pregnant." She sticks her nose up in the air and stalks off, her friends shooting me dirty looks as they sway across the room on four and five inch heels.

The bartender arrives with our drinks as if on cue.

"I ordered you a coke with lemon," Trudy says. "Like always."

I force a smile. "Thanks."

No one brings the topic of Luke up again. In fact, after we finish our drinks, Addy, Paisley, and Trudy all beeline for the dance floor. We pretend Foster's fiancé and her friends aren't there, which is sort of hard with their stupid sashes proclaiming "Bride," and "Bridesmaid," but we persevere.

By the time we're heading home though, I've thought about nothing but Luke and my breakup with Foster for almost three hours. When we all slide into the seats in my car, I hit the seat warmer button, and then I clear my throat.

"Maybe you guys are right. Losing Foster knocked me on my rear end. I don't want to go through that again. If someone told me Foster wanted kids, and no dice without them, it would have saved me a lot of time, and a lot of heartache."

Addy pats my knee. "This is the right call, you know. We all love you. We want what's best for you."

I nod. "I know that. Maybe Luke was the palate cleanse I needed, and after the holidays, I'll be ready to date someone for real."

Trudy and Addy both reassure me that it must be true. I drop them off at home, first Trudy and then Addy. Since Paisley picked them up, only her car is at my house, so she'll spend the night with me. I swear, drinking is such a hassle, I don't know why people do it at all. They hug me tightly and tell me I'm being smart, and I know they're right. By the time I reach my house, I've heard a ding on my phone. I pull into the garage and pick it up in front of her.

I smile when I see it's from Luke. HOPE YOUR GIRLS' NIGHT WAS FUN. YOU LEFT SO FAST I COULDN'T ASK. PLANS TOMORROW?

I close my eyes and set the phone down. Paisley snatches it from the cup holder. "Oooh, lover boy himself."

"Give me that," I say, tired and cross all of a sudden.

She wiggles her shoulders. "You'd love it if I jumped out

and weaved my way inside right now so you can dump him via text. You big chicken."

Before I can snatch the phone back, she starts texting. By the time I wrestle it away, she's already hit send.

NO PLANS YET. WHAT DID YOU HAVE IN MIND?

Three tiny dots indicate Luke's typing a response. Paisley and I both stare at the phone, like a dog watching a squirrel. Finally, the text pops up.

LET ME MAKE YOU DINNER. FOUND A BABYSITTER. WE CAN DO YOUR PLACE OR MINE.

Paisley shakes her head at me. "You can't do someone's house, not if you're dumping him. It'll be too awkward. You've got to suggest a restaurant."

She's right. CAN WE GO OUT INSTEAD? I DON'T WANNA DEAL WITH CLEANUP.

SURE, Luke texts, STAPLEHOUSE. MEET ME THERE? OR SHOULD I PICK YOU UP? 6:30 OK?

"Uh, how is he going to get into Staplehouse?" Paisley asks. "It's booked up like a month out."

I shrug. "Maybe he doesn't know that. He's not from here. But even if we can't get in there, we can hit another place close."

THAT'S FINE. MEET YOU THERE.

"If he can get into Staplehouse, maybe you shouldn't break up with him." Paisley smirks, but then her face turns serious. "Addy and Trudy mean well, but they aren't you and they have no idea, not really. Are you sure you want to do this?"

I shake my head. "No, and that's exactly why I need to."

CHAPTER 17

I dress in a dark blue sheath dress that hugs me all over, and my favorite pair of dark brown Frye boots. When I reach Staplehouse, Luke's pacing outside, on the phone with someone.

"I told you already. I don't want to do that."

Pause.

"Because I hate that kind of stuff, which you know."

Pause.

"It's like this. You handle this part, and I'll do my part. I've got the prototype, and it's perfect. But you'll have to do the sales pitch without me."

Luke glances my way and notices me, a smile spreading across his face, erasing the frown lines creasing his forehead. "Look, I've got to go. We can talk more in the morning."

Pause.

"Fine. Yes, but not now. Tomorrow. She's here."

Luke hangs up and holds out his hand to me. "You look like a young Emilia Clarke. All you need is a dragon on your shoulder."

"I left the dragon at home," I say. "I know how you feel about pets."

"Oh," he says. "Amy would appreciate your burn." He takes my arm in his and leads me through the front door, where I'm fully expecting we'll be turned away.

"Mr. Manning, please, come right in." The maître d' greets us in a black suit and waves us inside.

Which is super weird.

"How did you get us in here," I whisper.

He squeezes my arm. "I may not be a fancy trust baby like your ex, but every store in town has lights, and I do quality work. I helped wire this entire place back when it was going in. I know the owner, and the head chef."

"In fact," the maître d' chimes in, "Mr. Manning helped the Giving Kitchen, back when it started. None of us will ever forget his boundless generosity."

Well, color me impressed. "Maybe karma is real," I say. "I've had a lot of clients who have brought me fruit cake, or a plate of cookies. I think I need to branch out a little."

Luke snorts. "Stick with me kid, and you won't need to."

My heart twinges a bit, knowing that I'm here with a purpose, and neither of us is going to like it. Why didn't Paisley just let me do this via text? I'm going to kick her in the shin next time I see her. Hard. Like I'm going to leave a bruise.

After we're seated, I have no idea what to say. I could break up with him now, before we've even gotten a basket of bread, but that seems kind of awful. Plus, I've never eaten here, and I kind of want to try it. Or is that even worse?

"How was your girls' night?" he asks. "What did you do? Since you don't drink, I was wondering."

I shrug. "First we paint our toenails, and then we braid each other's hair."

"Is that before or after the big pillow fights?"

"So you can tell when I'm kidding now?" I ask.

He taps the side of his head with one finger. "Prepare to be impressed with my powers of observation. I noticed. . . your hair isn't braided."

Before I can reply, a waiter places a menu in my hands. I glance down at the words, and then they draw all my attention. No prices, not categories, nothing I can make sense of in the slightest. It's just a list of ten or fifteen words.

"Uh," I say, "what in the world is this?"

Luke smirks. "It's a tasting menu. You get ten or eleven courses, all of them so good you wish there was more to each one."

"Wait, we don't get to pick what we're eating?" I bite my lip. "This is weird."

He splays his hands out in front of him. "We can leave if you'd like, but I think even if you don't like a few of the options, you'll like enough to get full."

"It might be good for me to try some new things," I say. "I have a tendency to eat the same burger and fries every time I go out."

I can't help but wonder what Trudy and Addy would think. Is this evidence that he's trying to change me? Should I be upset?

But the thing is, I'm not.

We chat and laugh, and every single time his fingers brush mine, my heart rate spikes and my mouth dries up. We're on the kombucha course, with only two dessert courses to follow and I decide I can't wait any longer. I open my mouth to break up with him, but he's faster than me.

"I've been thinking about your Sub-for-Santa conundrum, and how your ex-boyfriend is essentially shutting you down."

"It's not actually—"

He holds up one hand. "Hear me out. I think you need to go over his head. This guy's not doing his job, and you need to tell his boss."

"He may also just be distracted, or possibly sick of having me in his office." I think about Jessica last night, her sneer, and how she knew my name. Maybe it's not even Foster who's the real impetus.

"Whatever the reason, if you love this program, don't let it go without a fight."

I shake my head. "I can't fight it, Luke. I don't have the funds, and after I start my new job, I won't have the time, either."

"It's all a matter of delegation. If you can get things rolling, I bet you can find volunteers to help out."

I sigh heavily. "I'd need a miracle."

"So go ask Foster for his help. Unless he's a real monster."

"Nah, he's a decent guy."

"Why did you two end things, if you don't mind me asking."

I need to just break up with Luke. I don't want to have to go into all of this, moments before I dump him. It's a waste, but maybe Luke needs to know.

"He wanted kids," I say flatly. "I don't."

"That was it?" Luke's eyebrows rise. "And neither of you would budge?"

I press my lips together. "Guess not. Although, now he's getting married in like a few days, and I ran into his fiancé at our girls' night. She was really, really drunk."

Luke tsks. "Never great to be too smashed, but if it was her bachelorette party, I think she gets a pass."

"You don't understand," I whisper. I have no idea why it's so hard for me to say this, but it is. "Foster told me she's pregnant, and that's why he proposed so fast. They only met a few months ago."

"And she was drunk?" He leans back in his chair. "That's not good. In fact—"

I nod slowly. "I told her as much. I warned her about Fetal Alcohol Syndrome and the damage it can cause, which is when she told me she *isn't* pregnant."

Luke whistles in disbelief.

"I don't know if that means she made it up so Foster would propose, or whether she's lost the baby. I wonder if I should say anything to Foster."

"Absolutely not," Luke says.

A waiter shows up at our side, and looks pointedly at Luke. "Sir? Did you need something?"

"What?" Luke glances at me and then back to the waiter. "Oh, because I whistled? Sorry, wasn't calling for you. I was surprised by something, is all."

The waiter gives a little half bow and takes our glasses. He glances down at mine. "You didn't enjoy the Kombucha?" he asks me.

"I don't drink alcohol," I say.

"It barely qualifies," the waiter insists.

I stare at him calmly. "I appreciate your opinion, but for me, barely is more than enough. Thanks."

"You weren't kidding when you said you don't drink, huh?" Luke asks.

I shake my head. "I'll never drink."

"Just like you never want kids?"

"Or we could talk about how you won't get your daughter a dog. We all have our lines in the sand."

Luke frowns. "Dogs aren't the same as kids."

"No, they aren't. And drinking too much alcohol isn't

the same as moving every few months, either. But both could damage a child, leaving them unable to form proper relationships."

The corners of Luke's mouth turn down. "What are you saying? That I'm as bad as an alcoholic father, because my job takes me from place to place?"

"How long have you been moving, Luke? Your entire professional life?"

"What does that have to do with anything?" he asks.

"I know you didn't move like this for your entire career. In fact, I'd hazard a guess you've been moving for four years, give or take."

Luke crumples his linen napkin in his hand. "Who told you that?"

I smooth my napkin flat on the table, trying to exude calm. "Amy. She said you've been moving since her mother died."

If I'd known how wounded Luke would look, I'd have kept my mouth shut. "Do you have any idea what it feels like, to have an epic love, to meet your perfect match, and then to watch her die doing the one thing you both wanted? Trying to grow your family?"

Luke looks away from me, away from anything, and he struggles to regain his composure. "Of course you don't," he whispers. "You'll never understand because you don't even want a family."

The waiter approaches, oblivious, with two plates and places them in front of us. "White chocolate tart, with hibiscus infusion and ginger reduction."

Luke nods at him stiffly and he walks away.

"I'm sorry I brought it up, Luke, but Amy told me all she wanted for Christmas was a puppy. I told her that seemed unlikely. She said if she can't have a puppy, she wants to live somewhere in a house with no wheels. She wants to make friends, and keep them."

I don't mention her asking me to be her mom.

Luke practically bites each word off as he speaks. "Amy is fine. She has a father who loves her, a brother, and all the finest tutors. Frankly, I'm teaching her a valuable life skill, how to build new friendships quickly."

I clear my throat. "Which is all fine. You're her dad, and I'm sure you know best. I bet you'll make sure she has an excellent education, even if it's from tutors in a trailer. I'm sorry I interfered."

Luke's eyes snap when he meets mine. "What would you have me do, Mary? Call and back out of my job? Stay here instead?"

My lips part in surprise. "No, I'd never dream of telling you what to do. I'm sorry I even brought it up."

"Because it's not like you're facing your demons. You're letting your mom and dad ruin not just your childhood, but also your entire life. You're giving them the power to incapacitate you."

"Excuse me?" I ask.

"You're a hypocrite," Luke says. "You chastise me for not staying put, for running from my problems, but you dump anyone who wants to talk about kids, because you won't make the sacrifices it takes to raise one, and at the same time you blame your parents for being selfish."

I slam my fork down on the table. "You have no idea, no idea what you're talking about. I don't want kids because I won't mistreat them the way my parents did. I won't, but I love my job, and I love accomplishing something outside of the home. I know myself, and I set healthy boundaries."

"Oh?" Luke asks. "And what kind of boundaries do you set, exactly?"

I push my chair back from the table. "I came here tonight to set one with you. I can't date you, Luke, not anymore. We want different things, and we just aren't compatible."

"I want something different? What, to take care of my kids? To put food on the table? And you want to be a saint who helps every poor kid in the city, but doesn't actually love any of them enough to change your life in the slightest."

I grit my teeth. "I should have broken up with you via text. I'm sorry I came tonight at all." I stand up and my voice is woodenly stiff when I say, "Thank you for dinner. I wish you and your family all the best."

"Now who's running away?" Luke asks.

"It takes a runner to spot one." I turn on my heel and walk out of the dining room and through the front door before the first tears spill, hot and fast, down my cheeks. The man outside with the Salvation Army cauldron swings his arm back and forth, back and forth.

"God bless you," he says.

I could use some blessings. I haven't had too many lately. I don't even look at the wad of bills in my hand before stuffing them into his red bucket.

I drive home on autopilot, barely noticing familiar landmarks as I pass them. When I finally turn into my own driveway, I stop on impulse at the mailbox and grab the weekend's pile of letters. Maybe the stack of bills will distract me. Sometimes routine things help me clear my head.

After I park, I toss the pile of letters onto my kitchen island and start working my way through them. Coupon mailer, bill, bill, coupon, flier, bill. Thick, heavy, embossed envelope. I tear it open carelessly, cutting my finger in the process. Blood stains the edge of the luxe paper.

A wedding invitation. From Foster and Jessica. A tiny

scrawl on the corner in Foster's handwriting. "Sorry this is late. Jessica didn't want to invite you until she realized you had a plus one. Hope to see you there."

Blood rushes to my head, my ears ringing. I'm invited, now that I have a plus one, huh? I close my eyes and shake my head slowly. I couldn't have waited until after Christmas to dump Luke? I could box Trudy and Addy's ears for this. Now, tomorrow, I'm going to have to march into Foster's office and tell him Luke and I have broken up.

I'd rather eat a bowl of glass shards.

Maybe I could RSVP and then claim I was ill or injured, instead. Or in the hospital! I could get a fake cast to really sell it.

I shake my head. Grow up, Mary. You can do this. Tomorrow, I'll simply march into Foster's office. I'll fight for Sub-for-Santa, and I'll tell him I won't be attending his wedding as an unwanted single, or with a plus one. And if he's a real jerk about it, I can always tell him his future wife lied and she isn't pregnant at all. I hope he got a good pre-nup.

Actually, if I'm being honest, I kind of hope he didn't.

CHAPTER 18

Heather smiles beatifically when I walk through the front doors of the United Way office, and I wonder why. It's too bright, too cold, and far too early for anyone to be that chipper.

"Morning," I mumble.

"It's a beautiful winter day," Heather says. "And we're less than a week away from Christmas. If you check the break room, you'll see a surprise for everyone from me."

I close my eyes and breathe in and out once. I need to find my Christmas joy. I'm letting men steal it from me. First Luke, and now Foster. No more. From today forward, I'll channel Heather's holiday spirit until mine regenerates.

"Thanks, Heather. I'll be sure to check it out. Is Foster in yet?" I ask.

She shakes her head. "He may be pretty late today. I think he had his bachelor party last night."

Of course he did. I massage my right temple and walk down the hall to my office to take some Tylenol. It's not fair that I feel horrible this morning, because like always, I didn't have a single drink. Even so, I tossed and turned with dreams of Luke and dreams of Foster, and dreams of Luke with Foster's head, or Foster's voice coming from Luke's mouth.

All in all, I've never wanted to turn my alarm off as badly as I did this morning. I did hit snooze once, and pull the covers up over my head. But I only gave myself six extra minutes, because I have too much to do today, and they're things that can't wait. Besides, my cleaning lady was coming by this morning to make sure everything's ready for Trudy to start moving in. I only have her come once a month usually, but she squeezed me in once she found out about Troy.

I slide into my tall, black, leather backed desk chair, a gift from Foster for my birthday last year. I make a few calls to Trudy's landlord to confirm he received her notice, in spite of the place being rented in Chris's name. I also call the moving company I hired to get her stuff packed and shifted over today, and they confirm they'll be at her house by nine a.m.

Once I'm done with my messy personal stuff, I dig in to the Sub-for-Santa work. This week's officially check-in week. I call each volunteer family to make sure they've found appropriate gifts and are wrapping them. I confirm they've been able to reach their family and schedule a delivery time, usually on Christmas Eve. This year, Christmas falls on a Sunday, which puts Christmas Eve on a Saturday, and sometimes that complicates matters.

I work my way down the list, chatting with some people, leaving messages for others. A few of them haven't bought all the gifts yet, but are going today. A few have had everything purchased and wrapped for almost a week. The over-achievers make me smile.

Of course, that smile that drops off my face when I reach the bottom of the list of names. Lucas Manning. Aka,

Luke Manning. Penciled in as a confirmed sponsor. I pick up the phone. It's business, not personal. I take a deep breath, because I can do this.

The phone rings.

Luke's deep voice intones, "Hello?"

"Mr. Manning," I say, trying my best to remain detached. Professional. "This is a courtesy call from the Sub-for-Santa organization. We'd like to remind you that your family's gifts need to be wrapped and ready to deliver for Sunday. Have you been able to touch bases with the family to confirm a time and place for delivery?"

"Mary?"

"Uh, yes, this is Mary Wiggin."

Luke's voice bristles more than a porcupine in a needle factory. "You dump me, and then you call me the next day and pretend . . . what? That you don't even know me?"

I sigh. "I have a job to do Luke, and I wasn't sure, er, I mean, this has never happened before."

"What, dating a sponsor parent? Or dumping someone because you're scared?"

My hand clenches on the receiver. "I'm not scared. I'm sensible."

"Sensible? What are you, British? Is your real name Mary Poppins?"

"Luke, I'm not trying to pick a fight here. I'm just trying to check in with you, okay? I've got a holiday party Wednesday that I'll have to attend alone because I'm getting a promotion I don't want. And I got invited to a wedding on Thursday for my ex-boyfriend, which would suck on a normal week, but now I'm dreading it because I don't have a plus one anymore, but he's put one on my invite. I don't have the time or energy to argue with you anymore."

"I'll still go with you, if you want me there," Luke offers.

"I'm sorry I said what I said last night, for what it's worth, and it sounds like it would suck to go alone, to both of those. Of course, if I help you out, you'd have to come to my red ribbon ceremony on Friday morning."

I want to tell him yes so badly, but everything the girls said is still true. He has kids, and I can't deal with them, I just can't. And he's still leaving, and on and on.

I clear my throat. "As much as I'd love that, Luke, and I really would love to have a gorgeous, funny, smart man on my arm at both events, but I can't do that. I can't learn to lean on someone who won't be here in a few weeks. And I can't keep spending time with your kids when they won't ever be my kids, and they can't be."

"The kids love you. It doesn't hurt them to spend more time with you."

I shake my head, but of course he can't see that through the phone. "I think it does cause them pain. Or at least, it shows them what they're missing. Did Amy tell you what she really wants for Christmas?"

"I know she wants a dog. Everyone in the entire RV Park knows she wants a dog."

"Amy told me what she really wants is a mother, right before she told me she wanted a home that's not on wheels. She said since she knows she can't have that, she asks you for a dog."

Silence on the line.

"Luke?"

"I'm here. I'm sorry, I was processing. She's never said anything like that to me. Not ever."

"My sister's son is sick, and they're moving in with me today. Plus my promotion is taking up a lot of time, plus this week is my last big push to get the United Way to keep Sub-for-Santa on its docket. I'm going to beg off on the wedding, I hope. And either way, I've got to be able to handle these things alone, just like I'll have to when you move away in a few weeks."

Silence again. I think about hanging up.

"Well, thanks for checking in," Luke says. "We've got all the gifts purchased, and we'll be wrapping them all tonight."

"That's wonderful to hear," I say. "And you've talked with the family?"

"I called the number twice. No answer the first time and no machine, but on the second try, I connected with the father. He only speaks Spanish, but I speak enough to make things work. I'll be dropping them off on Sunday at noon. His kids will be at mass with their grandmother. He has a shed we can store the presents in."

"Perfect," I say. "Thanks so much. I'll make note of it. And don't forget to keep all your receipts. You can deduct them."

His receipts. I smack my forehead. "Oh, Luke, I'm so sorry. We never divvied up the cost of the gifts that were for my family. You have the receipt. Can you text me the amount and I'll mail you a check?"

"You paid for Chuck-e-Cheese. As much as I'd love to lure you over under the pretense of dividing up a check, we're square. Don't worry about it."

Not a chance. I'll guesstimate and send him twenty percent more. "Uh huh. Okay."

"Mary?" Luke asks.

"Yeah?"

"It's really good to hear your voice. I really am sorry for what I said last night. I don't know what you went through, and I don't think you're running away. Quite the opposite. Your sister's moving in with you, and you're taking a promotion you don't want to help her with her son. You couldn't be more different than your own mother, from what I can tell."

My throat closes off and I can barely breathe, much less talk. I choke out a few words. "Thanks, Luke. Goodbye." Then I hang up the phone. A moment later, I hear a familiar voice booming from down the hall.

Foster's here.

"Precisely," he says, his voice moving from the hallway into the conference room. "Please, come right this way. I'll show you the plans for the new healthcare supplemental access for children. Once we've reallocated funds like you suggested—"

Foster stops speaking, presumably because the person he's with asked him a question.

"Right, yes, I have a list of programs we'll be cutting. Of course. I'll have Heather grab that for you right now."

I grab the stack of papers off the corner of my desk, and jog down the hall to Heather's kiosk with them under my arm. I need to catch Foster's eye. It's almost time for me to leave, but I need to make my case for keeping Sub-for-Santa, and I need to tell him I can't make it to his wedding.

Foster turns to face me when I reach the receptionist desk. "Mary?" His eyes search my face, looking for my purpose in chasing him down the hall. "I'm a little busy right now."

"I can see that you are," I say. "I only need a minute. I think you're making a huge mistake letting corporate cut the Sub-for-Santa program and I've got evidence to back up my claim."

Foster exhales heavily. "Not right now, Mary, okay?"

"What evidence do you have, exactly?" A short man, balding, with thick black-rimmed glasses stands in the doorway of the conference room.

I glance from Foster to the man and then back again. "Uh, Foster?"

"Uh Mary?" Foster asks me, his tone so condescending that my hand itches to slap him. "Answer Mr. Peters, He came all the way out here from Alexandria, and I was about to hand him a list of underperforming charities we should eliminate to make room for a larger initiative for sick kids. So go ahead. Show him your evidence that giving kids some toys at Christmas is more important than, say, providing them with a prosthetic limb, or glasses that will enable them to see the chalkboard and learn how to read and add and subtract."

I frown. I wasn't expecting to present to the Vice President of the United Way. And with that glowing introduction, Mr. Peters isn't likely to listen to a word I say.

"My name is Mary Wiggin. I've been spearheading the Sub-for-Santa program for years, for free. It meant so much to me as a child. In fact, before I get into the evidence I brought, I just wanted to say that I was a recipient of Sub-for-Santa for many years, from the age of seven. Most years, it was the thought of Christmas that helped me survive and thrive in school. That's why I've been giving eighty to a hundred hours of my time free each year in support of this program. I know hope and excitement and wonder don't manifest as tangibly as medical care, but Sub-for-Santa's very low resource, and I don't see why the two initiatives would be zero sum."

Mr. Peters' eyebrows rise. "Zero sum?" He laughs then, a great big belly laugh. "Of course they aren't zero sum, except that our funds are limited and if we spend the money we've raised on one thing, we can't spend it on another. Last week, I tasked Foster here to cut enough programs to make room in the budget for our top priority, which is aiding sick kids."

Foster walks back toward the conference room. "We can talk more tomorrow, Mary. Stan and I have a lot of work to do now."

"Let her come show me her evidence," Mr. Peters says. "I'd be most interested to see why she thinks United Way needs this program. After all, our goal is to maximize good for the funding we have. Shouldn't we listen to a self-proclaimed expert on it before we decide? And, frankly, her excitement has me questioning Sub-for-Santa's removal."

I jog behind Foster and Mr. Peters and into the conference room, spreading my notes, articles and spreadsheets out in front of them both.

"Okay, first we've got the chart here that shows how many kids have been helped, and the total cost per family to United Way. If you average our costs out by family, we only spend $11.40 per family at Christmas. It's very low budget, because in fact, it's a fundraiser all its own. The families who sign up pay for almost everything."

Mr. Peters hums quietly to himself. "And where does that eleven dollars go?"

I point at another chart, a budget break down. "We have promotional materials we provide to churches, clubs and schools. They help us identify families, which we then screen for eligibility. Beyond that, we also have mailers, paperwork fees, and whatnot. And while I work for free, I need an assistant to help me manage all of this, and she can't afford to work for free. I pay her half what she makes at my firm, and she's the best secretary I've ever had, but her salary composes about half of the expense for the administration."

"If I agreed to let this continue, but I insisted on cutting your budget by half?" Mr. Peters stares into my eyes. "What then?"

I wring my hands in my lap where I hope he can't tell. I'd need to do Sub-for-Santa without a secretary or assistant, and I have a new job where I'll be working even more. I want to keep it alive, but I'm not Atlas and I can't carry the whole globe. Tears well up in my eyes. "I don't know, sir. Maybe we could make that work. Would we be allowed to do additional fundraisers, and use any funds we generate to pay my assistant?"

He shakes his head. "Against policy."

Of course it is. "I could pay the assistant instead."

He shakes his head again. "If you donate to United Way, it needs to go into the general fund. It's against our charter to have you pay an assistant on your own. In fact, it might invalidate our 501(c)(3) status."

I close my eyes. "Sir, we're talking about a very small amount of money here. And I have more evidence of the benefits. Look at these articles about our program. This program is marketing and publicity gold, sir. People love the stories and the good we do generates a lot of positive buzz for the United Way. It's hard to quantify the exact benefit, but it's got to help people be more generous in donations. Families love participating, and obviously the recipient families love knowing someone cares about them. It fosters exactly the kind of goodwill and general kindness that's missing in the world."

Mr. Peters flips through my fliers and my clippings. He lays his huge hand across the top of the clippings and leans back in his chair. "I hate to tell you this Mary, because I admire your excitement and your passion, but even though this certainly seems like a worthy cause, I have to evaluate everything as good, better, best. I would place this squarely into the "good" category. It's good, but our money can be better or even best used elsewhere."

I knew this was coming. Foster told me resisting was

futile, but somehow, here, looking this man in the eye, I can't quite believe he's turning me down. I think about the little girls out there with nothing to look forward to all year. I think about the little boys who only ask for a baseball and a glove. No glove for their dad, because they have no dad. I remember at last year's drop off, one mother fell at my feet and wept. Her husband was sick and the care for him was more than she could manage. Food stamps kept them alive, but there was nothing left over for the children.

"You're making a mistake, sir." I reach across the table in front of him and gather up all my press clippings, thank you letters, emails, and charts. None of it mattered, not in the end. "But because your family knew the right people, and donated to the right groups, it's your mistake to make. I wish you the very best in your admirable and more impressive goals of healing sick kids' bodies. I hope that one day you'll see the value in instilling hope and love in kids' hearts, too."

I head back into my office long enough to check my voicemail and make notes, grab my coat, and finish up my phone call notations. I'll be calling all day tomorrow as well, hoping everyone has done what they were supposed to do. If not, I'll have a few extra families this year. I've had as many as six extra families in the past, but last year I only had two.

I slide my arms into the sleeves of my navy blue pea coat and button it up. I'm proud that I don't glare at Mr. Peters where he's still poring over letters in the conference room when I walk past. He's all alone in there, which leaves me wondering where exactly Foster went.

I slow down as I pass Foster's office, looking for clues of why he abandoned ship.

I don't notice her perfectly curled, shiny, blonde hair until I'm two feet from Foster's office door.

"Babe, when can we go?" she asks, one hand on her flat stomach. "I swear this baby is making me so hungry all the time."

"I just hope you can still fit in your dress at the end of the week." Foster grins down at her. "My parents spent a fortune on it."

She's not really pregnant, I want to shout. She lied to trick you into marrying her. But I don't say a single word. I think he may deserve someone like her.

I wave at Foster. "Hey boss. I'm headed out, but I wanted to let you know I won't be able to make it to the wedding. Unfortunately my funding for buying cute, wedding appropriate clothing and shoes has been cut and reallocated to my toilet paper fund. I do hope you understand. Wiping butts is more important than supporting friends. I wish you both the best of luck in the future."

"Don't be petty Mary," Foster says. "It doesn't suit you. And you know very well that the budget decisions are above my pay grade. I'm just doing my job."

When Jessica recognizes me, her eyes flash. "Mary Wiggin."

I bob my head an inch or so. "So nice to finally meet you," I say, daring her to say different.

"I told Foster not to send you an invite with a plus one. You've only been seeing this new guy for what? A week? That kind of thing falls apart as fast as it goes together, if you know what I mean. We didn't want to put any undue pressure on something so new, and although you're welcome to come alone, we didn't want you to feel conspicuous."

Her liberal use of 'we' makes me want to hurl in the big, black, pot next to Foster's fake Bird of Paradise plant.

I scratch my head. "I think Luke and I started dating about two weeks after you and Foster." I smile sweetly.

"But it's not my relationship status that's getting in the way of me coming. Actually, I can't make it because I'm getting a promotion at work, and my sister is moving in with me, along with her toddler son. Bad timing, is all."

"Wait," Foster says. "What's going on with Trudy?"

"It's nothing, really."

Foster opens his mouth, but before he can speak, Jessica, who's glaring at me says, "Well, in any case, thanks for letting us know." She leans against Foster and slides her hand down his arm to take his hand in hers.

"Sorry to tell you so late, but I just can't go."

Jessica's smile is relieved. I glance at Foster and he's wearing his plastic smile underneath pained eyes. Which means he's relieved too. If they didn't want me to come, why even bother inviting me?

I pull my phone out of my purse and pretend to be reading a text message. "On second thought, Luke is free and we'll be there. With bells on."

Jessica raises one eyebrow. "What wonderful news."

"Yeah." I drop to a whisper. "Speaking of wonderful news, I heard you have some great news to share. When I guessed, Foster told me to keep it to myself, but of course I can congratulate you." I stare right into Jessica's eyes. "Are you hoping for a boy or a girl?"

She flinches and her face falls. At least she has the decency to pretend to feel awful about her lie. I consider telling Foster, but I keep my mouth shut.

Foster wraps his arms around her shoulders from behind. "We don't care about the gender as long as it's healthy."

I think about Troy, who isn't healthy, and I frown. "What does that mean? If it's born with Down's syndrome, you won't want it? If it's born with a bad heart, or another condition, will you walk away? What if he or she isn't that smart, or very talented? Will you still love them then?"

Foster leads Jessica out of his office and back toward the conference room. "Such a nice chat. We're glad you'll be there for our wedding. But for now, Jess and I are taking Mr. Peters to lunch."

"I have to get to work anyway," I say. "I'm way behind now that I've got a new role to train for."

All I can think about the entire drive over to my tax firm is. . . how in the world will I skip the wedding, or go alone, without confirming their suspicion that I can't hold a relationship together for more than a month? It's been a long month already, but I can't bear the idea of facing them without a plus one. Yuck. What's wrong with me? Why didn't I let it go?

I reach for my phone, about to text Luke, when another message pings.

YOU OKAY? Trudy asks.

HOW'S THE MOVE COMING? I text back.

ALL MOVED OVER ALREADY. THOSE GUYS WERE FAST, AND IT HELPS OUR PLACES ARE CLOSE TOGETHER.

What a relief. WONDERFUL NEWS.

I NEED A BREAK AFTER THIS.

Me too. In the past year, Foster's managed to find the perfect girl for him, a beautiful, money loving, raging liar. Meanwhile, I'm still completely single, unlovable, and married to my job. Actually, Foster's and Trudy have always been oil and water. She's probably the perfect person to be my plus one, if I have to go, and I feel like I do.

WOULD YOU COME WITH ME TO A WEDDING?

Trudy texts back immediately. WOULDN'T MISS IT.

Peace settles over me like a warm blanket, fresh from

the dryer. I've got a plus one, and I don't have to worry about upsetting Luke or reopening that can of worms. THANKS T.

ANYTHING FOR YOU. YOU'RE THE BEST PERSON IN THE WORLD. I'M LUCKY YOU'RE MY SISTER.

Unlike the polite platitudes friends throw out, I know Trudy means it from the bottom of her heart.

CHAPTER 19

I carefully hang my keys on the hook by the door from my garage into the house and head inside, but I only take three steps before stopping dead in my tracks. There's literally a box blocking my entrance, no matter which way I turn.

"Trudy?" I call out.

"Aunt May May?" a small voice comes from behind a box blocking my way into the kitchen.

"Hey Troy. Any chance you could find your mom and let her know I can't get inside my own house?"

"Yeah, yeah, I will." Troy takes off skipping, which I know, because I hear his sneakers squeaking on the tile, but also because once he moves into the living room, his happily bobbing head bounces into view.

I try shifting a triple high box stack while I'm waiting, but it's no good. I'm about to give up and circle around to my own front door, when I see Trudy's dishwater blonde hair over the pile I couldn't budge.

"I need to work out more," I say.

"I'm sorry." Trudy starts shifting boxes out of the way. "I

was going to put most of this in storage, but then the storage unit I called tried to triple their price."

Any increase would be more than she could afford.

"That's okay. I have lots of room in my garage and even more in my attic. It's probably better this way. You and I can sort through all of your stuff and figure out what you want to keep and what needs to be donated, and we can do it at our leisure."

Trudy smiles. "Thanks."

A knock from the front door reminds me I ordered pizza on my way home. I've been eating too much pizza lately, but I do not have the energy, nor apparently the space, to make anything tonight.

"Umm, if you can run grab that, I'll start shifting some of these into the garage. We can go through them all and repack what you're not going to move inside."

We spend the rest of the night tag teaming the unpacking, watching Troy and cleaning up, but as soon as Troy's in bed, she pounces.

"And?" she asks. "Did you break up with him?"

My stomach turns and I collapse on the couch. The feeling of cotton balls stuffed in my throat keeps me from talking, so I simply nod.

She sits next to me. "So right after you broke up, you got Foster's wedding announcement, right?"

"How did you know?"

She shakes her head. "It's the way stuff like this always happens. Remember the time Miss Fitzgibbons cut my bangs two inches too short?"

I stifle my laugh. "The day before senior prom. You thought your life was over."

"This will be funny in a few years, too. If you don't want to use me as your plus one, you can always beg off and skip the wedding entirely."

I rub my face with both hands. "It's not even just the wedding. I got final confirmation today that United Way won't renew the Sub-for-Santa charter, which means this is my last year."

Trudy puts an arm around my shoulder. "It's amazing you've done this for so long, but maybe it's the right time to move on."

Is she right? Should I give up on all the kids who need a little cheer, the kids like me who just need something to hope for? When I speak, my words come out very softly for some reason. "Am I using Sub-for-Santa as a way to avoid forming lasting relationships with children in my life?"

Trudy narrows her eyes at me. "Who said that?"

I shrug. "Me, I said it. Why would you think someone else would say that?"

Trudy scowls. "It was this Luke guy, wasn't it?"

"I might have attacked him and said he's doing his children a disservice by moving them several times a year. It could even have gotten personal. I might have impugned the trailer."

"That sounds kind of harsh, and unlike you," Trudy says.

"Someone needed to tell him, because Amy hates it and she loves him too much to say anything."

"Now you're advocating for his kids. You form meaningful relationships with anyone you've been around for thirty seconds. And you've been the best aunt in the world to Troy."

I lick my lips. "I wasn't fishing for compliments. I really want to know."

Trudy groans. "No, Mary, I don't think you're avoiding meaningful relationships with anyone, but you definitely *are* avoiding becoming a mother, and that's your prerogative."

I've never asked my sister this, because I didn't want it to sound critical. I don't want her to think I'm judging her, but I need to know. "After how Mom and Dad raised us, how could you have ever wanted a child? Don't get me wrong, Troy is wonderful, but aren't you scared?"

"Kids are so hard," Trudy says, "and the hard things about being his mom change every day. It's like he's quicksand. In a diaper. Slipping through my fingers one minute, and sucking me under the next."

"Gee," I say, "still not getting why you wanted to have a baby."

Trudy leans her head on my shoulder. "We both had horrible parents. The worst I've ever seen, maybe. One left us and never looked back. The other drank himself into a stupor every day and didn't even notice when we left. But I had something better than them. I had an older sister who took care of me better than they could. I won't make up a bunch of fortune cookie truths about how fulfilling it is to be a parent, and how wonderful Troy is when he's sweet, and how I love and hate raising a mini-me. Because I don't think parenting is about me. In fact, I think the main reason I needed a child in my life was to learn to serve someone else. Mom and Dad were selfish. They only cared about what they wanted, their own desires and pains."

"Dad's sick," I say.

She nods. "Yeah, he's an alcoholic, and that's hard to figure out, right? Is he selfish, or sick? But at least that first time he picked up that bottle instead of taking care of us, he chose himself."

I sigh. "And I don't want to be a mom because it will be easier for me, so I'm like Mom and you aren't."

Trudy jerks back. "Exactly the opposite. I was super selfish when we were growing up."

"No." I shake my head. "You weren't selfish before you had Troy. I was there, remember?"

Trudy laughs. "That's sweet of you to say, but wrong. I spent all my time doing whatever I wanted. Work, play, entertainment. Now I break my back for this little demon child, and I'd do so much more if he needed it. The real reason I could have a child is that Mom and Dad *weren't* my examples. They were, and are, selfish to the core. No, my example, the person who gave me hope I could do better was my surrogate mother. The best mom I've ever met." A tear pools in Trudy's eye.

"Who?" Maybe she means Mrs. Fitzgibbons of the horrible haircuts. Or her favorite fifth grade teacher who kept going to all her plays long after she left elementary school.

Trudy rolls her eyes. "You're so dense sometimes. I'm talking about you, Mary. You were the best mother anyone could ask for. It wasn't fair to you, and it wasn't right, but you're still my fill-in-mom. You're still my model of what I one day hope to become if I try really hard."

"You're not my daughter," I say. "I've just been a good sister."

"Fine," Trudy says. "Then you've shown me what family should do. All I'm saying is, you don't need to have kids, because you're already the most selfless person I know."

"Actually that reminds me," I say. "I wired the money for the clinical trial for Troy to the hospital today, so he should be fine to begin tomorrow, like we planned."

Trudy gives me a big hug, and it was totally worth the expense, knowing she's okay, knowing Troy gets his best chance.

The next two days pass in a blur, between unpacking, wrapping, checking in on families on either end, and coordinating the details of taking over for Shauna.

I'm dressing for my company holiday party, when my phone bings. I pick it up. It's a message from Luke.

AMY HAS BEEN INSISTING I TELL YOU THAT YOU'RE STILL INVITED TO COME DROP OFF GIFTS WITH US ON CHRISTMAS EVE. SAT @ NOON.

My heart flip flops. I dumped him on Sunday, and I know three days isn't a long time, but it feels like forever. I miss him, and I want to beg him to come with me tonight, and to the wedding tomorrow. I want to see his red ribbon cutting, and play with his kids, and tell them how amazing it is that their dad made that building possible.

Trudy and Addy were right. I'm way too invested in this.

I APPRECIATE THE INVITE. I'D LOVE TO COME, BUT THERE'S ALWAYS A LOT OF LAST MINUTE DETAILS, AND I HAVEN'T QUITE FINISHED MY OWN SHOPPING YET. I'LL TEXT YOU IF BY SOME MIRACLE I CAN MAKE IT.

I shove my phone in my purse and walk into the mostly clean living room. "How do I look?" I spin in a circle for Trudy and Troy.

"Amazing!" Trudy says.

"Sparkly," Troy says.

I'm wearing a dark green business suit, but my camisole underneath is red with sequins. I don't wear them together usually, but it's Christmas. And as Troy pointed out, it's sparkly. Much like a child, I love sparkly things.

Trudy gives me a big hug, and before she lets go, she whispers, "I hope you love this new promotion, but I think maybe you accepted it for me. I'm not sure why exactly, but I promise I'll pay you back for what you've given up one day."

"Having you in my life is my payback," I say. "I love you."

My drive to the holiday party takes me past the same Pet Smart, and I'm sad to see that there's no SPCA event there today. I think about that beautiful dog. I've done some research on Great Pyrenees, and they're excellent pets. When I pull into a parking space outside the Hyatt, I rummage around in my purse until I find the card with the rescue lady's number on it.

I may not be able to keep Luke, and I may not be willing to give up my career to have kids, but I could make room for a dog. I know I could. Plus, Troy will love it. Right? Before I have time to overthink it, I dial. After several rings, a man picks up.

"Hello?" he asks.

"Uh, yes, my name is Mary Wiggin. I stopped at Pet Smart a few days ago, and there was a dog there, a Great Pyrenees, and this might sound crazy, but I think I fell in love with her. I keep thinking about her. I was told you might know where I could locate her?"

"Faith," the man calls with his mouth still near the receiver. He nearly bursts my eardrums.

"Hello?" a woman says.

I explain again why I'm calling. "You're talking about Andromeda. She was chipped, but we contacted her former owner and they said she's a good dog, but the husband has cancer, and they were gone too often with his treatments. They gave her to a friend, who apparently let her go."

"That's horrible," I say. "I'm very interested in her. What would I need to do to adopt her?"

Faith walks me patiently through the entire process. "Can you come by to see her tomorrow around lunchtime?"

"Oh," I say. "So soon?"

"She's too polite to do well here with my four other

dogs," Faith says. "She's not getting enough food and she's already terribly malnourished. If you're serious, and you're responsible, you can take her home tomorrow."

We work out the details and I hang up.

I expect to feel shaky or nervous at the thought that I might be a dog owner tomorrow morning, but I don't. I didn't want a dog last week, but it's not like I'm with Luke anymore. Which means I'm excited to adopt this dog for me, not for anyone or anything else. I may not be able to be a good mom for real, but I think I can handle a big fur ball.

No one expected me to bring a date to the company holiday party, so when I square my shoulders and walk inside alone, no one bats an eye. The entire night goes smoothly, perfectly even. I don't spill anything on my dress, and before I've even used up my third accounting joke, I'm being summoned to the stage.

"Some of you may be surprised to hear this," Shauna says, "but I've taken a position running our London office. It puts me back at home, near my in-laws." She makes a face and everyone laughs. "Actually though, I prefer them to my own family."

Everyone laughs except for me. If I ever get married, I'm sure that will be too true for me. Her joke hits a little close to home.

"Although we're excited to move back to the UK, I'm heartbroken at the idea of leaving all of you."

Shauna reaches over and takes my arm, tugging me near the microphone. "Corporate initially wanted me to help them choose an outside hire. I convinced them they should offer my job to one of our own."

Everyone cheers. Eighty accountants, fifty something support staff, and loads of significant others.

Shauna holds up her hand to quiet my co-workers. "As I'm sure you've already guessed by her presence on stage, it's my pleasure to inform you that with just a little bit of cajoling, and a good amount of well-intentioned arm twisting, Mary Wiggin has agreed to take my place. I'm sure you'll all welcome her and help her with patience and understanding during this transition."

Everyone claps again, more loudly than before, if that's possible.

After the announcement, drinks flow freely, and I'm suddenly surrounded by a bunch of sloppy, goofy, and gleeful dancers. I start for the exit, shaking hands and accepting congratulations as I go. I've almost reached the back door when Shauna stops me.

"Are you leaving?" she asks.

I nod. "Today was our firm's last day before Christmas, but I've got a full day of work ahead of me tomorrow."

"Right, your charity stuff." She nods. "Well, I do have some bad news. I got an email from corporate a few hours ago. They've instituted a vesting plan for the corporate bonuses."

I reach my finger into my ear and wiggle it around. Maybe I've got earwax in there or something. "I'm sorry," I say to Shauna, "but it sounded like you just told me that the bonus you guys promised me won't be accessible. For years."

Shauna's lips press tightly together. "They've had a problem this year with poaching. Other firms steal their talent during the training phase when things are rough. No real incentive to stay once you've already gotten your huge bonus."

"How many years does it vest over?" Before Shauna can even answer, I shake my head. "I guess it doesn't matter. I emptied out my retirement accounts to pay for my nephew's treatment. I needed that bonus money so I could roll it over. To prevent my penalties, etc. Now I won't be able to."

Shauna closes her eyes and shakes her head. After a moment, she reopens them. "Mary, I am so sorry. I had no idea you meant to do that, but my hands are tied. I'm one vote among two hundred."

"It's fine." I force a smile, and make small talk for a few more minutes before someone wanders up to ask Shauna questions about her timing. I take my chance to sneak away.

I run numbers in my head all the way home. Any way I slice it, I'll have to take out a home equity loan to pay the additional tax penalties for early distribution of my retirement fund.

By the time I reach the driveway, I've put things in perspective, I think. I had the money to help Troy, and with a home equity loan, I'll have the means to pay my taxes. I'll also be making more going forward, so I can catch up on retirement savings. I hope.

I put on my game face before I walk through the garage door. I won't let Trudy know what's happened, because she'll never forgive herself. The guilt she'd feel about a debt of that size would destroy her.

One of Shauna's favorite sayings comes to mind. 'It's only money,' she'd tell me, whenever I had a bad return to discuss with a client. It's not health, it's not livelihood, it's not a beloved family member in trouble. It's only money.

When I walk through the door, I'm so focused on my own drama, that I barely register that Trudy's on the phone. Tears roll down her cheeks from where she's curled in a ball in one of my chairs.

She has to be talking to Chris. I want to reach my hand through the receiver and pop him on the nose, but that probably wouldn't help things, and it's not scientifically possible anyway.

Trudy shakes her head. "Of course not. You were so busy that I didn't want to upset you."

I can hear him yelling and swearing through the teensy phone microphone. I stride across the room and snatch it out of her hands. Chris continues to rant, and I'm glad I snatched the phone when I did. He's off the rails.

"You think you get to make all the decisions about my son? Well, you don't. You're pathetic, and you'll always be pathetic. That's why I left, you know. It was like, having Troy broke you."

"Are you quite finished?" I ask.

"Excuse me?" Chris swears. "Who is this?"

"Merry Christmas to you too, Chris. This is Mary, Trudy's older sister."

"Give the phone back to Trudy."

"I acknowledge your request, but as you're an abusive, unfaithful loser, I decline to honor it. In fact, I won't be honoring any requests from you. Today, or at any point in the future. Trudy has been afraid to tell you about Troy because you told her she's a drag now. She was afraid to tell her son's father about his condition, because you're so selfish, she worried you'd like her even less if you knew Troy was sick. I'd suggest you think about that, but I doubt it would penetrate your tiny brain. Now she's finally gotten the nerve to call and dump you—"

"She can't dump me. I already left her."

"Have you ever heard the saying, Chris, that behind every little sister is an older, crazier sister? People laugh about that like it's a joke. Except for us, it's true. I've got a baseball bat, a handgun, *and* a shovel and Trudy and me were raised to take care of problems ourselves. Keep it up, and I'll let you pick which one I use on you first."

"Oh please." Chris swears again. "Like I'm scared of a little girl. I could kill you both without breaking a sweat, except then I'd have to take care of Troy, which I don't wanna do."

"Fine," I say. "You may not be scared of me or Trudy, but you'll be very afraid of the lawyer I hired to ensure you only see Troy under limited visitation. Possibly only supervised custody once I play this recorded call. Thanks for being so creative with your threats and curses."

Chris lets off a string of curses that are, in spite of what I said, more creative than I expected from him.

"I never understood why people said profanity was the crutch of the uneducated. I know plenty of educated people, and most of them swear. But after talking to you today, I'm starting to understand what they meant."

"You stupid—"

"I think you're drunk, Chris. And as such, this conversation isn't going anywhere. But here are the main talking points. Get a pen, and write them down. Number one, my sister's new lawyer, Ann Stephens, obtained a temporary restraining order against you. With the holidays upon us, the judge granted it for two full weeks. If you call my sister, if you text her, if you come near my house, I'll call the cops so fast it'll make your head spin. And you'll get a restraining order against you for the duration of the pendency of this divorce. Bonus for me. Number two, when you realize you want to win Trudy back because your new girlfriend is a steaming pile of poop compared to my lovely sister, don't waste your time. She's done with you, and poop is closer to what you deserve. Number three, you will never criticize Trudy regarding her timing in telling you about Troy being diagnosed with diabetes. You left them. You were busy shacking up with a new lady and you didn't care about your family. I won't have you unloading your own guilt onto Trudy. Am I clear?"

Chris gives me the oral equivalency of the bird and hangs up. I text him to reiterate my three points and then toss the phone on the island in the kitchen.

I manage to get Trudy up off the chair, and onto her bed. I lay next to her until she's asleep. It gives me a long time to think.

I have a shiny shovel that's never been used, but I don't have a gun or a baseball bat. Maybe I should buy one of each.

CHAPTER 20

I want to text Foster and tell him that I'm sick. I almost text Luke and ask him to come with me after all. Taking my sister along instead of my supposed boyfriend is embarrassing, but I can't quite bring myself to use Luke that way. And if I see him again, well. There's no telling what pathetic thing I may say or do.

"So are you going to this thing?" Paisley asks me Thursday morning.

"Wait, are you going?"

She grins and shakes her head. "I'm a lowly peon, remember? There's no way his royal highness Prince Foster would condescend to asking me along."

"The way he treated you was always one of the things that bothered me the most about him."

Paisley collapses into a chair in my office with an exaggerated sigh. She puts the back of her hand to her forehead. "I lost so much sleep, tossing and turning, wondering what I might do to impress Foster and his snooty family so he'd think I was worthy of being your friend."

"No you didn't."

She sits up straight and grins. "No, I didn't."

"I've been thinking," I say.

"Uh oh, that always gets you in trouble."

"Shaddup." I mock-scowl at her. "Maybe I can use last minute Sub-for-Santa details as an excuse."

Paisley shakes her head, her strawberry blonde curls bouncing around her shoulders. "Not a chance."

My bottom lip sticks out a little in a pout. "That was my best idea. Why not?"

"Look, when someone close to you dies, you need to go the funeral. It's like, cathartic. It helps you accept that they're gone, and process the information so you can move on."

"Oh good grief. Foster didn't die."

"More's the pity," Paisley mutters. "But your relationship died, and you haven't moved on, not in over a year. It could be because you kept seeing each other intermittently thanks to your role here. Or maybe not, but I think watching him marry the most idiotic woman I've met this month, and I've been to Wal-Mart four times already so that's saying something, might help you grieve and move on."

In spite of Paisley's absolute certainty that I should go, I make up and discard various excuses all day. I've got a cold. My nephew's back in the hospital, which is a lie, but it did happen last week. My dad's liver is failing, which is almost certainly true, although I'm not sure we'll even know when it happens. I haven't heard from him since I dropped off a basket of presents and hygiene products last Christmas.

Even with my waffling back and forth over my RSVP to the wedding, Paisley and I finish our calls in record time. I start the process of taking out a home equity loan so that I can afford to pay my tax penalties in the spring. Afterward, I run to the store and do some shopping for Troy and Trudy, for my dad, and for Paisley and Addy. I even run by Pet Smart and pick up large breed dog-essential items. A crate, dog food, treats, rawhide chews, bowls and a leash. I toss a dozen different toys into my cart on my way out, unsure what exactly Andromeda might like.

When I reach the address Faith gave me, and walk up the sidewalk, my heart pounding, my hands shaking, I hear the barking of thirty dogs coming from inside the house.

Maybe this is a big mistake. Plus, I didn't even run it by Trudy, and she's living with me.

I reach my hand up to knock, and then drop it by my side. Again, for the second time in a week, the door opens without me even rapping it once.

"You must be Mary." An older woman, with her hair in a frizzy white ponytail, sporting a floral print caftan, opens the door. Her face breaks into a smile, and I notice a few of her teeth are dark brown. I don't shudder, or even squirm. Or at least, I don't think I do.

Appearances aside, Faith is one of the nicest people I've ever met. She puts her other four monstrously large dogs outside. Andromeda trots right up to me and sniffs my thighs, and then my knees, tail wagging the entire time.

I crouch down at eye level with her.

"Sit," I say.

She sits.

"Down," I say.

She flattens to the ground.

"She adores you," Faith says. "Did you bring the papers I asked for?"

I nod and pull them from my purse.

She looks over them while I wrap my arms around

Andromeda's neck. She smells like oranges now. So much better than the vomit smell she exuded that night at the Pet Smart.

"Did you miss me, girl?" An enormous pink tongue licks me from chin to forehead. "Ewww, gross!"

Faith chuckles. "She likes to lick."

I try not to imagine where else her tongue has been. Now that she's clean, it's clear I underestimated her beauty. She may be the most beautiful dog I've ever seen.

"You know she'll require grooming several times a week?" Faith asks.

I bob my head. "I've been researching."

"The great news is that she never barks, even when surrounded by the horrible miscreants from my mob, and she's already housebroken. Usually the first few days are rough, but she's been perfect."

An overachiever. I should've guessed. I scratch her behind her ears and after another twenty or so questions, she follows me happily outside and hops into the back seat of my car. Of course, as soon as I put it in drive, she tries to climb into the front seat.

I shout, "No!"

She ignores me, and I shove her into the back. I feel kind of bad about it, but she's too big to hog the front seat. She tries to climb over a half dozen more times, but once we reach the highway, she settles down.

When I reach my house, I'm surprised to discover Trudy isn't home. I spend the afternoon acclimating Andromeda. She sniffs every square inch of the backyard, though what she can smell in all the ice and mud, I have no idea. She lays at my feet while I wrap presents on the dining table. I usually sit down on the floor to do it, but I'm not sure whether Andromeda would chew on anything when my back was turned so I keep the operation up high.

We watch *The Miracle on 34th Street,* and *It's a Wonderful Life* while I work, and I swear she's paying attention. She looks from me, to the screen and back again. I've got everything wrapped, including family and friend gifts, and gifts for my assigned family. I leave Andromeda inside while I run out in my slippers to take the trash out to the big black can just outside of the garage when I realize I missed something at the bottom of one of the bags.

The horse plush Amy and I chose for the girl in her family looks up at me accusingly from the inside of one of the bags. My heart stops. I ought to take it to Luke's house. Maybe I should do that right now, and he'll probably still be at work so I could go without seeing him.

Unless he's all done. The ribbon cutting takes place tomorrow morning. He could be working right up until the deadline, or he could be relaxing at home. I think of him playing with Chase, catching balls, or building a tower with blocks only to knock it down. Or maybe he's reading Amy a book.

I shake my head to clear the delusional thoughts. I want to see Amy and Chase again, but I shouldn't. And I have no idea where he is right now. Work? Home? Shopping?

Or maybe he's on a date with someone else. My heart sinks, but I'd have no right to care, even if he was. I stand outside, frozen in thought until I'm almost frozen in body. A bark from Andromeda, probably upset I left her inside, returns me to my senses. Horse or not, I shouldn't see Luke or his kids again. I can't run it over without the risk of seeing him.

Besides, I'm almost out of time. I glance at my watch and realize I have barely more than an hour to get ready before I need to leave for Foster's wedding. I have to decide whether to dress up and go to this stupid wedding like

Paisley thinks I need to, or stay home and feign sudden and dire illness.

I'm waffling between the two when Trudy arrives home, her hair up in a fabulous French twist, and a dry cleaner bag in hand. No three year old anywhere in sight.

"Where's Troy?" I ask.

She bites her lip. "Well, I didn't want to hire a normal kid babysitter because he's so complicated right now. We lined up the continual monitor and a responsible adult needs to take regular reads."

"Okay. . . So where is he?"

"Chris' parents' house."

I slap my forehead. "Is that wise?"

Trudy shakes her head. "I don't know. They're upset about the divorce, but they know it's all Chris' fault. They've apologized to me a lot, and begged to babysit Troy whenever I need help." She lowers her voice. "I think they're worried that they won't get to see Troy anymore, and they're really the only grandparents he has."

"I hope you told them about the restraining order, at least."

She bobs her head. "Of course I did. They understand they can't have Chris over. Troy was sitting on grandma's lap watching *The Grinch* when I left. Lemme go change and then I'll be ready to go."

If Trudy's gone to all this trouble for me, I can't back out.

I trudge back to my closet and put on my favorite formal dress, a champagne colored silk sheath dress slit up to mid-thigh. I pair it with my only pair of Louboutins, an almost boring, classic black heel with patent accents to spice them up. Dark hair, dark shoes, champagne in the middle.

Trudy gushes when she sees me. "Oh Mary, no one will

pay any attention to that lying loser once you walk in. Foster's going to wish he'd hadn't been so intractable."

I doubt it, but I certainly hope she's right. Even now, even today, I can't help feeling like Foster sent me a message when we broke up. Without the promise of children, I wasn't enough for him.

I'm grabbing my purse when I hear a blood-curdling scream from the family room. I rush toward the noise, my heart beating its way out of my chest. Is Chris here? Does he have a gun? I should never have threatened someone so crazy. What was I thinking?

When I reach the family room, Trudy's standing on the back of the sofa in four inch brown high heels, clutching my flimsy blinds for dear life. Andromeda's standing in front of the sofa, tongue lolling, tail wagging.

"Whoops, I forgot to tell you." I scrunch my nose up and hunch my shoulders. "I got a dog this morning, the one I told you guys about. She's a rescue. Her name is Andromeda, and she's the sweetest thing you've ever seen."

"That thing is a *dog*?" Trudy asks. "Are you sure?"

"She's a Great Pyrenees, and they're infamously good with children, so don't worry about Troy."

Trudy's chest rises and falls rapidly, but after she's thought about what I've said, her erratic breathing slows, and she climbs down from the sofa. "Now I feel foolish, but it never occurred to me it might be a pet. I thought a wolf had gotten into your house somehow." She puts her hands on her hips. "You hate animals."

"We never had any, and they seem like they'd be a lot of work, but when I went into that Pet Smart on a whim, she had been surrendered by a family who didn't want her anymore, even though she's a wonderful dog."

I sit on the floor in my fancy dress and Andromeda lies down next to me, her head in my lap. I rub her gorgeous head and scratch her ears. "I never thought I'd get a pet either, but I swear, meeting her felt like fate. I miss Luke a lot more than I thought I would. In fact, I miss his kids too. Having a dog helps my heart not feel so empty."

Trudy drops onto the sofa with a whump. "When you dumped Foster, you know what you never, ever said? Not even once?"

I shake my head. "No. What?"

"You never told me you missed him."

I recoil. "That can't be right. I was devastated when we broke up."

Trudy smiles. "You were. But you said things like, 'I'll never find someone who's fine with just me. Someone who doesn't care whether we have kids. Someone who thinks I'm enough."

"I did say that," I admit. "But I missed him too."

Trudy shakes her head. "You were uncomfortable at the United Way office. You lamented how miserable it was being alone all the time. But you never, ever said you missed him. You never said your heart hurt when you thought about him. Nothing like that."

I narrow my eyes at her. "Are you saying I never loved Foster?"

She shrugs. "I don't know how you felt. I'm only telling you what I saw. I guess you'll probably know when you see him today. If you're depressed and weepy watching him walk down the aisle, you'll know you did love him and you need to move on. If you're fine, well."

Armed with the hope that perhaps Foster never meant as much to me as I hoped he would, I lock sweet Andromeda in the laundry room with her food and water, and head for the wedding.

Trudy and I watch the ceremony from the very back row. Foster's Catholic and either his soon-to-be wife is too, or else she didn't mind a traditional Catholic wedding. Altar boys walk up the aisle with incense, waving it to and fro. The priest rambles on and on about the power of God and how we should emulate God's example. Except, as far as I know, God's not married.

And I don't care at all that he's marrying a very young, very immature, and in spite of her fake pregnancy, a very attractive girl. In fact, I hope they're happy. I won't be in the United Way offices anymore where he'll rub my face in it, but even if I weren't being cut, I don't think I'd care. When I look at Foster now, my boyfriend of a year and a half, I don't feel anything at all.

The most exciting thing that happens during the ceremony is that the octogenarian in front of me dozes off and begins to snore. It takes three different people jabbing her to wake her up. Not a bad way to get married, I guess.

The reception afterward is a different story.

We're seated at a table for eight, next to all of Foster's couple friends. I introduce my sister to all of them in turn. I've missed hanging out with a few of them, like Brittany and David. They're all perfectly polite to me, in spite of my date being my sister, and the food is bland, but I don't mind.

After the cutting of the cake, Foster circles around to our table to chat. The first words out of his mouth are, "Where's your boyfriend, Mary? I thought he was coming, but I see your sister here with you instead."

I open my mouth to answer, but before I can, Trudy interjects. "Luke's building opens tomorrow. He got stuck reviewing his team's work on a bunch of punch list items and called and asked me to fill in for him."

Foster frowns. "He has your phone number? I don't think I have it at all and me and Mary were together for way longer."

"What can I say?" Trudy asks. "I like him a lot more than I ever liked you."

Foster snorts. "You're telling me he hasn't finished everything on a hundred million dollar building the day before the ribbon's being cut, and he's down there doing what? Reinstalling electrical outlets?"

Trudy licks her lips. "I'm not telling you anything Foster, and I don't have to. See, you've never had a real job, not one you earned yourself. All your jobs were dropped in your lap by your daddy. But for those of us without a cushy trust fund, sometimes work comes first, before things we'd rather be doing, even if it's the day before our job is done."

"He's the perfect fit for Mary then," Foster says. "The girl who picks work over her boyfriend, and won't even have kids because she loves her job too much."

"You didn't hear?" I ask. "Luke has two children. Adorable, precious children."

Foster's jaw drops. "What?"

"Maybe the problem wasn't my job after all. Maybe I had other hang-ups that kept me from agreeing to marry you and that was just an excuse. Maybe it was the unsteadiness of our relationship that got in my way, not that it matters anymore. I'm so glad you found someone who's a perfect fit, and I wish you all the best."

Foster splutters. "She is a perfect fit."

Trudy coughs into her napkin. "Hey Romeo, I hate to interrupt our witty banter here, but perhaps you ought to check on your perfect wife. She's pounded at least three chardonnays while you've been over here chatting with us." Trudy's voice drops to a whisper. "I hear that's bad for the baby."

Eyes widen all around the table, and Foster practically jogs across the room to where Jessica's standing, goblet in hand.

Those two deserve each other.

After a moment, the conversation at our table recovers, and it's like Foster never came over to hurl insults at me. Trudy handled him so well that Foster's words rolled over me like water down a glass pane, and I realize something. I wasn't just being contrary with him. Our relationship was unsteady. Did I use my fear of children as an excuse?

Once the wedding starts to wind down, Trudy and I make a mad dash through the sleet out to my car. It's been such disgusting weather lately. Once we reach the car, I turn on the wipers and they fling the ice chunks away. Before I pull out of the parking lot, Trudy pulls out her phone. When her face falls, I know she's heard from the loser himself.

"What did he say now?" I ask.

"Chris used to tell me his biggest fear was that I'd turn out like our mom. He said he was always waiting for me to bail and leave him with Troy. But he's the one who left."

I pull out onto the main road. "I think we've established Chris is a moron, with poor judgment and even poorer insight." I want to take Trudy's hand in mine, but the roads are intermittently icy, so I keep my hands at ten and two.

Her voice is small enough I can barely make out her next words. "I've never thought I was much like mom, but maybe I'm like Dad."

I shake my head. "You're nothing like either of them. You picked a lousy husband, but other than that one error in judgement, you're nothing like Dad. You care for your son, you sacrifice for everyone around you, always putting them first. You're an artist who takes a run down space and turns it into something beautiful. And most of all, you'd never quit on your loved ones, and you'd never leave."

"Everything you said about me is true for you too, Mary."

I think about that for most of the way home, which is easy because Trudy stares quietly out the window. I've been terrified that if I had a child, I'd fail them. I believed I couldn't pursue my career and raise children at the same time, because my mom didn't do both. She bailed.

"You don't think I'm like them at all?" I hate how uncertain I sound. I always told myself the reason I couldn't have kids was that I didn't want to sacrifice my career, and if I had kids I would, which would make me resent them.

Maybe my real fear is that I wouldn't sacrifice my career, and I'd be as bad a mom as my own Mom was.

Trudy shakes her head. "If Foster's loony wife ever actually gets pregnant, they won't be excellent parents. I try my hardest most days, but I'd still say I'm mediocre at best."

"Don't say that," I say. "You're amazing with Troy and you've given up everything for him."

Trudy says, "No, no, no, I'm not fishing for compliments. I'm telling you, you'll be better than me, and I'm okay. Head and shoulders above where Mom and Dad were with us."

"You're already head, shoulders, torso, thighs, calves and ankles above Mom and Dad."

Trudy laughs. "Sadly that's true, but earlier when I told you I thought of you as my real mom, I wasn't kidding. For more than twenty years you've done everything for me. You taught me to read and helped me with my homework. You made my lunches, my snacks, and signed all my school forms. You walked with me door-to-door selling stuff for every fundraiser. You combed my hair, bathed me, and helped me write papers, albeit kind of awful ones. A writer you are not."

"Hey, that story about the little spot of air was brilliant."

"Whatever you say," Trudy says. "But you woke me up

and brushed my teeth and you told me bedtime stories, and you did all of that while working part time, and working on your own school work. You stayed close for college instead of taking that fancy scholarship to Brown. You helped me manage college while you were in grad school, and—" Trudy chokes up and wipes at her eyes.

"Hey," I say. "It's okay, I get it."

Trudy shakes her head and can't meet my eye. "You told me Chris was an idiot and you said I shouldn't date him, but when I ignored you, you helped me plan a wedding which you paid for, never once complaining. You even sobered Dad up and brought him to walk me down the aisle. When I had Troy, and I was drowning, and I had no job, and I felt like a loser, you were there to help with him, and assure me I could do what needed to be done. And now that you're proven right about Chris, and Troy's sick, you're there again."

I put my arm around Trudy. "I'll always be here for you."

She nods. "I know that, in my whole soul. I watch you help those other kids, children you don't know, trying to bring some hope to other kids like us, and I'm so proud of you. Mary, you can do anything, which I know because I've seen you do *everything*. I didn't want to move in with you, because I'm embarrassed to be a burden. Again. But when I needed somewhere to go, you opened your home to me and Troy without reservation."

"You're always welcome with me, you know that."

"And you paid for Troy's hospital stay, and this new medical treatment, which I'll never have the words to thank you for. In fact, the one thing I don't think you'll ever do is become like either of our parents in any way."

I hug Trudy tight, thinking about her words, her certainty. If she's right, I might have made a catastrophic mistake with Luke. I can't stop thinking about him, or his children, but I already shoved them away pretty hard.

Not that it matters, I remind myself, since they're leaving in two weeks.

I almost wish I was a little more like my mom. If I was more like her, this might hurt a lot less.

CHAPTER 21

With a wrapped, stuffed horse in hand, I pick my way through the crowded streets of Atlanta toward the red ribbon ceremony for the new Citibank building. After yesterday's miserable flurries, it's a surprisingly gorgeous day, almost fifty degrees outside and sunny.

I 'excuse me' and 'pardon me' and 'can I squeeze past you?' my way to somewhere near the front of the crowd. I know it's a long shot, but I'm hoping to see Luke, and with the gift I inadvertently kept in my hand, I have an excuse to talk to him.

I look for Luke during Mayor Overton's speech without luck. After the Mayor, the President of Citibank starts talking too. Commerce for Atlanta, a new age of banking, blah, blah, blah. What about the lights guy? He's gotta be there, right? My eyes scan the people sitting on risers behind the makeshift podium. Maybe I need glasses, because I cannot make him out anywhere.

After the ribbon's cut, a band starts playing. I tap my foot to the music, wondering if there's somewhere else I should check before I throw in the towel and leave. I'm turning to go when I finally see him. Luke's standing on the dance floor, twirling a stunningly beautiful blonde woman, her hair curled perfectly under an adorable knit cap. She's sporting gorgeous, knee-high boots over tight black pants, and a sparkly grey sweater tunic that hugs her curves perfectly.

I stand there watching them, transfixed, and inexplicably unable to look away. I may have to tear my eyeballs out so I can leave. I imagine how I'll sprint back to my car so I don't embarrass myself, sobbing and messy, to every passerby. I'm starting to spin on my heel when Luke locks eyes with me. Too many emotions cross his face for me to read any of them. His eyes widen and he stumbles a little, his partner frowning at him. She's gesturing and saying something I can't hear. He turns toward her, and I take the chance to dash away.

I sit in my car, breathing in and out, in and out. Who was she? I realize that I don't know Luke well enough to have any idea. It takes me a good fifteen minutes to get my car out of the parking lot I found, but that's probably good. I didn't care that my boyfriend of more than a year married someone else last night. In fact, I wish them the best.

Conversely, I wish nothing good for that blonde woman. In fact, I'm gripped with a strange and savage urge to march right back to the City Center and claw her eyes out. Which is ridiculous for many reasons, but first and foremost because I don't even know what she means to Luke.

Once I've calmed down, I drive home, numb and full of sorrow I can't even share. My family and friends don't approve, which makes me feel worse. I pull into my garage at home and lean my head against the steering wheel. Once I walk inside, I'll need to talk to Trudy, and play with Troy.

I'm so happy she's living with me, but I miss the quiet time and space I used to have.

If Luke did change his mind, and if he did want to stay here and find a more steady job, and if I did decide to try managing his kids and my job. . . It hits me that I'd never have peace, quiet, or a neat house ever again. Boom, insta-family.

I can barely handle the sister and nephew I've got.

But the thought of never seeing Luke again, or even worse, bumping into him somehow and seeing that he's married and someone else is holding Amy's hand. . . I hate that idea even more.

I sit up and reach for the handle on my door, pausing when I hear my text message notification. My hands shake when I pull my phone from my purse. Which is stupid. It's probably Paisley confirming our drop off time tomorrow. Or maybe Trudy asking where I went. Or Addy confirming that Trudy and me will be coming to her house on Christmas Eve.

Except it's none of them. The message is from Luke. I close my eyes, unaccountably nervous about what he has to say. When I finally force myself to look, I'm not sure how to respond.

WHERE DID YOU GO?

My fingers freeze. What do I say? I finally settle on the truth. Sort of. HOME. I ONLY CAME TO BRING THE STUFFED HORSE AMY PICKED FOR YOUR FAMILY. Which sounds really stupid. He knows where I live, which means he knows I could more easily have driven that by his trailer. Of course, I don't think about that until after I've hit send.

WHY DIDN'T YOU GIVE IT TO ME?

Time for the real truth. If I can't be at least a little honest, he'll never realize I've changed my mind. YEAH,

SORRY. I SAW YOU WITH ANOTHER WOMAN AND FREAKED OUT A LITTLE.

He responds with a 'laughing so hard he's crying' emoji.

THAT'S TOO BAD. MY COUSIN REALLY WANTED TO MEET YOU. AMY TALKS ABOUT YOU NON-STOP.

My heart executes a perfect cartwheel. His cousin. Amy misses me.

ONLY AMY? I type the words, but I can't quite get myself to hit send. I look at them for a count of ten, and then start to delete them.

Before I can, a new text pops up from Luke. YOU STILL THERE?

When two big, furry, paws slam against the glass of my car window, I jump in my seat, and my thumb hits send. ONLY AMY? My needy plea zooms through the ether and to his phone, and there's nothing I can do to stop it.

I swear.

Trudy's eyes widen from where she's standing behind Andromeda. "Sorry I scared you." Her voice is muffled but I can make it out. "Troy, Andromeda and I heard the garage door, but you never came inside. We wanted to make sure you were okay."

Family is nosey. Family is annoying. Family gets all up in your face.

And at least I know someone cares. I pretend I'm not freaking out over having sent a text basically asking Luke if he misses me.

I open the door and follow Trudy up to the steps into my own home, listening all the while for a ping from my phone. Troy's waiting at the top, his chubby arms outstretched, bouncing on his toes. "Aunt May May. Pick me up!" He's so adorable that part of me hopes he never masters the baffling secrets of the letter 'r'.

I toss my bag into the utility room and swing Troy up into my arms. "I'm going to have to stop calling you Troy and start calling you Tank if you gain any more weight."

"Why Tank?" he asks.

"Tanks are like really big, really heavy trucks. It still starts with the letter 'T' like your name, but it means you're a big boy."

When he grins, I notice his mouth is full of goldfish, the chunks rolling around in there like wet laundry in a dryer of slime. Gross.

Which isn't even why I want to put him down and stare at my tiny phone screen. But I will not be the pathetic person who hunches over her iPhone, watching and waiting for a response. I won't be that needy mess. I won't. I have a sister and a nephew and they're welcoming me home enthusiastically. I'll play with them and maybe later, when I have nothing better to do, I'll see if Luke ever replied. Maybe, or maybe not.

I glance around the room, and a smile lifts the corners of my mouth. I've been so busy, I've barely had time to decorate for Christmas this year. Today Trudy and Troy did it for me.

"I hope you don't mind," Trudy says. "I found the decorations in the garage when I was shifting stuff around in my boxes."

"I'm delighted," I say. "You decorated my pitiful tree, and put up the garland, and all my other trinkets and nativity sets, and signs. Wait, what am I smelling? Is that Wassail?"

Trudy points at Troy and he beams, paper-mache-like blobs of goldfish goo dribbling from the corner of his mouth. "I ask and ask Mom to make it."

"I also started the clam chowder." Trudy bites her lip, like she's worried I'll be mad.

"Hey, I said my home is your home, so don't look worried. All of this is wonderful." We've had clam chowder for dinner on the day before Christmas Eve for years, ever since a neighbor brought it to us. It was the best meal I'd ever had when I was nine years old. She gave us her recipe and we've followed it faithfully ever since.

"I know it's rough having someone else in your house, and even harder when that person has a toddler who makes messes, draws on things, and leaves toys all over. And then we pounced on you when you were trying to have a second alone in the car. I'm sorry."

My chest feels heavy, because that's exactly what I was trying to do. "I love you, Trudy and I'm so glad you're here. I mean that."

"Would you like some Wassail as a peace offering?" Trudy asks.

"I'd love some." I set Troy down on a chair and I'm about to sit next to him when I hear a tiny ping from my bag in the laundry room. In a move that would impress Trinity from the *Matrix,* I rotate on one foot and practically leap into the laundry room.

So much for not being the pathetic person who waits for a text.

"Are you okay?" Trudy lifts one eyebrow accusingly. "What's going on? Why did you wait in your car for so long?"

I swipe my phone, and read his text. I THINK ABOUT YOU EVERY DAY. I HAVEN'T TALKED ABOUT YOU AS MUCH AS AMY, BECAUSE AS AN ADULT, I KNOW THAT WOULD BE PITIFUL.

I laugh, but I notice a toe tapping in front of me. "What's going on?" Trudy asks.

"Since last night's wedding, I've been thinking that maybe my moratorium on children stemmed from my fear that I'd do a bad job with them. That I'm like our mother. But you seem to think that's not the case, that I'd be a good mom."

Trudy sits on the floor, and Troy comes bouncing across the tile, Wassail sloshing over the corner of his mug. Andromeda follows behind him, lapping up spilled apple cider like a Roomba mop with a shaggy tail. Dogs have benefits I didn't even consider before now.

"Honey, no. Stay at the table. Look, you're spilling," Trudy says.

"You have it." Troy points at the two mugs Trudy's holding.

Trudy surrenders and moves her arm so Troy can climb into her lap.

"Who are you texting?" Trudy asks.

"Santa Claus?" Troy's eyes widen and his mouth drops.

I shake my head. "No, not Santa Claus, sorry."

He exhales heavily. "I'll never find him."

I frown. "Did you not get to see him this year?"

Troy shakes his head slowly. "I was sick and we moved."

"I found Santa years ago," I say slowly. "And I saved his number in my phone. I'm happy to text him what you want."

Trudy's eyes well with tears and I watch as she turns away.

Troy and I talk for a few moments and firm up the details of his list. I text Trudy's phone with his official list. A nerf gun, a basketball that's not little, and a bean-bag chair. All of which we can accommodate, I'm sure. Trudy wipes her eyes. "Thank you for your help, Mary."

"Anytime." I tap Troy's nose. "Now Mr. Inquisitive, take that mug back over and drink it at the table. You can't have food anywhere else other than the table until you're eighteen years old."

His eyes widen. “Are you that old?”

I nod my head. “Yes, exactly that old.” Andromeda barks, and I roll my eyes. “Fine, I might be lying. I'm thirty, okay? But who's counting?”

Trudy laughs, and Troy narrows his eyes in suspicion, but he walks back to the table, only sloshing a little more over the side in the process.

“I have to mop every single day,” Trudy says. “You do know that, right? If you're texting Luke again, just keep that in mind.”

“Thanks for the reminder, but he's just being nice.” For some reason, I don't want to admit to Trudy that I'm hoping he'll change his mind. That I'm hoping he and Amy and Chase might stay. Maybe because they disliked him. Maybe because I now have a dog, and if I pick up with Luke again, they'll assume I got the dog for him. Maybe because it might be nothing. It probably is nothing.

Or maybe I'm selfish enough to want to have something that's just mine, not shared with a dog, a sister and a nephew who are all less than a foot away from my face, trying to sneak a peek at my phone screen.

“I'm going to take Andromeda for a walk.”

“We need to come up with a nickname,” Trudy says. “Because saying four long syllables every time we mention that dog is almost worse than Gertrude.”

“Nothing's worse than Gertrude. Mom sure saddled you with a doozie before she left, didn't she?”

Trudy laughs. “How about Dromy?”

“It fits the theme.” It's a long running joke that anyone who's anyone in my life has to have a name ending in y. Paisley, Addy, Trudy, Troy and of course I'm Mary. “But it's not very cute, and it sounds like a boy.”

“Well, what then?” Trudy asks.

I glance down at Andromeda's squishy, shaggy, grey

and tan and white face, and her black nose. "How about Andy?"

"Andy, Andy, Andy," Troy says.

"I think we have a winner." Trudy smiles.

"Andy and I will be back. I may see how much she might want to jog."

I've scarcely jogged around the corner, carefully avoiding sloppy wet patches, when my phone dings again. WHAT ARE WE GOING TO DO ABOUT THAT HORSE?

Andromeda pulls and pulls on her leash when I stop, whining a little, but I take the time to respond before jogging again. I CAN BRING IT BY TONIGHT AND LEAVE IT ON YOUR STEPS. I start jogging, and my poor, bony dog bounds ahead with me, frolicking as much as the leash I bought allows her.

BUT THEN I WOULDN'T SEE YOU.

My heart rate spikes, and not from the jog.

YOU CAN COME TO DINNER IF YOU WANT. MY SISTER AND HER SON LIVE WITH ME NOW, SO THEY'LL BE HERE. YOU CAN BRING AMY AND CHASE.

The response this time is immediate. WHAT TIME, AND WHAT CAN WE BRING?

CAN YOU BRING ROLLS? SIX P.M. OKAY?

WE'LL BE THERE WITH ROLLS. PROBABLY NOT WITH BELLS ON, THOUGH. IF I'M LUCKY, CHASE WILL BE WEARING PANTS.

He's so cheesy, but I guess I like cheesy things. I grin like a mental patient for the rest of my three-mile run, but at least Andy doesn't seem to mind.

CHAPTER 22

Poor, emaciated Andy poops out about half a mile before we reach my house and we walk the last few blocks very, very slowly. I feel a little guilty, actually, but it's good to know two and a half miles is about her limit. I'm whistling *Jingle Bells* when we walk through the front door at noon.

"Why are you so happy all of a sudden?" Trudy asks.

"I should've asked you about this, and I'm sorry." I try and try, but I can't seem to wipe the smile off my face.

"What is it?" Trudy turns greenish. "Is Chris coming over? Did he call you?"

"Oh my gosh," I say, "No, nothing like that. I'm so sorry I frightened you. I was texting Luke back and forth and, well, I invited him to dinner."

Trudy drops the bowl she's holding and it clatters to the floor. Thankfully it was plastic, and empty.

"You're excited, clearly." I laugh. "Sorry I didn't run it past you. Are you mad?"

"Not at all. It's your house," Trudy says. "You don't need my permission to invite someone over."

"It's your house too, now," I say. "If you're upset, I can text him back and beg off."

"Not at all. I'm actually really happy to meet him. But Paisley and Addy are going to lose it if you don't invite them, too."

"Well, they may just have to lose it. I can't deal with Addy's negativity and Paisley actually likes him, but she's a loudmouth and I have no idea where we are."

Trudy nods. "True. Mums the word for now."

"He's bringing his kids," I say.

Troy claps. "Kids, kids, kids."

"How old are they again?" Trudy asks.

"He has a four-year-old boy named Chase, and a precocious five-year-old girl."

"Party, party, party!" Troy yells.

"He's bringing rolls," I say, "but I can run grab whatever else we might need."

Trudy gives me a list and I head for my car. Andromeda barks and scratches on the garage door after I close it, so I open it back up. "You can't come with me, Andy." I scratch her ears. "But I'll be back. Eventually you'll realize that I will always come back."

She licks my hand and then lays down in front of the door, face forlorn, resting poutily on her paws. I ruffle the hair on her head and she sneezes.

"I am sorry I'm leaving again so soon." I reach up to the top shelf and grab a rawhide stick. When I close the door this time, she's eagerly engaged in chewing it to a pulp.

I reach Super Target quickly, and while I shop for the items on Trudy's list, I keep my eyes peeled for something for Amy and Chase. And Luke. He's the hardest, and I can't find anything that perfectly suits how I feel about him. I finally check out, frustrated and confused.

How do I feel about him?

I want to see him every day. I want him to kiss me. I like his kids. I like that he supports me in the things that matter. I like what a great dad he is. I like that he's polite and generous, and that he's persistent, but not overbearing. I like that he's funny and quotes Dr. Seuss.

I'm not as nervous about the children part anymore. In fact, I'm looking forward to seeing Amy again, and Chase too. I mentally note that I should hide all the balls.

But they're moving in a few weeks, with no way of knowing when or if they'll be back. Normally I'd say whether he was here or not, I wouldn't see them in the winter and early spring. I'd be far too busy with tax returns. But now, with my promotion, my months will be largely the same.

By the time I reach my house, it's time to make dessert. Troy and Trudy asked for my chocolate layer cake, and that takes some time to make, bake, cool, and frost. We listen to Christmas music while we bake, and I trip over Andromeda fifteen times. I need to remember to call her Andy, but my heart is full.

"My house is so much nicer with you and Troy in it," I tell Trudy. "I know it's easier to have your own space, but for now, I'm so happy you're here."

"You're just happy because Luke's coming over." Trudy winks at me.

"It's not only that," I protest. "It's having my family here with me."

Trudy hugs me, and then we both run to our rooms to change into presentable clothes. I pick a red and green plaid tunic, shot with gold threads, and dark green leggings. I pair them with my favorite pair of knee-high, flat-bottom boots. I even have time to touch up my make-up.

Trudy whistles when I walk back out. "Wowsa! I hope Luke knows how lucky he is that you like him."

I roll my eyes. "You're so biased. But thanks."

Trudy cleans up pretty nice, too. She lost all the baby weight she gained in the year after Troy was born. She hates running, but she does little workout videos during his nap religiously. She's got sandy brown hair, which she highlights, and the same greenish eyes as me. She's taller than I am, and somehow curvier too, which just isn't fair, and she's got dimples I'd kill for.

"You look beautiful too, Trudy. You deserve better than . . ." I don't want to name Chris in front of Troy. I'm not sure how much he understands. "Well, you know. And you'll find the right guy too eventually, I know you will."

Trudy grabs Troy under his arms and swings him up to her hip. "I've already got the only guy I need, and the first and last man I've ever loved without reservation." She kisses Troy all over his face, and his giggles fill the room.

He's laughing so hard snot runs down his face when I hear the door. My stomach flip flops and I want to run and hide in my room. The last time I saw Luke, I said awful things. I told him he's failing his kids. What do I know about raising kids, or losing a spouse? I'm such an idiot. What if he only came to shut Amy up and pick up the dumb gift?

Trudy waves me over to the door. "Hurry up, it's cold out there."

Duh. I jog across the room to the front door and pull it open. For a moment, my eyes lock on Luke's impossibly handsome face, his dark honey hair, streaked with dark grey around a face that's usually smiling.

"Hi," he says. "Merry Christmas."

I can't help myself from grinning, and he smiles back at me. I hear the clicking of Andy's claws on the tile behind me, and then a squeal from waist level. "You have a dog? But you said you didn't!"

I want to smack myself in the forehead. I should've warned Luke. He's going to think I've gone insane. "Well, I didn't have a dog until yesterday."

Amy hugs Andromeda around the neck. "It's the prettiest dog I've ever seen in my whole entire life. I didn't even know dogs this beautiful were real on the earth!"

I grin, and Luke does, too.

"Her name is Andromeda, but we are going to call her Andy. I came across her by accident, and found out her family didn't want her anymore. They said they didn't have time to care for a dog. The pound would kill her if she wasn't adopted before the week was up. A nice woman from a rescue agreed to take her until they could find her a home, but the other dogs were eating all her food and bossing her around. When I heard that sad tale, and she behaved perfectly for me, I decided to adopt her."

"Are you only helping out with her, then?" she asks.

I shake my head. "No, she's my new dog. I'm not a fan of puppies. They're too chewy and barky, and jumpy, and they aren't house broken so they pee all over, but this lovely lady is only three years old, and she has impeccable manners. Once we get her fattened up a little, I think she'll be about perfect. I took her for a jog today and she did great for about two and a half miles. I think as she gains strength she might be able to go a little further. We'll see, I guess. I don't wanna hurt her paws."

"Oh, Dad, did you see? I told you Mary was perfect. She even adopted a dog."

Chase is hiding behind Luke's leg. "Hey buddy, would you like to pet Andy?

He bobs his head, and I hold out my hand. He takes it, and lets me tug him around to where he can pet Andy. His little hands ball up in her fur and she whimpers. He lets go, but she doesn't growl, or snap or even whip her head around. I'm impressed.

"We may need to go over some rules for how to treat a dog, Chase, okay? I had to go over the same rules with my nephew Troy. Speaking of, he's right inside, waiting on you two. He's been dying to show you his room and his toys."

I stand up and make the introductions, and then go over some basic rules of dog etiquette. Troy, who had been chattering about this visit all day, grows a shy side and hides behind the couch for a full five minutes before we can lure him out, but eventually, Chase and Troy warm up and run off to his room. I take a seat at the kitchen table, and Luke and Trudy do the same.

"I'm not sure we'll be able to pry Amy's hands off of Andy in time for dinner," I say. "Speaking of, are we almost ready to eat? Trudy?"

"Sure, yeah, the soup's been on a low simmer for a while. The fruit's cut up, and I've got glasses out, and the dining table is set."

"Perfect, thanks."

Luke slaps his knee. "Oh, the rolls!"

"Did you forget them?" I ask. "It's no big deal. I'll toast some sliced bread." I stand up and walk toward the cabinet.

"They're just in the car," he says. "I'll only be a minute."

"Oh, and don't forget the stuffed animal." I point. "It's wrapped and sitting on the end table there."

Luke nods, and when he heads for the front door, I call out to the boys. "Chase! Troy! Wash your hands, it's time to eat."

Amy doesn't move. She's still lying on the rug next to the sofa, an arm thrown over Andy. I crouch down by Amy, intent on getting her to wash her hands. "Sweetie, Andy's not going anywhere, and you clearly adore one another, which is great. But can you come wash your hands so we can eat?"

Amy sits up and exhales. She pats Andy's fluffy head and stands up. "It's going to be so hard for me."

My eyebrows crinkle together. "What's going to be hard?"

She walks toward the bathroom with me, slowly. "Going back to my house after being here." She throws her arms around my waist and squeezes me tight. "Why can't you just be my mom?"

So that idea hasn't shifted at all. I drop to my knees, and I hear the front door open, so this will have to be quick. "Sweetheart, I'm sure your dad has lots of lovely friends who are girls, and one day maybe he'll want one of them to be your mom. But it's really his choice to make."

"And yours too, right?" she asks. "Because I've never met any other friends who are girls. Dad never ever brings any of his friends home, except you."

My heart takes flight and I want to dance around the room. Which is stupid. If he isn't sure whether he likes me or not, my terrible dance moves would bump him solidly into the anti camp. "Amy, I promised you before and I'll promise you again. No matter what, I'll always be your friend. You guys are moving soon, but if you ever come back to visit Atlanta, you're welcome to stay here with me, or come to dinner."

"Unless you marry someone else," she mutters.

She's way too smart for a little kid. "Well, then it might be kind of weird."

"Not for me, it wouldn't be."

"You have so much to look forward to right now," I say. "Let's enjoy playing together and seeing the dog while we can, okay?"

"I wrote Santa a letter," she whispers.

"Oh?" I ask.

"I asked him if you could be my mom, and we could get a dog. The perfect puppy."

"Well, maybe you'll get a puppy," I say. "Who knows?"

She shakes her head. "I think Santa knew there was something better than a puppy. Andy is the best dog I've ever met. Now I just need the other part." The corner of her mouth curls up into a smile and she scampers off to wash her hands just as the little boys come barreling into the room, each of them holding a truck.

Troy and Amy love the clam chowder, but Chase won't even try it.

"It looks yucky," he says.

I make him a peanut butter and jelly sandwich. "Here you go, sweetie."

He beams at me.

"You'll regret that precedent," Luke says. "At my house, if they don't like dinner, they go to bed hungry."

"You can't be serious," I say.

He nods. "It's the only way to make sure they learn to eat new things."

"When they get hungry enough, they'll eat what you offer," Trudy says.

I suddenly feel left out, like the only person here who knows nothing about kids, and has no right to an opinion.

I stand up and grab the cake from the fridge so I don't have to meet anyone's eye. The frosting was a little runny, so I tossed it inside to firm it up. I start slicing pieces and passing them out. When Chase sees the cake, he bolts his sandwich in three bites.

"Whoa there, slow down," I say. "You might choke."

Chase chews and swallows. "I love chocolate cake."

Luke laughs. "To be completely fair, Chase loves any kind of cake."

"I'm glad I picked this for dessert, then," I say.

"Mary doesn't cook dinner very often," Trudy says. "She always hated it when we were kids, but she's a gourmet dessert chef."

"Hey now, don't set the bar too high." I carry the slices over to the table and set them in front of everyone.

Amy takes a big bite and coos. "Oh, Mary. Can we save some of this for Santa Claus? I bet he's sick to death of cookies, and this is really good!"

"I think that can be arranged," I say. "I'll send your dad home with some."

"Wait!" This time, it's Chase objecting. "Won't we see you tomorrow? We're having a big party!"

I pat his sticky hand. "It's wonderful you'd like me there, but I have a party to attend tomorrow, too."

His face falls. "Oh no."

Amy chimes in. "Can't you skip it? We're moving soon."

My heart constricts and I want to tell them I'll miss it, but I can't do that. "I'm so sorry Amy, but I'm sure I'll see you again before you move." I glance at Luke and he reaches over and takes my hand in his.

"You certainly will if I have any say in the matter."

"Oh fine," Amy says. "But you'll be sad when you hear how good Uncle Paul's pumpkin pie and Dad's ribs are." Her eyes widen. "Not as good as your cake, but really close."

I don't care as much about the ribs or the pie, but I do wish I could be in two places at the same time. When dinner's over, we let the kids play for a bit while we chat.

"So tell me about this Uncle Paul," I say to Luke as I stand up and move to the sofa. "Is he your brother?"

Luke follows me and when I sit down, he sits right next to me. "You have one sibling, a sister. I have one sibling, and it's a brother."

"And?" I ask.

"And what?" He puts his arm around me.

"Is he older or younger? Taller or shorter? Are you close? What does he do, and where does he live?"

"Call 911," Luke tells Trudy, who has followed us over. "I'm being interrogated by the Gestapo!"

I roll my eyes. "Seriously. You've met my sister now, but I'm just hearing about Paul."

"I'm older than him, by five years. I didn't want to admit it, because then I'd have to admit that I'm forty."

"Oh no." I hold my hand to his forehead. "You didn't tell me you were on death's door."

He takes my hand in his. "I didn't want to scare you off, but I managed to anyway."

"I toughened up," I say. "I won't be scared so easily again. Not that I'm at risk, with you leaving in like three weeks."

He nods. "Not much time left for scaring, I'm afraid."

"But we do have time for you to tell me more about this younger brother."

He grins and leans back in his chair. "He's smarter than me, by a wide margin. I was always good with my hands, and he always had his nose in a book. When he wasn't reading, he spent a lot of time in science labs, blowing things up."

"Sounds like a real dork," Trudy says. "But I'm not sure I believe you. Older siblings are a little too critical sometimes."

"You're both welcome to come tomorrow. You could meet him yourself," Luke says. "He lives in Atlanta, so he's around pretty often. He travels all the time for work, but when he's here, he comes to play with my kids."

"Does he have any kids?" I ask.

"Oh, I know where this is going." Luke puts his arm

around me. "He sounds like a better candidate than I do, is that it? He's local and isn't planning to move, he has no kids, and he's brainy. Well, I got news for you, sister. I already called dibs."

"I'm not the last drumstick." I feign displeasure, but really I'm floating on cloud nine. "You can't call dibs on me."

"Watch me."

Luke leans forward, with Amy on the floor curled up with Andy, and Trudy sitting in the chair next to us, and kisses me square on the mouth. When he pulls back, I can't help sighing. I've missed Luke. A lot.

"Dibs," he says. "Witnessed, right?" He glances over at Trudy and she giggles.

"Yep, I saw it. Sorry, Mary, but you'll never be able to date his brother Paul. It would violate the rules of sibling ethics."

"Phew," Luke says. "Glad we got that cleared up."

I lean my head against his shoulder. Before too much longer, my eyelids get heavy. Luke and Trudy are talking and laughing, but I'm so tired, I just want to curl up and go to sleep with Luke by my side.

Gentle hands shake me awake. "I fell asleep? Again? I'm sorry."

Luke's breath on my face makes me want to close my eyes again. "You've been working two jobs. I don't blame you."

I rub my eyes and notice that I'm not the only one. Amy's asleep with her head on Andy's belly. Luke picks her up, and Andy sits up, looking at him with mournful eyes.

"You know, before you came over," I whisper, "I was Andromeda's favorite person. I have a feeling that's no longer true."

"Don't worry. You're still someone's favorite person."

Luke brushes his lips against mine, careful not to jostle Amy. "Thanks for inviting us over."

I slip into a pair of Hunter boots, but don't bother with a jacket. I scoop up Chase, and Trudy hands me a Tupperware with chocolate cake for Santa. I walk out to the truck, and notice the temperature has dropped again. I buckle Chase in while Luke shushes Amy, who has awoken thanks to the freezing night air, and buckles her in, telling her it's going to be okay.

Her whimpers turn into tears when she realizes they're leaving. "I don't want to go, Dad. I want to stay with Mary. Please! I'll be so quiet she won't know I'm here."

I walk over and give her a hug and a kiss. "I'm sure I'll see you soon."

"Tomorrow?" she asks.

I bite my lip. "I'm not sure. I've got my delivery to make, and some last minute presents to wrap."

"Christmas day, then?" Her tiny hands grab mine, and she squeezes. "Please?"

"You just want me for my dog," I joke.

She shakes her head, deadly serious. "Even if you didn't have Andy, I'd still love you."

I want to unbuckle her and give her a marathon hug. It's like her words are gluing the fragments of my broken heart back together. I kiss her forehead. "It's time for you to go now, but I promise I'll see you soon. And in the meantime, I put some of my cake for Santa in a container underneath Chase's feet. Okay?"

She nods, and I step away, turning back toward the house. Instead of climbing into the driver seat, once the door shuts on Amy, Luke grabs me gently, spins me around and pulls me into his arms. He's fast this time, not slow. He kisses me urgently, his lips covering mine, his arms wrapping all the way around me. The ground beneath me spins, my heart beats a staccato rhythm, and my arms twine around his neck. I don't ever want him to stop.

But of course, eventually he does. He can't let his kids sit in a running truck forever. I stand outside while he backs out, ignoring the freezing gusts of wind as long as I can still see his truck. Once he's gone, I walk back inside. I notice the wrapped horse stuffed animal is still sitting on my end table.

I text him right away, in case he wants to turn around. YOU LEFT THE HORSE TOY.

Ten minutes pass. Then another five. No response. Which probably means he's a responsible driver, which is good.

Finally, I hear a bing. UH OH. GUESS THAT MEANS YOU'LL HAVE TO COME HELP ME DROP OFF TOMORROW.

WAIT, DID YOU DO THAT ON PURPOSE?

He replies with a single word. COSTANZA.

I show it to Trudy. "What the crap does that mean?"

A quick Google search shows me that George Costanza is a character on an old sitcom, Seinfeld. Trudy and I stay up half the night watching episodes until we figure out what he meant. In one episode, George Costanza leaves an alarm clock at the home of a woman he likes. He confesses it's part of his plan. Ladies may not like him initially, but if he spends enough time around them, he grows on them. He leaves things intentionally, so he can have a reason to see them. He does this over and over until they've fallen under his bizarre and awkward spell.

It's a cute reference, but Luke doesn't need gimmicks. He's already grown on me. In fact, I think he's more than grown on me. I think I might love him.

CHAPTER 23

My Sub-for-Santa drop off takes place at seven a.m. The girls' mother wants to hide the toys before her daughters wake up. When I return, filled with a sense of elation and excitement, I take Andy for a short two-mile jog.

When I drop her off at the house to run another three miles, she glares at me.

"You couldn't do more than two and a half miles yesterday. Be patient, we'll work up to more, okay?"

She drops her head on her paws and exhales dramatically. What a diva!

By the time I return home and shower, it's nine a.m. I spend twenty minutes picking up the gift I thought of for Luke. I'm proud of my idea, but a little nervous he won't understand it. I wrap the presents I picked for Amy and Chase, and do the best I can with Luke's oddly shaped present. I spend the rest of the morning making sugar cookies for tonight's party at Addy's house. I've made and taken sugar cookies on Christmas Eve for a decade.

I glance at my clock. Fifteen until noon. I have just enough time to meet Luke over at his drop-off. I text him.

I'LL MEET YOU AT YOUR DROP OFF?

He replies immediately. LUNCH AFTER?

WHAT ABOUT YOUR KIDDOS? I ask.

MY COUSIN HAS THEM UNTIL TWO.

I THOUGHT AMY WAS GOING?

Three little dots. I wait. THEN I FOUND OUT YOU WERE GOING, AND I WANTED MORE TIME WITH YOU. WITHOUT MUNCHKINS. I MAY HAVE BRIBED THEM WITH PEPPERMINT ICE CREAM. I'M NOT ASHAMED.

My smile is so wide, my mouth starts to hurt, but I don't want to seem too eager. I'LL MEET YOU AT THE DROP OFF AND WE CAN SEE FROM THERE.

Let him think he'll have to convince me.

I park behind his truck, and when I hop out of my car, Luke jumps out of his as well. He's wearing a dark brown leather jacket and dark jeans over a golden polo shirt. I almost forget to grab the wrapped horse, I'm so distracted by his presence.

He waits for me to reach him and snags my hand. "Uh, how are we going to carry all these presents while holding hands?"

Luke takes my face in his hands and kisses me softly. "Fine, fine, I'll let you go. But only for a moment."

We carry the boxes inside one at a time. I notice several of the boxes are addressed to the parents, and I'm even more impressed by Luke's generosity. He must have a lot of expenses, what with his upcoming move, and Christmas for his own children, but he's gone above and beyond anyway.

Once we're done, the father in the family rushes over

and hugs me, his eyes watery. "Thank you, muchas gracias. Díos te bendiga."

"You're welcome," I say. "We're happy to help."

Luke takes my hand to walk me back to my car, and this time I don't pull away. "You never answered. Do you have time for lunch?"

"Sure," I say. "As long as we're fast."

He beams. "Pick the place. Anything's fine with me."

"How about Boston Market?" I ask.

His eyebrows rise. "I give you carte blanche, and you pick a fast food place?"

I shrug. "I love their food at the holidays. Turkey, dressing, mashed potatoes, and yams. Cinnamon apples, and best of all, their cornbread."

He pulls me in for a hug. "Boston Market it is, then."

We drive over separately since we arrived that way. Luke and I walk through the line and tell them what we want, and then we carry our trays over to an empty table. There aren't too many people in here on Christmas Eve.

"I know it's Christmas, but is there any chance me and the kids can come by tomorrow?" Luke asks. "I know it's a busy day, but we'd all love to see you. In fact, Amy packed a bag this morning. She informed me that when I leave for my new job, she's going to stay with you."

I shake my head. "No, she didn't say that."

Luke purses his lips and exhales. "She did indeed."

"Well, I'm sorry she's giving you a hard time. I know I was rough on you before, but I promise I won't encourage that kind of nonsense."

"I know you won't. But she helped me pick something for you, and we'd love to come and drop it off. We can be fast if you're super busy."

I grin. "I've got something for you guys, too. Nothing

big, and I really hope you're not upset when you see what I bought for the kiddos."

He shakes his head. "As long as it doesn't have a heartbeat, it's fine with me."

I frown. "Uh oh. I'm not sure whether elephants are returnable. I think the tent I bought this one under had a sign that said, 'Absolutely no returns or exchanges.'"

Luke snatches a bite of my cinnamon apples.

"Hey," I object. "Those are mine! You should've gotten your own."

"It's more fun to take them from you."

His eyes sparkle, and his smile fills me with joy, and the words just tumble out of my mouth uncensored. "I love you."

Luke's bluish-grey eyes widen and his mouth opens half an inch. He blinks at me several times. I want to curl up into a tiny ball and disappear into a crack in the floor, but there's nowhere to go.

"I'm sorry," I say. "I—"

He puts one hand over mine, and the other over his heart. "Say it again."

"I'm sorry."

He shakes his head. "No, not that, goofball. The other part."

I look at the wall and then back at him. "I don't think—"

He squeezes my hand. "Please."

I sigh and force the words out. "I think I love you, Luke Manning, fixer of closet lights, frenetic tidier, phenomenal father."

He breathes in through his nose and closes his eyes. When he opens them again, he's beaming at me. "I love you too, Mary Wiggin, genius with numbers, philanthropist, surrogate mother to so many, and devoted friend."

"I don't want you to move," I say, "and I know that's

selfish of me. I know you like the change of pace, and you're showing your kids the world. I'm sorry I said you're a bad father for moving them. Really you're a great father. I just wanted you to stay, and I didn't know how to ask, so I tried to make it about something else."

He takes my other hand in his, too. "You were right. I was hurt, I was offended and I didn't want to hear it. When my wife died. . . She died from eclampsia an hour after delivering Chase. We were visiting her family in the middle of nowhere when she went into labor, several weeks too early, and we had no idea anything was wrong."

He closes his eyes, but doesn't let go of my hands. "I loved her so much, Mary. Losing her decimated my heart, pulverized it. I took care of my kids and I worked and that's all I did. About a year ago, I decided I missed doing adult things. I started going out with friends and family, but they kept trying to pair me up with people. Ridiculous people. Clingy people. Annoying people. It made me nuts."

"Sounds like your friends care about you, but I've been there too. Setups suck. In the last two months, I've gone out with a computer nerd so awkward he never met my eye in the entire two hours we spent at dinner, a taxidermist who pointed out to me every single animal we passed and how he'd preserve it after it died, and a slick corporate lawyer who didn't talk about anything but money. I'm also pretty sure the lawyer can't keep straight the things that actually happened in his life, and what things he's embellished. Either that, or he really did hike Mount Everest a week after arguing a landmark case before the Supreme Court. Which would require he have mountain goat blood."

Luke releases my hands and starts eating again. "Oh man, before I met you, I went out with a ballerina who wouldn't consume anything but veggie sticks and fruit juice, a psychologist who spent the entire date analyzing me, which was painful and ridiculous, and a Mary Kay lady, who honest to goodness, gave me a skincare kit for my hands. I still get text messages from her every week or so advertising the deals of the week."

I laugh. "I think my friends stopped setting me up with people they had considered and thought were a good fit a few years ago. Now I'm like that pasta trick, you know the one to test whether the noodles are ready?"

Luke shakes his head.

"You throw noodles at the wall and if they stick, they're good. They started just setting me up with anyone who was single, and a few people whose divorces weren't even final." I pull a face. "For most of the people I've met in the last year, all we had in common was that we were both single."

Luke chuckles. "Actually, one of my setups wasn't even single. Halfway through dessert, she mentioned her husband was very understanding." He wipes his mouth. "I practically sprinted out of there."

"You're kidding."

He takes my hand in his. "My miserable dates over the past year were bad enough to make me want to go dig a hole and bury myself."

"I'm glad you didn't do that," I say.

"Me too." He grins at me. "I haven't been this happy in more than four years. You're like finding the puzzle piece I didn't know was missing."

"I'm happy when I'm with you, too. And for what it's worth, I'm sorry about your wife. I can't even imagine what that must have been like for you."

"I'm glad you can't imagine it. I wouldn't wish that kind of pain on anyone." He points at my leftover macaroni and cheese and cinnamon apples. "You done?"

I nod. "Go right ahead. But next time, you'll know to order some yourself."

He bobs his head sheepishly. "I will. And speaking of pain, how was your ex's wedding?"

"Actually," I say, "going to that helped me out."

"Oh? How so?"

"This isn't going to make me sound very good, not compared to your declaration of how deeply you loved your wife, but...I realized I never really loved Foster to begin with."

Luke's face stretches out. "Really?"

I look down at my hands. "Not in the same way as I care about you." I force my eyes up to his, and they're shining at me, which makes me brave. "I loved the idea of Foster, but I didn't trust him, or myself. I'm still nervous I'll turn out to be like my dad, or my mom. They were the worst parents ever. But more than that, I didn't believe Foster would support me."

Luke lifts one eyebrow. "I thought the guy was a spoiled rich kid."

I shake my head. "Not like that. I mean, support me, and help me achieve my goals. My dad never supported my mom or me and Trudy, and my mom never supported my dad, or any of us." I look back down at my hands and my voice drops. "I didn't trust Foster to be there when I needed him, or be okay with me not being who he wanted me to be, but who I really am."

"You're saying you weren't filled with regret, watching the one that got away?"

I run my hand through my hair. "Uh, no. I actually couldn't decide who I felt more sorry for. The girl lying to her boyfriend so he'd propose, or the guy whose fiancé isn't actually pregnant. She couldn't even maintain the lie long enough not to get 'stumble and pass out drunk' at her own wedding."

"I wish I'd been there to see that," Luke says.

I squeeze his hand. "I do too, but I'm also glad I went with Trudy."

"Ouch," he says.

I shake my head. "No, not like that, but it was good for me to face up to the fact that I didn't trust him, and I wasn't me around him. It helped me realize I've been myself around you."

Luke leans across the table and my heart accelerates because I think he's going to kiss me. Only, he doesn't. His forehead touches mine and his gorgeous eyes are so close, it looks like he's a Cyclops. "I'm glad you decided you can trust me."

Then he backs away an inch or two and kisses me. I forget where we are until someone behind us clears her throat.

"Sorry," Luke says sheepishly.

I glance at my watch and gasp. "Oh man, I've gotta get back. Trudy and Troy will be waiting on me."

Luke carries his tray of discarded plastic and napkins and mine to the trashcan, and then walks me out to my car. Before he lets me duck into my seat, he leans down and kisses me, like a kid in a candy shop. Eager, insistent, and joyful. When he finally pulls back, I'm dizzy. His hands steady me.

"I'm glad you accidentally said I love you," he says. "But I'm saying this on purpose, and I'm going to repeat it whenever I see you. I love you, Mary. Drive safely and think of me at your family party."

I touch my fingers to my lips. "Give your kids a hug for me." I climb into my seat and turn on the car. Luke taps gently on the window until I roll it down.

"I think you forgot something."

I glance in front of me and behind, but I don't see anything. I've got my keys and my purse. "I don't think so," I say.

He tilts his head. "I love you, Mary." He widens his eyes and bobs his head. "This is where you say..."

I chuckle. "Right. I love you, too, Luke. You super hot, immensely polite and irritatingly persistent man."

This time when I roll up my window and put my car in drive, he grins that gorgeous grin of his, and waves as I drive away.

CHAPTER 24

Christmas Eve at Addy's is the same as it always is, except I feel like I've been blown up like a balloon. Instead of helium, I'm full of joy. I float from dinner to the little family and friend Christmas pageant we always do. Troy is the cutest shepherd, and Addy's twins make perfect wise women, holding a doll between their hands as the missing third. I play my typical role of narrator, and it takes far longer than it should with Paisley cracking jokes the entire time, but none of the toddlers melt down, so I count it as a win. I eat too many desserts after that, and when we watch *Home Alone,* it's funnier than usual.

The shiny halo of love that surrounds Addy and her husband doesn't irritate me this year. The person they love most sits right here under their own roof, their two daughters are safe and happy, and they're content.

When we sing carols, I miss Luke. When we unwrap presents, I miss Luke. When we all say goodnight, I miss Luke the most of all.

By the time I reach my car with Paisley, Trudy, and

Troy in tow, it's quiet enough for me to hear my phone bing, and I whip it out.

An hour ago, Luke sent me the first message. MISS YOU.

Forty minutes ago, he sent another. SEND ME A PHOTO. I MISS YOUR GORGEOUS FACE.

Ten minutes later he sent the third and final text. PAUL THINKS I'M MAKING YOU UP. HELP A GUY OUT. LOVE YOU.

I hold my phone out and snap a photo.

"What are you doing?" Trudy asks.

I fill her and Paisley in on the details of my lunch date and my accidental blurting of I love you.

"Oh my good—" Paisley says.

"Look, it may still turn out to be nothing. Not many relationships can withstand the strain of long distance, and Luke's leaving, remember?"

"You need to ask him to stay," Paisley says.

"I can't ask him to do that." I shake my head. "He has to decide for himself. He's a big boy."

"You're killing me," Paisley moans.

I text Luke the photo with this message. I'M REAL, AND INQUIRING MINDS HERE WANT TO SEE YOU, TOO.

INQUIRING MINDS? Luke asks. WHO EXACTLY ARE YOU WITH? SHOULD I BE JEALOUS?

A smile spreads across my face.

"I've already seen him," Trudy says.

"Well I haven't seen him in days and days," Paisley says.

I'M WITH PAISLEY, TRUDY AND TROY. I insert a laughing face emoji. I DIDN'T WANT TO SAY I MISSED YOUR FACE. I WAS TRYING TO BE COY.

COY IS OVERRATED, Luke texts, but he doesn't send a new photo.

I pull up the photo Luke sent me of him with his kids and set it as my background.

"Santa's coming," Troy says. "We go home!"

"Aunt Mary is busy swooning up here, sweetheart. Be patient."

I put the car in gear and pull out of Addy's driveway.

Trudy rolls her eyes. "I can't believe you two said I love you before you even took your first picture as a couple." She shakes her head. "Neither of you are on Instagram?"

"Nope." I tilt my head and frown. "Actually, maybe he is. I didn't ask."

A few minutes later, my phone bings. Paisley and Trudy don't even complain when I pull over to check it, but Troy does.

"Go home," he says.

"We are headed home," I say. "I just need to check something."

I swipe my phone to see a photo of Luke, with Amy and Chase huddled up next to him. Their faces all beam at me. A few seconds after that, another photo appears of Luke with a taller, skinnier guy. Shiny chestnut hair without a hint of grey, and the same grayish blue eyes, but not as obviously handsome.

"I bet that's Paul," I say.

"Uh, I'm sorry," Trudy says.

I spin my head to stare at her where she's sitting in the backseat by Troy. "Sorry for what?"

She narrows her eyes and looks at the photo again. Then she looks at Paisley, whose face reflects my bafflement.

"I'm sorry," Trudy says, "that Luke already called dibs, because his brother is vastly more attractive."

Paisley and I exchange a glance. It's nice to know we're on the same page.

"Uh, well," I say. "I think I'll bear up under the disappointment as best I can."

The girls make me repeat our lunch conversation over and over until we reach my house. They love hearing all about it, and thankfully Troy's sound asleep by the time I park in the garage. While Trudy unloads Troy quietly, I turn to Paisley.

"Are you sure you don't want me to take you home? It's a little more crowded than usual, with Trudy in my guest bedroom, and Troy in my office."

Paisley shakes her head. She has no family here in Atlanta, so for the past three years, she's slept over at my place. "I told you already, the sofa's fine."

After Trudy gets Troy tucked in, we all help her put out the Santa gifts for Troy.

"It's exciting he's old enough to understand this year," I say. "Or at least, kind of understand."

Trudy smiles. "Luke's kids are darling, by the way, in case I haven't already said so."

"I wish I'd met them," Paisley says.

"Well, stick around long enough tomorrow, and you will."

"You couldn't pry me out of here with a crowbar," she says. "In fact, maybe I should make popcorn tonight?"

I swat her on the shoulder. "Very funny."

"I'm not kidding. This is better than a Hallmark movie."

I finally go to bed, but before I'm quite asleep, I hear a ping. Normally I'd ignore it, but my heart speeds up, because it might be Luke.

SWEET DREAMS, ANGEL.

I rub my eyes so I can see well enough to text a reply. I'M NO ANGEL, BUT THANKS.

ALL THOSE KIDS ARE GOING TO WAKE UP

TOMORROW WITH GIFTS, FEELING LOVED, AND FEELING LIKE SOMEONE CARES, THANKS TO YOU.

I choke up a little thinking about it, so it's good we're communicating via text. EXCEPT I DROPPED THE BALL, AND UNITED WAY IS CUTTING THE PROGRAM.

Luke's reply comes fast. THAT WASN'T YOUR FAULT. BESIDES, SOMEHOW IT WILL WORK OUT FOR THE BEST.

For the first time in a long time, I think he might actually be right.

The next morning, I wake up way, way, way too early to the squeals of an excited little boy. I haven't even sat up yet when he climbs up on my bed and starts to pat my face. "Wake up, wake up, wake up. Santa here!"

"He's not here," I say. "Do you mean he left presents?"

"Yes, yes, yes!"

I blink, and blink and blink, and grab my robe as I stumble out of bed. Christmas morning passes too fast, like it always does. I've barely cleaned up the mess from breakfast and changed into appropriate clothing when I hear a knock at the door. I glance at my watch. Nine in the morning.

I yawn on my way to open the door, only a little bummed this means I can't take a nap yet. Even so, I hope it's Luke, I hope it's Luke.

Luke's big grin is the first thing I notice. The second is that he's wearing a Santa Claus hat. The third is that he's the hottest thing I've ever seen. I feel like I've been waiting for years and years, and I've finally found someone who embodies the same magic for me as Santa always did. He fills my heart with the same verve, the same excitement, and the same love. I found out years ago that Santa didn't really exist, and it became my job to take his place for other children who needed hope. But today, when Luke walks inside, I realize something wonderful.

I've finally found my Santa.

"Come in." I wave Amy, Chase and Luke inside.

Troy bounces up and down, screeching about his presents while Luke kisses me quickly. "Merry Christmas, Mary."

"There are still three presents under your tree," Amy says with a glint in her eye. "Who are those for?"

"You sly little thing," I say. "One of them is for you."

"Is it the big one?" She rubs her hands together and bounces up and down.

I nod, and she rushes over to grab it. She pulls up short less than a foot away and turns around. "Is it okay if I open it now?" She looks from me to Luke and back again.

I make a shooing motion with my hands. "Of course, go ahead."

She tears the wrapping paper off to reveal a painted, red, wooden chest, with gold trim. The lacquer on it still shines.

"What is it?" she asks me.

"Open the latch," I say.

She fiddles with it a moment before she figures it out, but then she throws the lid back, and dresses and tiaras and gloves spill out. She coos in delight.

"I noticed the other day that you don't have a dress-up chest. It was one of my most beloved toys when I was a girl."

"Are these your old dresses?" Amy asks, her eyes wide with wonder.

I shake my head. "No, my old dresses were yucky. I threw them out a long time ago. But that's my old dress-up trunk. I called it my Princess Wardrobe. I thought you might want to have it."

I watch her mouth the words, "Princess Wardrobe" a few times, as if she's trying her best to remember it. Then she leaps from the ground and runs over to hug me around the waist. "Thank you so much!"

"You're welcome," I say. I whisper the next words. "Think your dad will forgive me for how much space it's going to take up?"

Amy bites her lip, and Luke puts his arm around her. "We'll work something out, won't we?"

She nods.

"Chase?" I say, "You're next, sweetie." I reach under the tree for the smallest gift, and pass it over to him.

He rips the paper off like a pro. Once he's uncovered the nerf gun and extra darts, he hoots and pumps his fist in the air. "A gun, Dad, she got me my own gun!"

"Oh no," I say, "are you a no gun family?" I want to curl up in the corner and hide. I should have asked first. Why didn't I ask?

Luke puts his arm around my shoulder this time. "Not purposefully. It's fine, and clearly I'm behind on getting him the exact toy that he desperately wanted."

I breathe a heavy sigh of relief. "You're next, then."

Luke leans over and pulls out the last present. The wrapping paper couldn't look uglier. The present's a weird shape and I didn't want to ruin it, so I wrapped half a roll underneath, bunched it up, and tied it with ribbon at the top. Luke plucks the card off first.

He reads it silently, but I know what it says. It's a simple message, just one line. *Merry Christmas Luke. I didn't know what to buy you, but in spite of everything I've always done to keep people at bay, you're growing on me. Love, Mary.*

He unties the bow and the paper falls to the sides of the big, leafy, Philodendron plant I chose. I like that it looks happy, easy going, and full of life.

"It takes up a lot of space, but I figure once you reach your new job, you can put it on the little porch area most of the time."

Luke sweeps me up in his arms and spins me around. "You're growing on me too, Mary." He kisses the tip of my nose.

"Dad, can we give her the presents now?" Amy's grinning, with her hands balled into fists at her sides, nearly vibrating with excitement.

"Wait," I say, "gifts?" I shake my head. "No, I only got you each one small thing. I refuse to open more than one present."

Amy takes my hand and her eyes plead with me. "We spent a long time on these. Please? Please open them all."

"How many are there?" I ask.

"Only three," Luke says. "One from each of us."

I lift one eyebrow, and Luke pulls out a long, flat box. I take it from him and shake it. I'm really good at guessing things. "The shape is right for clothes, but the sound is too clunky." I glance from Luke to Amy and back again. "You got me a book?"

He shakes his head. "Not exactly."

"This one's from me." Chase smiles for miles.

"Thanks, sweetie." I pull the wrapping paper off and open the box. It's a stack of paper, folded in half."

"Uh," I say. "What is this?"

"Read it," Luke says.

I glance over the paperwork, and as I do, my jaw drops. "This is the paperwork for the creation of a foundation, Luke. It's funded up to a quarter of a million dollars."

Luke points at the name on the paperwork. "My lawyer thought Santa's Aid Society conveyed the point, but no one could come back and complain later. He said we can change it for three more days, if you hate the name." Luke unbuttons his jacket to reveal a green shirt with the words Santa's Aid Society printed across the front, and an image of an elf.

Amy unzips her jacket, and she's wearing the same green shirt.

Chase tugs his sweater up, and almost pulls off his shirt and sweater both. Luke laughs and helps him, and of course he's got a matching green shirt.

"This is too much," I say.

Luke sets the box down. "Oh come on, it's tax deductible."

"Luke," I say. "That's not the point."

"Ooh, ooh, open mine next." Amy hands me a tiny box, much narrower than the first, but just as long.

"We're not done talking about this, Luke." I point at him until he meets my eye and nods.

His face is more sober than I've ever seen it. "Of course not. I named you the President, and I'm the Vice President. I imagine we'll talk about this a lot. Or that was my plan."

I had no idea electricians made enough money for this kind of donation. I open the next box. It's a set of keys, one large, and one small, on a silver keychain that has the word "Winning" engraved on the oval plate.

"Uh, I think this one might need an explanation."

"You need to sleuth better." Luke winks. "There's a paper underneath it."

I pull the paper out and start reading. It's a warranty deed for a house, and the address seems familiar. I flip to the next page, and there's a photo. Of my dream house for the past twenty years. The house that wasn't even for sale. The one with a pool, a beautiful yard, the perfect floors, and mica flecked counters. The old, white, colonial home I've wanted my entire life.

I read the deed more carefully. Now, somehow, it's mine.

"What is this?" I ask. "It's way too much, Luke. I can't accept it."

Luke hugs Amy and Chase and then whispers, "You two go play for a minute so I can talk to Mary, okay?"

I grab my jacket and Luke and I walk to the front porch. "I should probably have told you before the presents," he says. "But I hate having this conversation."

"Oh my gosh, you're a drug dealer or something." My stomach feels like it's full of rocks. "Or a smuggler? A thief!"

He laughs, deep and loud. "Nothing of the sort, but I'm glad to know you go straight there."

"Then what?"

He throws his hands up in the air. "When we were both young and stupid, my brother Paul and I wanted to start a business. I'd identify things that the world needed by working at real jobs. Paul would do research in a lab to try and make them. We collaborated on something, and it turned into the main component of LED lights. That was our first project. Since then, we've created and patented more than a hundred new inventions, most of them electrical in nature."

I recall him telling Foster he invented the LED light. I thought he was joking, so I didn't even think about it a second time.

"But. . ." I splutter. "You live in a trailer."

Luke puts an arm around me. "After Beth died, I didn't

care about money, or possessions, or houses. All I wanted was to feel numb enough not to think. But then you pointed out that big, white, columned house, and explained what it meant to you. When you told me why you loved it, I don't know. I just had to see it for myself. I called my realtor and set up an appointment."

"Wait," I say. "It wasn't even on the market. You can't set up an appointment for something that's not for sale."

He tsks. "Oh, dear Mary, everything's on the market for the right price. But as it turned out, the Bennetts had been thinking of downsizing for years. I didn't even have to pay much over the appraisal value for it."

I don't even have words.

"Do you have any questions?" he asks. "Anything at all?"

"So you're like a billionaire or something?" I ask.

He laughs heartily again. "Not even that close."

"What are you worth, then?"

He shrugs. "It fluctuates, you know, but somewhere around 600 million, last I checked."

He could buy and sell Foster a hundred times.

My jaw drops.

I stand up and turn to walk back inside my modest little three bedroom home. Luke jumps up after me and slips on the step, falling backward on his butt into a bush. I shouldn't laugh, but I can't help myself. Mr. Richy Rich himself, bent double and stuck in a brown holly bush.

Once my giggling fit subsides, I offer him a hand and help him stand up. He doesn't let go of my hands once he's standing again. He pulls me close and kisses me until I can't think anymore. Numbers don't exist, money isn't real, and nothing matters except Luke, and me, and his darling children. When he finally lets me go, he drops to one knee and holds up a big black box.

If the box was small, I'd think he was proposing. As it is, he's handing me a big present in a really strange way. Maybe his fall damaged his brain.

"You've done way too much already," I say. "What's this?"

He arches one eyebrow. "I'd hardly find the woman of my dreams, and the house of my dreams, and then buy her that house and drive away to a job in the Midwest."

I take the box and unwrap it. "This bag says Prada."

He nods. "There's a note."

I pull a yellow post-it off the gorgeous black Prada bag. "Perfect Mom Bag."

My heart races. "You bought me a mom purse?"

He grins. "Look inside."

I reach inside and pull out a little blue box that says Tiffany's on the top.

Luke pulls me into his arms. "If you hate this, you can go pick out something else, but I wanted to surprise you. You've never had the life you deserved, not even close."

"I love my life."

He kisses my forehead. "And that's what I love about you. Life gave you a pile of crap, and you rolled up your sleeves and got to work. You've made the life you deserved for yourself, and as far as I can tell, you never even complained."

"Oh, I complained alright."

I open up the blue box and gasp at the enormous emerald inside, flanked by two large, sparkly, diamonds.

"Is this because of our joke?" I ask.

He frowns. "What joke?"

"Green eggs and ham?"

He laughs, and shakes his head. "I told the jeweler I wanted something that exactly matched your eyes. This is a little too green, but I figured you'd let that go."

My knees feel weak, so I'm glad Luke's arms are still around me. He slides the ring on my finger and I don't stop him.

"You've always taken care of everyone else, and never worried about yourself. I know it hasn't been very long for us, but I've watched you sacrifice and sacrifice and sacrifice for others. I've watched you care for your sister, your nephew, and hundreds of kids you don't know. I've watched you interact with my children, and I love you for all of that and more. Please, please, don't freak out about the money thing. Give me a chance, give us a chance, and I won't let you down."

The door opens behind me, and Amy's head pokes out. A second later, Trudy's head pops out just above it. "Did he do it yet?" Amy asks Trudy.

Trudy shakes her head and whispers, "He's doing it right now."

"Well, what did she say?" Amy asks.

"I haven't said anything yet." I huff.

Amy squeals. "The ring's on her finger, though!" She ducks back inside, and after beaming at me, Trudy follows.

"They're excited, that's all." Luke drops his hands. "So I know I slid that on there without you saying anything. Any chance I'll get some kind of answer out of you?"

I grab Luke by his shoulders and pull him up against me. I press my lips to his, and disappear into the feelings again. He's a good man, a hard worker, and a wonderful father. So what if he's sinfully rich?

Everyone's entitled to one flaw.

"Yes," I say. "I'll marry you and move into a big, old, white mansion with your beautiful children. On one condition."

Luke's smile nearly cleaves his face in two. "What's that?"

"You have to call and quit your job in Louisville."

He exhales dramatically. "Oh, please. It's like you don't know me at all." He winks. "I did that yesterday."

My eyebrows rise. "Before you knew my answer?"

"You said you loved me. Even if you said no the first time, I figured I could work with that."

I slug his shoulder, and he picks me up and twirls me around. The ring spins around my finger, weighed down by the enormously large emerald.

"Oh, hey," I say. "Maybe we ought to take this off until we get it sized."

"Sorry," he says. "My brother's a hopeless bachelor, but he offered me one piece of advice."

"What was that?"

"He said, 'make sure that ring's not too small. No woman wants to find out you think her fingers are fat.'"

I throw my head back and laugh. "I can't wait to meet your brother."

Amy comes bouncing out of the house like a pinball. "I picked it, I picked it. Dad said if I did a good job, you might be my mom. Santa didn't bring me one, but I think it's because he knew I already had you."

Her eyes, desperate with hope, lock on mine. I don't tell her that Santa brought her a mom after all, my Santa, because I don't think she'll understand. No one else will. But before I can think of what else to say, Luke takes the ring back and slides it into the box.

Amy's lower lip trembles. "You didn't like it?"

I pull her into my arms and hug her tightly. "You did a wonderful job, sweetheart, but the ring is a little bit big."

She closes her eyes and sighs. "That's Dad's fault."

I swing her around. "Yes, it is."

"Dad says the white rocks are what girls all want, but

the I picked the green one that really matches your eyes. I didn't think you'd want what every other girl wants. We comzimized."

"Compromised?" I ask.

"Yes!" She nods her head. "Exactly. What do you think?" She meets my eyes. "Also, not to push you or anything, but Dad says if you say yes, we don't have to move. We can live here in a house without wheels instead."

I think about the absurdly large ring. "I think I love the ring." And I can't wait to show it off to everyone I meet.

Chase comes running out next. "What does she say?"

Luke swoops me up in his arms and carries me inside. I whap his arm again. "You can't carry me over the threshold. We aren't even married yet."

"I'm practicing. So sue me."

Luke and his kids stay the rest of the day, and it's absolutely the happiest Christmas I've ever had. I tell Luke so.

"Oh Mary," he says, "I'm just getting started."

* * *

If you enjoyed Finding Santa and want more, don't worry! I'm working on the second book in the series and it will be out soon. In the meantime, check out my YA series, Sins of Our Ancestors, available now! You can read a preview of the first book in the series, *Marked,* next! Also, you can check it out on Amazon now!

Please sign up for my newsletter! Twice a month, I'll send you bonus content, updates on upcoming releases, and promotions from my friends.
Visit: www.BridgetEBakerwrites.com to sign up!

Finally, if you enjoyed reading *Finding Santa*, please, please, please leave me a review on Amazon!!!! It makes a tremendous difference when you do. Thanks in advance!

THE END (for now)

<<<<>>>>

CHAPTER 25

I'm a big, fat coward.

I've known this about myself definitively since one month before my sixth birthday. The night I lost my dad.

Case in point: I'm just shy of seventeen. I've been in love with the same guy for almost three years. Even though

I see Wesley a few times a week, I haven't said a word. But tonight I have the perfect opportunity to do what I've always feared to try. Tonight, to celebrate our upcoming Path selections, all the teens in Port Gibson play a stupid, risky game.

Spin the Bottle.

I glance around as I walk toward the campfire in front of me. Only thirty-five kids turned seventeen in the past year, so of course I know them all. My best girl friend, Gemette, waves me over. I try to squash my disappointment at not seeing Wesley. When I played this scene in my brain earlier, I was sitting by him.

"You gonna scowl at the fire all night, Ruby?" Gemette pats a gloved hand on the slab of granite underneath her.

"You couldn't have saved us one of those seats?" I point at the smooth, flat stumps on the other side of the fire. I sit down and shift around, trying to find a flat spot.

"I think what you meant to say was, 'Thanks, Gemette. You're the best.'"

Her straight black hair reflects the campfire flames when she tosses it back over her shoulder. It's against the Council's rules for hair to cover your forehead. Gotta make it easy to see anyone who might be Marked. Except tonight, no one's following the rules. Everyone's wearing their hair down, and Gemette's silky locks frame her face beautifully. I envy her sleek hair almost as much as I covet her curves.

"My bum's already hurting on this," I mutter.

"If you weighed more than eighty-five pounds soaking wet, it wouldn't bother you so much."

Instead of curves, I've got twig arms and a non-existent backside. I shift on the huge slab, trying to find a position that doesn't hurt. I arch one eyebrow, not that she can see it in the dark. "I weigh ninety-two pounds, thank you very much."

Gemette snorts. "That proves my point, you bony butt."

She leans toward the fire and picks up the glass bottle lying on its side. She tosses it a few inches up into the air before catching it again.

"Be careful with that." That bottle's the only reason I'm sitting here, sour-faced, stomach churning.

Slowly the remaining seats around the fire fill up. Wesley shows up last. There aren't any seats left, but before I can convince Gemette to squish over, he grabs a bucket. He turns it upside down and takes a seat a few feet away from everyone else. I guess that's fitting. His dad's the Mayor of Port Gibson and a Counsellor on the CentiCouncil, so Wesley's in charge by default tonight. He'll probably take over for his dad one day, which isn't as glamorous as it sounds since less than two thousand people live here.

He looks around the fire, and his gaze stops on me. He bobs his head in my direction, and I shoot him a smile. I'm glad he can't hear the thundering of my heart.

Although we're all huddled around a campfire, and I've known most of the kids here for years, we maintain carefully measured space between us. Tercera dictates our habits even when we're rebelling. Which we're only doing because it's a tradition.

Maybe Tercera's made cowards of us all.

"Are we starting?" Tom's sitting to my left. His parents are both in Agriculture and he's Pathing there, too. He has broad shoulders and tan skin from working outside most of the day. Gemette likes him, and it's easy to see why. Of course, he's nothing to Wesley.

I glance across the fire in time to see Wesley stand up. He straightens the collar of his coat slowly and methodically, like his dad always does before a town hall meeting. Wesley loves doing impressions, and he's usually convincingly good at them.

"I'd like to take this opportunity to welcome you all to the Last Supper." His voice mimics his father's, and he touches his chin with his right hand in the same way his dad always rubs his beard. Wesley himself is tall and lean with long black hair that he's wearing down, for once. It falls in his eyes in a way I've never seen before, and I feel a little rush. I want to touch it.

Wesley smirks. "I know you may be less than impressed with the culinary offerings for our gathering, but as I always say, Tradition has Value." He cracks a grin then, and everyone laughs. "Seriously though." He drops the impression and returns to his normal voice, which I like way better anyway. "I know the food sucks, but this whole thing started with a bunch of teenagers who were sick of rules and ready to throw caution to the wind for a night."

I look down at the three or four-dozen nondescript metal cans with the tops peeled back, resting on coals. Another few dozen are open but sitting away from the fire. Presumably they contain fruit or something else we won't want to eat hot.

Wesley leans over and snags the first can, his gloves keeping him safe from the heat. "I hope you'll all forgive me, but this was what we could find."

"This is a pretty crummy tradition." Lina reaches down and grabs a can with mittened hands. Her dark brown hair falls in a long, thick braid down her back, like it has every single time I've seen her.

"Traditions matter, even the silly ones. They help pull us together as a community, which is valuable when fear of Tercera yanks communities apart. We're stronger when we aren't alone. Thinking every man should look out for himself hurts all of us." Wesley takes his first bite right before Lina. I grab a can of baked beans.

The food really is as bad as it looks, but at least it's not spoiled.

Wesley talks while we eat.

"As you already know, we come from a variety of backgrounds. Before the Marking, Port Gibson housed approximately the same number of people, but not a single person who lived here before the Marking survived. We cleaned out the homes, burned some to the ground and rebuilt, circled the city with a wall, and made it our own. The Unmarked who live here are Christian, Muslim, atheist, black, white, Hispanic, Russian, German and Japanese. I could keep going, but I don't need to. Before the Marking, these differences divided humanity. Now, we know that what truly matters is what we all share. We embrace the traditions that bring us all together, because we're more alike than we are unalike."

I swallow the last spoonful of baked beans from my can and set it down on the ground by my feet. I'm almost the last one to finish eating, but several half-full cans are scattered around the campfire. A few people grab a can of fruit. I prefer the stuff my Aunt and I process and can ourselves, so I don't bother.

I rub my hands together briskly. Even in mittens, my fingers feel stiff. It's usually not too cold in Mississippi, even in January, but a late freeze has everyone bundled up. The Last Supper's supposed to be a chance to rebel, but I'm grateful that everyone's as covered as possible. It means I won't look as cowardly for keeping my mittens on. My aunt is Port Gibson's head of the Science Path, so I know all about how Tercera congregates first in the skin cells, even before the Mark has shown up on the forehead in some cases.

The wind moans as it blows through the trees, and we all huddle around the meager fire. Even though the flames have died down to coals in most places, it burns hot. My face roasts while my back freezes. The bottle lies stationary on the weathered flagstones by the fire where Gemette set it, light glinting off of the dingy glass at strange angles.

The quiet conversations die off and the nervous laughter ends. Eyes dart to and fro among the thirty something teenagers gathered.

"So." Evan's voice cracks, and he clears his throat. "Who goes first?"

"Thanks for volunteering," Wesley says.

I suspect no one else asked for just this reason. All eyes turn toward poor, gangly, redheaded Evan.

Evan gawks momentarily. Even though he and I work in Sanitation together, I don't know him well. I haven't been there long enough to guess whether he feels lucky or put upon. He sighs, and then leans forward and tweaks the bottle. It twists sharp and fast and skitters to the right, spinning furiously.

I really hope the bottle doesn't stop on me, and I doubt I'm alone in that thought. Evan's funny in a self-deprecating way, but he isn't smart, and he definitely isn't hot. I bite my lip, worried about what I'll do if it does stop on me.

It slows quickly and finally stops pointing to my left. I sigh in relief, which I belatedly hope no one heard.

Tom gasps, and then in a raspy voice says, "No way. I mean, you're nice and all Evan, but I'm not . . . I don't . . ."

"Yeah, me either. Chill, man." Evan laughs. "So, does it pass to the next person over?" Evan raises his eyebrows and glances at me.

I want to protest, but my throat closes off and I look down at my feet instead.

Evan stands up. "So Ruby . . ."

He may not have saved me a seat, but Wesley jumps in to save me now, thank goodness. "That's not how it works. If you get someone of the same gender, and neither of you . . . well, then your turn passes to him or her. Which means you sit down Evan, and you spin next, Tom."

"Who made these rules?" Evan grumbles as he sits.

Gemette smiles. "They make sense, Evan. I mean, it's not spin the bottle and pick best out of three. Your way, you'd basically pick someone in the circle who's close and kiss whoever you want."

Evan shrugs and glances at me again with a smile. "Sounds pretty okay, actually."

Tom snorts. "I don't hear Ruby complaining about Wesley's rules. I'd say that's your answer, man."

I look back down at my shoes, but not before I see Tom's wink. Jerk. Evan must feel idiotic, and I definitely want to sink into the ground.

I bite my lip again, this time a little harder. Tom's an obviously good-looking guy, but I have no interest in kissing him. I hope his wink was a joke about Evan and not some kind of message.

Cold air blows past me as Tom leans forward to spin the bottle, his body no longer blocking the wind. One thing jumps out at me as he reaches for the glass bottle. In spite of the cold, Tom isn't wearing gloves. He must've taken them off at some point. He's either a daredevil or an idiot. I'm not sure which.

Tom spins the bottle less forcefully than Evan and rocks back and forth as the bottle circles round and round. His eyes focus intently on the spinning glass as if he can somehow control where it stops. I wonder who he's hoping for and look around the circle for clues. Andrea seems particularly bright-eyed. My eyes continue to wander. One gorgeous, deep blue pair of eyes in the circle stares right back at me. Wesley. I've looked at him a lot over the past few years, but this feels different somehow. A spark zooms through me, and I quickly stare at my feet.

No luck for Andrea tonight, or Gemette. The bottle comes to rest on Andrea's best friend, Annelise, instead. She and I were in Science together a long time ago. Her dark brown hair hangs loose, framing high cheekbones and expressive chocolate eyes. She frowns. Tonight doesn't seem to be going right for anyone so far.

"Now what?" Annelise's voice shakes. "We just kiss, right here in front of everyone?"

"No, of course not," Gemette snaps.

"Who made you the boss?" Evan frowns. Judging by his sulky tone, he's still mad about losing his turn earlier.

"Unfortunately, I'm the boss," Wesley says, "and she's right." He points to a dilapidated shed at the top of the hill. "You two go up there."

"Romantic." Tom rolls his eyes as he stands up. He rubs his bare palms on his pants. Gross. At least I know I'm not the only nervous one here. Tom and Annelise trudge a path through clumps of frozen brown grass toward the rundown tool shed.

What a special memory for their first kiss.

Gemette sighs and I pat her gloved hand with my own. I'd feel worse for her, but Gemette likes every decent looking guy in town, including a few boys a year younger than us. She'll recover from missing out on a special moment with Tom.

I glance again toward Andrea, an acquaintance from my time in Agriculture. She and Tom trained together for years. She may have liked him as long as I've liked Wesley.

She looks into the fire while her foot digs a messy hole in the soil. I wonder how I'll feel if Wesley spins and gets Andrea. Or worse, Gemette. I'll have to sit here and twiddle my thumbs while I know he's in there kissing a friend. My stomach lurches. Coming tonight was a stupid idea. I clearly didn't think this through.

No one speaks to distract me from my anxiety. The shed isn't far. We could easily eavesdrop on them if the wind would shriek a little less.

"How long does this take?" Evan asks.

"Who the heck knows?" Gemette points at the bottle. "Impatient for another crack at it?"

Kids around us chuckle.

After another few awkward moments, Gemette grabs the bottle and gives it a twist. "No reason we have to wait on them."

"Sure," Wesley says. "Whoever it lands on can go next."

"Wait," Evan asks, "whoever it lands on goes next as in it's their turn to spin? Or goes next as in Gemette's going to kiss them?"

The bottle stops before anyone can respond, pointing directly at Wesley. His perfectly shaped brows draw together under disheveled black hair. Gorgeous hair. His lips form a perfect "o". His bright blue eyes meet mine again.

My heart races and the baked beans sit like a lump in my belly. I shouldn't have come. Of course Wesley will want to kiss her. Gemette's gorgeous, curvy, and smart. Ugh. Am I going to have to sit here while my best friend kisses the guy I like twenty feet away? This is all my fault. If I'd only told Gemette, she'd beg off.

I bite down a little harder on my lip and taste blood this time. I really need to kick this particular habit, especially with kissing in my future. Maybe. Hopefully. I'm such an idiot.

Wesley clears his throat. "I think I'm going to sit this game out. I'm more of a moderator than a participant."

"No," I blurt out. "You can't. You're here, you're seventeen, you have to participate." What am I doing? Why am I shoving him at my friend? But if I don't make him play, I'm flushing my chance to kiss him down the toilet. I want to cry.

"Well, then I guess it's my turn to spin." His deep voice sounds completely different than any of the other kids here tonight. My stomach ties in knots when I hear him speak, which is ridiculous because I've heard his voice a million times.

I glance at Gemette. She looks disappointed and I want to cry with relief, but I don't blame her. He could've kissed her but didn't pursue it. I imagine most any girl here would be disappointed. He glances up and his eyes lock with mine again. Caught. I start to shiver and try to stop it. This look is different somehow from any before, like something shifted. Wesley clears his throat, looks down at the bottle, gracefully reaches over, and snaps it between his fingers.

It spins evenly, not moving to the right or the left. It spins on and on, and I wonder if it'll ever stop. It slows, whirling a little less with each rotation, the butterflies in my stomach swooping and swirling with each pass.

Until it finally stops. On me.

My eyes snap up reflexively, wide with shock. Wesley doesn't even seem surprised. He simply stands and inclines his head toward the shed.

"Isn't it still..." I clear my throat. "Umm, occupied?"

"We can wait over there." He gestures at the hill to the right of the shed. One side of his mouth lifts in a smile and

I feel an answering grin form on my lips. Which makes me think about what we're about to do with our lips.

Swarms and swarms of butterflies flutter in my chest.

"Sure," I say.

I stand up, and without even thinking, I wipe my palms on my jeans. They aren't even sweaty and what's more, I'm wearing mittens! I really hope no one noticed. Okay, more specifically, I hope Wesley didn't notice. Gemette holds something out to me when I stand. I can't tell what it is from feel alone, thanks to my thick mittens, and in the dark I have to squint to make it out at all. A tube of something. "What—"

"Lip gloss," she whispers. "A gift from my mom. I was going to use it, but looks like you need it more, you lucky, lip-biting brat." She winks.

I'm glad Wesley's still across the fire from me and that it's dark. Maybe he somehow miraculously missed both the palm wipe and her wink.

I walk as slowly as I can toward the old shed, partially to avoid tripping, but also so I won't look overeager. I try to hide my face while I apply the fruit-scented lip-gloss so that Wesley won't notice. It's dark, but I don't want him to be put off by dry, scratchy lips, or worse, dried blood. Gemette's a good friend. I feel guilty for overreacting earlier when I thought she might kiss Wesley. Not super guilty, but you know, a little.

Neither of us speaks a word, but I feel the eyes of the other teens follow us toward the shed. We're only a few crunching steps away when the swinging door flies open and Tom and Annelise barrel out. I jump when it bangs shut behind them.

Tom looks as ruffled as I feel, his eyes darting back and forth. He ducks his head and reaches down to take Annelise's hand. They walk out and away from the fire and the rest of Port Gibson's teens. I can't tell where they're headed, but somewhere far away from here.

"Did you know almost a third of the couples in town trace their start to the Last Supper?" Wesley asks.

"No way."

He shrugs. "We've only been an Unmarked town for seven years, so it's even more impressive. Not all of them are matched up from a bottle spin, but I think the game helps people realize how they feel."

A thrill rushes through me. Does Wesley feel the same as me?

My hand reaches for the door handle and collides en route with his. I'm wearing mittens, of course, and he's wearing shiny, brown gloves, but a thrill runs through me when we touch, even through layers. He doesn't move his hand away, but instead draws my hand in his and pushes the door handle back in one fluid movement. My heart skips a beat and time stops. When the door's completely open, he slowly releases my hand. I lower my eyes and step over the threshold into the rundown little building.

Although there's clearly no power, and consequently neither heat nor an overhead light, the walls at least cut the wind. It's at once both warmer and quieter. Two tall candles burn softly on a pile of rusted metal boxes in the corner. Someone prepared this dump, I realize. I wonder whether it was Wesley. The flames provide enough light that I can see his face. His dark brows are an even more startling contrast to his dark blue eyes than usual, accentuated by his hair falling in his face.

"So," I say. "Here we are."

Wesley looks at me from less than a foot away. The shed's small and crammed full of moldering farm implements. The air around us practically hums, but that isn't new. It's always like the moments right before a lightning storm when he's near. Supercharged almost, like the electrons around my body might fly off at his slightest touch. The difference is that here, away from the town's work projects, away from my family and his, it feels like anything really could happen.

Wesley's so close I can smell him, the same citrusy, woodsy smell I've secretly savored for years. It's even stronger tonight, like he put on more of whatever it is he usually wears. I breathe deep, and all the memories of him re-imprint on my brain. Scrubbing, sanding, painting, digging, cleaning, hammering. Projects his dad made him attend, but I suffered through to be near him. When I'm with him, I belong somewhere for the first time in a decade.

When we become adults next week, Wesley's mandatory attendance at work projects ends. Wesley steps into his role as an administrator, and I'll become part of Port Gibson's janitorial crew. It's now or never if I want to make any kind of permanent place with Wesley.

I never thought I'd be close to him like this, and I know I may never be again. I lean toward him and tilt my face upward, eyes closed, ready for what comes next. Maybe I'm even a touch impatient. I have waited for this for years.

Except I keep waiting, and then I wait some more.

Not a single thing happens. The trouble with being ridiculously small is that Wesley, who's on the tall side anyway, towers over me. Even with my face angled up, his lips are pretty far away. I can barely make out his expression, but it looks guarded.

Maybe he doesn't know how to do it?

No way. Wesley must know. I mean, it's not hard, right? You just push your lips onto the other person's mouth. Why isn't he doing anything? This is the moment. THE moment!

Until it passes. And then another moment falls on top of it, and another. All passing. Even the butterflies in my stomach get bored and go look for flowers elsewhere.

I'm not sure exactly how much time has elapsed, but the seconds drag, heavy with my growing frustration. Soon, someone will bang on the door. "You've been in there forever," they'll say. "Make room for the next couple."

I want to smack them in their eager faces.

I know I don't have much time, and I want to say something, anything. I need to tell him how I feel, say the words, take a gamble. But like it always does, my tongue shuts down. My throat closes off. The words stick inside my throat. Why am I such a coward? Our perfect moment withers and dies. Tears well up in my eyes, and I can't breathe.

Wesley isn't similarly affected. He steps back and says, "We don't have to do this, Ruby. It's not safe at all. I don't know why my dad even lets these dinners happen."

"Why'd you spin the bottle in the first place?" I hear the desperation in my voice, but the words pour out in spite of myself. "I know you, and you know me. How's it dangerous for us?"

He takes another step back, his expression registering surprise. "People get Marked, Ruby. It still happens. Every few weeks, in fact. Maybe I'm Marked. You don't know. It happens, even here, even with all our rules. It may take years to die once you're Marked, but it's inevitable."

I roll my eyes. "Well I'm not Marked, if that's what you're worried about." I point at my forehead. "See? Clear."

"We shouldn't be taking these risks." Wesley scowls. "Not now, not right before our real lives begin. This whole thing's supposed to be a time to say goodbye to being a kid, not act like an idiotic five-year-old, breaking rules for no reason."

Our real lives? Maybe he never thought it felt right, the time we spent, the way we are together. Maybe I never belonged with him at all. "Why'd you even come, then? Why follow me in here if you're not going to kiss me?"

Was he hoping for someone else? Was he stuck with me and looking for any excuse to bolt? Am I Evan in this scenario?

I look up, but I'm too close. The hair cascading over his face obscures my view. I want to touch his hair; I want to kiss him; I want to tell him I love him, and that I always have. My fingers and toes and everything connecting them zings in spite of the bitter cold, in spite of the indifference of his words. Energy spins round and round in my body, a closed circuit with nowhere to go.

"Look, Ruby, I don't know what to say . . . but the thing is . . ." He sounds torn, confused.

Suddenly, I don't want to hear "the thing," whatever it is. I've been talking to Wesley for years, talking and talking, and working alongside him, but I don't want to talk to him anymore. I know what I want and I'll never have a better chance to play things off as part of a game, if he feels like I now suspect he does. The notion of an excuse appeals to my cowardly heart. I can't speak the words, but I won't stand here and do nothing, not anymore, because he's the real life I've longed for.

I stop thinking and step toward him instead. He tries to step back and slams up against the back wall. I quickly take one more step and use my gloved hand to pull his head down to mine. I push my lips against his. In my haste, I push too hard and pull a little too fast. Our teeth smack into each other and my tooth knocks against my own lip, splitting it wide open again.

It's the opposite of magical.

I look up at Wesley instinctively. He has blood on his

mouth, but whether it's his, or mine, I can't tell. And if it's not awful enough already, Wesley stiffens from head to toe like I mauled him, like I forced him into something torturous.

A tear rolls down my cheek and I inhale deeply. I won't cry over this. I can't, because there's no way I can play it all off as a game if I bawl my eyes out. I turn away from him. If I can't stop the tears, at least he doesn't need to see them. When did this go so wrong? I should be calm, cool, in control. I need to laugh it all off and tell him friends can't be expected to kiss well. Whoops.

Except my heart won't listen to the screaming from my head. I'm not calm. I'm the opposite of cool. I've lost all control.

He grabs my shoulder and tugs me around. I turn, but my eyes stay glued to the ground, too ashamed to meet his gaze.

"Ruby, look at me."

He puts two gloved fingers under my chin and lifts. His head comes down then, but slowly, too slowly. My heart stops pumping and I worry it might never beat again. His lips brush mine gently, then with more pressure. I ignore the discomfort of my torn lip and lean into him, connected to him in a way I can't explain. I need more air, but I want less, because that means more space between us. If this never ends, maybe it'll erase the moments that preceded it.

Suddenly, he lets me go and steps back. Emptiness fills the space where he stood. I reel again, sucking air in and blowing my breath back out to steady myself.

When I raise my eyes, our gazes lock. All my sorrow from before is gone, replaced with a feeling like I'm flying, soaring, floating on top of the world. His sapphire blue eyes reflect candlelight back at me. He's breathing as deeply as I am; he's as affected as me. I can't look away from his strong, almost hawkish nose, his square jaw, his flashing eyes and thick black lashes. I continue to stare as Wesley reaches up and brushes his unkempt hair away from his eyes.

I almost faint.

Such a simple movement. Small in the grand scheme of things, but also vast, earth shattering, all encompassing. My dreams crumble. My world spins out of control. He moves his hair off his forehead, and suddenly things make sense. His reticence to touch me, his skittishness, but also his quick recovery. Once he knew it was too late, he didn't hesitate to kiss me. Because we'd already touched.

There, on his otherwise perfect forehead, is a rash. Before it wouldn't have mattered. Before the Marking no one would care. Acne on a teen, a reaction to hair product. It shouldn't matter that his forehead has a blemish. It shouldn't terrify me, but it does. Because that small rash means Wesley is Marked, and in under three years, he's going to die terribly.

And now, so am I.

* * *

ACKNOWLEDGMENTS

My husband does almost all the laundry, almost never complains about all the time I spend writing, and supports me in every single way. He has been my biggest cheerleader, and my number one fan (other than maybe my mom!) through my crazy publishing journey. It was a lot of fun writing Luke and Mary's story, but I love ours even more.

My mom is a champ! She cheers when I need it, edits when I need it, and pays attention to the small details. Thank you for all your help, and sorry for all the late night calls and texts.

Esther, you helped me so much with my back cover copy! THANK YOU! Shauna, you're always there when I'm mopey or struggling, and you were a CHAMP on the cruise while I huddled over my laptop.

My kids are so patient when I say, "Wait! Just a few more things!" They fill my life with joy, and support me in my writing endeavors. I'm forever grateful for the joy they bring me. But Tessa, my own little precocious five year old, deserves an extra thank you here. If she wasn't quite so funny, or quite so bright, I wouldn't have had so many readers fall in love with Amy.

ABOUT THE AUTHOR

Bridget loves her husband (every day) and all five of her kids (most days). She's a lawyer, but does as little legal work as possible. She has a yappy dog, backyard chickens, and a fish. She makes cookies too often, and believes they should be their own food group. To keep from blowing up like a puffer fish, she kick boxes every day. So if you don't like her books, her kids, or her cookies, maybe don't tell her in person.

ALSO BY BRIDGET E. BAKER

Try her debut, YA Post apocalyptic novel, Marked

Or the dynamic follow up, Suppressed

Or… the finale to the fast paced series, Redeemed